BURIED ROOTS

TERRA WEISS

AUTUMN SKY
BOOKS

To Deena.
This book would
not exist without you.

Contents

1. The Gnarly Tree — 1
2. The Inheritance — 7
3. House and Home — 21
4. The Note — 26
5. The New Arrival — 32
6. The Search — 40
7. The Helper — 46
8. Cut The Cheese — 60
9. The Festival — 67
10. The Runaway — 78
11. Starry Night — 84
12. The Plunge — 92
13. The Reception — 99
14. The Restoration — 111
15. Twisted Tree — 118
16. The Loft — 122
17. The Ride — 131
18. The Trip — 141

19.	The Dinner	152
20.	The Old Friend	164
21.	The Bond	172
22.	Shattered Lines	177
23.	The Discovery	188
24.	The Tension	192
25.	The Code	199
26.	The Party	202
27.	The River	214
28.	The Call	219
29.	The Gray Night	223
30.	Long Way Home	228
31.	The Big City	233
32.	The Guest	238
33.	The Dock	245
34.	The Capture	251
35.	The Truth	253
36.	The Shock	258
Epilogue		265
Don't Go Quite Yet!		270
Books by Terra Weiss		271
About Terra Weiss		273
Thank Yous		275
Copyright		278

1
The Gnarly Tree

The car fishtails.

My knuckles go white as I pump the brake, but the tires have no traction. The car spins, and endless pine trees whiz by.

This is exactly how my adoptive parents died.

I don't have time to die right now—I have work crap piled a mile high on my desk that no one else can do.

After seconds that seem like hours, everything jolts to a stop. The car is on the shoulder of the creepy back road, and I scan my body for cuts and bruises. There are none, and relief washes over me.

Looks like I'm not dying, at least, not today—the day I'm driving into a strange town under stranger circumstances.

Still stunned, I glance out the windshield. The mist wafts through the air like an infinite ghost, but I can see it up close now—the thing that caused me to veer off the road.

"It's just a tree. Knock it off, Willow Dawson," I mumble, but my heart isn't listening as it thuds wildly in my chest. It's because it knows it's not just *any* tree—it's the one that's appeared in my night terrors for as long as I can remember. A monstrosity perched on a hill.

It's a magnolia, which makes sense. Georgia is full of them. But this one stands alone, high in a clearing, its trunk unnaturally large. What stops my breath is the enormous branch that leans so far to one side, it appears to float like a feat of gravity.

In my nightmares, it's always advancing, warp speed, then wrapping its limbs around me until everything goes black.

This *cannot* be a coincidence.

It's always eaten at me—why I'm haunted by a tree I've never seen. My legs feel like Jell-O as I step out of the car, so I shake them as I breathe in the thick air. It's my first time in the South, and they, whoever they are, aren't joking—it's stifling in Georgia, especially in July. Shards of sunlight appear through the splitting clouds, which remind me of the stretched cotton candy from Coney Island. I have fond memories there, but that was before.

I walk around assessing the damage, my stilettos sinking into the red-clay dirt with every step. Miraculously, the vehicle looks unscathed—only the left tires are stuck in a shallow ditch. It'll be ugly, but I can peel the car out. Pops taught me how... along with changing a flat, and all the other handy things that make me good at my job. "Happiness is dirty hands and a clean conscience, Willow," he'd say. And, as it turns out, I've needed both, just to survive. I miss him so much. Every day.

Through the haze, I stare at this hellish tree on the hill above me. I'm slow to approach this hideous oddity of nature, but I have to look at it. Even though everything in me pleads not to, my feet trudge up the hill.

Its bulging roots are so widespread, the surrounding earth is knotty, tangled. My heel gets stuck, and I stumble and fall, hitting the ground with a thud. Standing and brushing off my pants, I realize my knee should be smarting, but I feel nothing.

Once I'm in front of the tree, my eyes can't help but roam skyward—it towers over me like a gnarly monster. Something deep in my gut draws my gaze down, and I see a handmade wooden cross, weather-beaten and moss-covered, stabbed into the ground. When I kneel to study it, shivers rock my spine, and I fight to take in air.

It refuses to come.

Carved into the cross are the words, "In loving memory of our sweet Willow."

I can't even begin to wrap my head around what I just saw. Exactly no one wants to see her name on a cross, and, man, what a creepy introduction to the itty-bitty town of Violet Moon.

With the ache finally settling into my knee, I approach my car, and everything around me is echoey and out of focus. I just have to take one step at a time, the first being to get this car out of the ditch. Then, I need to be back on my way to sign the deed on a property. It's my first place, and it's one I've never heard of or seen before... except from the pictures on Zillow and Google Maps, which show only a grove of trees. A perfect stranger willed it to me, and it's probably a moonshine shack—but it's *mine*, so I was following the GPS to the address the probate lawyer gave me, 55 Lilac Lane.

A windowless white van slows to a crawl as it swerves around me. Nerves clench in my gut as the driver pulls onto the shoulder just up ahead. A stranger driving a kidnap van in this desolate place? *Hell no!* I already have a raging fear of the woods.

When the driver steps out, I grip the pepper spray on my key ring. So what if he's got a killer bod and shock of black hair? Who cares if he's wearing a faded t-shirt and rugged jeans, like some Hallmark movie hottie? I know better than to be fooled by looks.

I check the highway, scanning for other cars. Of course, this country road is empty. When he gets closer, I see the oily black streaks on his face, the filth on his hands, and the dirt on his clothes. And he's wearing mismatched neon socks. That has to be ironic, no? But his smile is wicked sexy when he says, "Can I help you, ma'am?"

Ma'am? Is he for real? I force a smile and a wave when I say, "No, thank you. I've got it." Translation: don't come an inch closer.

"You've got it?" His voice is incredulous.

"Yup. All good."

His eyes bulge as he stops and glances at my stuck tire. "All good? Looks like you're in a bit of a pickle."

On closer inspection, he has muscles everywhere, and the light scruff on his carved jawbone is annoyingly sexy. Which again, will not stop me from pepper spraying his fine ass. Hello, stranger danger—in the middle of nowhere. "Pickle? Nah."

He rakes a hand through his hair. "Look, this isn't a sexist thing. I have a mother and three sisters who could kick everyone's ass. But this road doesn't see much action, and I can't leave someone out here."

"I appreciate that, I really do. But I won't be stuck long—I'm handy." That's a stretch. I restore homes, so I *am* handy, but with cars, I only know the basics.

He raises a brow as he studies my face. "Handy or not, getting a car out of a ditch is a two-person job. At least." He cocks his head and hitches up his voice a notch when he adds, "Out here, there's no Triple A."

"I don't need Triple A. But thank you."

His lips quirk up as they appear to search for a response. "Once I leave, you might not see another car for hours."

"I'll figure it out. I'm a New Yorker."

"Ah. That explains it."

My hand lands on my hip. "Explains what, exactly?"

"Nothing." His mouth curves in a patronizing grin.

His amusement pisses me off. It's *really* hard not to sound condescending when I say, "I'm sure you've got places to be."

He hesitates before he hitches his thumb over his shoulder. "Okay, then. I'm leaving."

Our gazes lock, like we're in a game of eye-chicken. That's fine, bring it—I don't mind studying his. They're part ocean, part storm cloud—sparkle tinged with despair. Like mine. I don't look away, don't blink when I say, "I see that, and good for you. Enjoy your day."

He steps away in defeat. "I'm really leaving this time. You'll be out here in the backwoods. All by yourself." Another step back. "When you could have a mechanically inclined, super handy guy give you a hand."

I put my palms up. "Again—mechanically inclined, super handy hands right here." I wiggle my fingers and paint on a smile. "Sir."

"All righty, then. Good luck." That grin is back. "Ma'am."

I hate to admit it, but damn it, smug is sexy on him. Our gazes lock again, and I enjoy looking at his smile, looking at *him*. Forget eye candy—this country boy... or man, with distinguished light creases on his temples—is more of an exquisite eye confection.

And now, I'm staring. I attempt to run my fingers through my auburn hair, which I've forgotten is bobby-pinned. My hand gets stuck, and I try to play it off as a head scratch.

He waves. "I'm Owen Brooks, by the way. It was nice meeting you."

"You too." I'm *not* giving him my name. I point at his feet and say, "Nice neon socks, by the way."

That smug grin is back when he runs a hand over his dirt-stained tee. "Pulling this look together wasn't easy."

I smile, and for the first time, it's genuine.

When he turns to walk away, I catch a glimpse of his backside, a work of art so fine it belongs in the Met.

When he opens the door to his truck, a tiny bulldog comes flying out and rockets toward me. Owen yells, "Demon, no!" before looking at me with terror in his eyes. "Don't touch him, he bites!"

"Aw, look at that baby." In a flash, the dog is at my feet, rolling on his back to display his pot-bellied stomach. I give it a good scratch and say, "That's a good Demon."

"Demon, git back here!" Owen's jaw is slack. He's shaking his head, dazed, when he says, "I've never seen that dog nice to anyone. Including me."

"Maybe that's because you named him Demon."

Owen's palms go up. "That wasn't me. The shelter gave him that name—appropriately, I might add. I'm fostering him until he learns his manners."

Tongue hanging out sideways, Demon has his paws on my leg as I give his head a scrub. "Aww, they've got you in finishing school, huh?"

When Demon runs back to Owen, I give them both a wave. "Bye, Owen. And be gone, Demon."

After the dog jumps in the white van, Owen steps inside too, then sits... and sits. This guy is seriously stubborn. He may be charming, but so was Ted Bundy. When I give Owen the hand signal to go, he finally starts his engine and inches away.

"I showed him." My lips split into a grin. But when I glance at my car, my stomach plummets.

I'm all alone, in the backwoods, with no Triple A... and stuck in a ditch.

2
The Inheritance

A broken heel, a ripped button-up silk shirt, and two sweaty armpits later, I have this godforsaken car back on the road. Pops didn't lie—the floor mat for traction worked... eventually. So, yeah. After changing heels, I'm back on the road with a trashed floor mat. I'll have to get a new one.

When I drive around a bend, I see the white van ahead, pulled off to the side of the road.

Oh my god.

Owen stayed and waited for me, which is ridiculously adorable or totally creepy. Both? I slow to a crawl as I drive by him, waving when our eyes meet.

Shock passes over his face, and I give him a two-finger salute before driving away. The GPS says I'll reach my destination in two minutes. After a few more curves in the road, a long driveway appears with a canopy of giant magnolia trees, its leaves blushed in shades of pink. No kidding—it's 55 Lilac Lane, so I pull onto the bricked road, like I'm entering some storybook castle.

This *can't* be mine. It must be the probate lawyer's place. Or maybe this is all some con job—I should be careful. But after living out of my car for a few months in Queens, I know how to take care of myself. With my finances and my fists.

I inhale as I take it in. Grand columns flank the white Victorian mansion with arched sash windows and wrought-iron Romeo and Juliet balconies. But it's the extravagant turrets on both ends of the home that give it the castle look. Crape myrtles blooming in ivory and the evergreen mountains make the place inarguably storybook.

There's a vintage Rolls Royce parked in the turnabout driveway, which probably belongs to the lawyer, too. I grab my purse and step out of the car in my fresh pair of heels. The warm wind hits my face as I brush off my ripped shirt, and my hair whips, something I normally don't like. But right now, it's sublime. "Wow," I say to no one.

Peering around, I inspect the aging mansion in front of me, realizing it actually needs a lot of TLC with its peeling paint and fallen shutters.

"Willow Dawson?" It's the voice of the lawyer, Roy Livingston, whom I've had several phone conversations with.

I turn to see a fragile, balding man wearing a bow tie and linen suit shuffling along with a briefcase. He extends his hand, a genuine smile spreading across his face when he says, "Roy Livingston. It's nice to finally meet you in person."

Okay, so he doesn't look like a swindler, not that I expected that from his gentle, hoarse voice. I approach before shaking his hand. "Yes, I'm Willow. It's nice to meet you too, Mr. Livingston."

"Please. Call me Roy."

"Okay, Roy." My eyes continue to roam the scene behind him, spotting a lake in the distance. "It's beautiful here."

He inhales sharply. "Well, glad you like it, young lady—because this place is yours."

"*This* house?"

"The house… and the fifty acres around it."

"*What?*" I squawk, my brain short-circuiting. I fight to inhale as I go still, but my heart definitely doesn't. A starburst of gratitude explodes inside me, and I stammer, "I don't know what to say. This is too much." People like me don't get things like this.

Roy pats my shoulder, a light chuckle whisking out of him.

I *have* to be related to the owner, Bo Underwood. I Googled him, and outside of finding an obituary that said he was preceded in death by Lily, his loving wife, along with a statement about the buildings in downtown Violet Moon he constructed, I found nothing. But I know too good to be true doesn't exist, as I've learned the hard way. "I just can't believe it."

Roy points to the swing that hangs on the home's expansive weather-beaten porch. "Sit with me?"

"Of course."

Once we're seated and I've shown him my driver's license and social security card, he takes a packet out of his briefcase and holds out the paperwork. Pointing to a few line items, he says, "That's your name. And your social security number matches."

I study it. "Yes. Both."

The lawyer shuffles through the papers, stopping on a page full of scribbles. "So, unfortunately, Bo hand wrote his will, and his penmanship left a little to be desired. Some places are a bit hard to decipher." Roy points at a line on the page. "For example, here, he wrote, 'Lily's wing,' but I think that's supposed to be 'ring,' which we couldn't find, by the way."

"Okay..." I trail off, thinking. I told Mr. Livingston about my closed adoption. When he didn't know why Bo willed me property, I asked him if he'd do me the favor of sending in hair samples of Bo and Lily to see if their DNA matched mine. After finding their hairbrushes last week, kindly, Roy did. My mouth curves when I say, "I don't have the

DNA results yet, but thank you so much for helping me out with my odd request."

"Sure, of course."

As my eyes roam "my" stunning estate, a shock-induced numbness spreads over my face, lips, and limbs, making it difficult for me to continue a coherent conversation. My mouth utters, "So, are we really, *really* sure this all belongs to me?"

"Since it's your name and social security number, and no one came forward during probate, I reckon so." Roy's big smile deepens the creases around his eyes. "So, Willow Eloise Dawson, you're the proud owner of this 6,500 square foot house and accompanying fifty-acre barley farm with a barn, two silos, a horse stable, a lake, four purebred Gypsy Vanner horses, and six goats."

My vision blurs, and I blink to clear it, but it's useless. A buzzing erupts in my ears, and I feel like I won the lottery.

I guess I just did.

This kind of thing happens to other people, not me. *Never* me. I'm the one who had to take a job cleaning toilets at sixteen while I quoted restoration jobs—for three years—before making enough to start my own gig. I begged the owner of my parents' apartment complex to let me replace my father as the super after he died. Since I was so young and had no references, I had to pay six months' rent up front for my studio. I've worked myself ragged for everything. Well, until now.

"Are you okay, Ms. Dawson?"

I shift my gaze to him, mumbling, "I don't know. Why didn't you tell me this was the place I was inheriting?"

"I had to see the whites of your eyes first. With an estate this valuable, I couldn't risk any funny business."

"Right." I see his point, but I don't think two weeks' stay is going to cut it. "And please. Call me Willow."

"Surely. Would you like to look around, Willow?"

Hell, yeah, I want to see inside this castle house that, apparently, belongs to me. I mean, come on—I'd want to see it if it didn't. And it'll hopefully provide clues as to why Bo Underwood left me this magnificent estate. "Absolutely."

After Google didn't give me much info on Bo, I became a member of a records website where I found birth and death certificates for the Underwoods along with the rest of their families. Bo had one older brother who's now passed, along with his parents. Lily's maiden name was Sheffield, and she had a brother who died a few months back, and a sister who died very young. Bo and Lily had no children, but as a Hail Mary, I looked up adoption records for a "Willow Underwood" and a "Willow Sheffield." I found nothing.

After an exhaustive search of property records, I found Bo had a New York address for a few years in the mid-eighties, which could link him to my father. But that doesn't make sense. If Pops and Bo were close, Pops would've told me.

Still. That freakish tree.

When Roy and I step inside, my jaw falls to the scarred oak hardwood floors. "Oh, wow."

Roy peers around, sighing as he fingers the dust off the ornately carved entry doors before shutting them. "Bo bought this estate because the original owner started this town with his barley farm, selling to bread companies. Then, Bo turned the place organic and began supplying the burgeoning breweries of Violet Moon. This house is a historic landmark, and with his skills, he began restoring it. He only got about halfway there when his wife got sick. A shame because he wanted to turn this place into a visiting ranch with horse lessons, hayrides, and goat milking—for the tourists and the kids of Violet Moon."

"I read that Bo was a talented builder." But neither this house—nor the work he did here—was in his obituary. Probably because he never finished it.

"Yes, ma'am. Bo had quite the vision, which you'll see when you visit downtown Violet Moon."

I approach the banister of the spiral staircase, which flows to an end with a delicately whittled horse, then run my fingers along the ridges of its mane. "Amazing."

My gaze floats around as I take in the two-story foyer with a magnificent marble fireplace in dire need of a deep cleaning. The elaborate trim work—aching for a fresh coat of paint—looks like art. The two-story windows, caked in dirt, provide a lush view, and the sunlight streaming in sets the room aglow.

A literal ache to restore the place clutches my chest, and it's not just because its rich beauty shines through the wear. It's the feeling blanketing me right now—the intangible one I tell people they should have when they're about to move into a place. It's instantaneous—the quieting of your soul when you've found home.

I stop myself because I can't go there. My home is in New York, and as magnificent as this place is, I need to get back. Lost in my thoughts, I realize the antique oil-bronze chandelier of an intricate metalwork design has captured my stare. "Incredible."

Roy rubs his brow as he looks up at it. "That was hand-crafted by the original owner of the home, and it was in rough shape. Bo refurbished it."

We make our way to the outdated kitchen. But the tattered art-deco cabinets are rosewood, which means they can be refurbished. With pointy black handles and off-white finishes, the nineties-flashback appliances are freshly cleaned. There's only one small window, making the space dark.

This room needs more windows and light, but the view is phenomenal—endless trees, mountains, and a lake in the distance. "So much potential," I utter, my mind filling in all the things that could be done—quartz countertops with an oversized island, maybe two. Top stainless-steel appliances. A chef's kitchen.

As we continue our tour, I only fall harder for the place. It boasts seven bedrooms, the oversized primary with coffered ceilings and a fireplace. The aging walnut-paneled office with wall-to-wall shelves comes complete with a rolling ladder. There are only three bathrooms, which makes sense. In older homes, they didn't put many in because of cost, and according to records, this home was built in 1932. But it has such amazing bones with the trim-work, views, and hand-carved doors. And there's even another spiral staircase in the back of the house, which is not only beautiful, but a great way to fire-safe a home with a second escape route.

The thought makes me feel closer to Bo Underwood. He had impeccable taste, and a pang hits my gut. I wish I could've met him.

When we tour the vast, empty basement, I'm shocked. How is there absolutely *nothing* down here? Did Bo have some sort of estate sale before he passed?

When Roy and I shuffle out to the back patio, I try to sound casual when I ask, "Do you know anything about the memorial cross on that massive magnolia tree? It's about three minutes south on Pineview Road."

He stops and looks at me. Tapping his dimpled chin, he says, "I know the tree, but nothing comes to mind about a memorial, sorry."

I bat a hand and whisk out a nervous laugh. "No worries. Just caught my eye."

Roy waves to a woman in boots and bib overalls approaching, and she's carrying a notebook. "There's Frankie. She's your neighbor, and she knows what's going on here a lot better than I do."

"Afternoon," she says gruffly, without a smile. She measures me out of steely eyes that are more gray than blue.

I approach her and extend my hand. "I'm Willow. Nice to meet you, Frankie."

"Same." She briskly returns the shake, and the rough calluses on her palms remind me of my Pops.

Roy says, "Frankie's been kind enough to take time away from her own farm and family to care for this place while it sat in probate."

I study her, a simple yet pretty woman, taller with heart-shaped lips and a jagged scar that runs along her chin. She looks to be in her late forties and fit enough to take care of the place. I nod. "Thank you—I'm sure that wasn't easy."

"We do what we can around here. The animals aren't gonna feed themselves."

"Would you mind getting Willow up to speed, Frankie?" Roy asks. "As soon as we finish up?"

"Of course."

As Roy talks me through the rest of the paperwork, I discover there's no cash in the estate—the little that Bo had was left to Frankie to pay for the transition period. So, I have zero liquidity to update the place before selling it. Which is for the best, I remind myself, because I absolutely cannot stay.

I've landed the most critical account of my career—Klein Homes, an influential New York building firm. They purchased a vacant apartment complex in Brooklyn and subcontracted my company, RevitaHome Contractors. We're the experts on restoration, and they need our help with all two-hundred luxury apartments. And even after collecting a third of the payment upfront, it's maxed out my borrowing limits. But I need it to save my business. Right now, I'm over leveraged with the skyrocketing prices of materials.

I have to get back to New York and the Klein account ASAP.

I sign on the dotted lines, then Frankie and I bid Roy goodbye from the front porch.

After he pulls away, a flash of red on the back road catches my eye, and I realize it's a truck creeping by. The windows are down, and the driver, a woman wearing a red polka-dotted dress and her salt and pepper hair in a poofy bun, gawks at us.

"Mind your business, Ms. Mary Louise!" Frankie calls out, then looks at me. "Don't pay her any never mind. She can't stop herself from sticking her nose where it don't belong."

"Afternoon, Frankie, ya old grump!" Mary Louise yells back with an exaggerated smile and wave.

I return the wave and smile, not sure what to do.

When the truck disappears down the road, Frankie says, "Let's get started."

"Sure. I'm just gonna grab my tablet to take notes," I say before snatching it from the car. As we walk to the pasture, my heels sink with every step, and I scribble, "New shoes" on my tablet.

"You from up North?" Frankie asks.

I fight to keep up with her brisk pace. "New York City. How'd you know?"

"You pronounce your 'e's like 'a's." She opens the gate, and five goats rush over. Roy said there were six—where's the last one?

Frankie gives them each a scrub between the horns. "Cool your jets. It ain't feeding time—you know that, now."

The tiniest one appears, clearly a baby, and stuffs his nose into my hand. There's the sixth. "Hi, there, little goat." This clearly encourages him because he continues to nuzzle me... all over my silk blouse. "Oh, no. Not the shirt." Although it's ripped now, anyway. Who cares?

He bleats as if to tell me off.

I meet his bright blue eyes with odd rectangular pupils in a stare off, trying to show him who's boss. But I'm finding it difficult to play hard ass with this creature that has ears like my favorite gray Angora sweater and a tongue that hangs out sideways.

Frankie opens her notebook and unclips a pen. Pointing the tip at the bulleted items, she looks at me and says, "You have three farmhands whom you'll meet tomorrow when they arrive at dawn. They manage the big stuff, like running the combines and collecting the bales of hay. It's summertime, which means you're gonna need to stay on top of pest control. It's your job to fill the troughs for the goats and the horses. The stables need cleaning weekly. And you've got a foal on the way, arriving any minute. You need to have the vet come by—"

"I'm sorry," I interrupt, trying to process her words. My brain's so fried, it's practically smoking. "I don't know how to do any of these things."

Her face is emotionless. "Then you're gonna have to learn in a mighty hurry. I can't help you right now—my daughter's getting married this weekend."

"Congratulations." Can I really do all this with my work responsibilities? I could hire more farmhands, except I'd need the funds to pay them, which are nonexistent. So, I have no choice—I have to do the work here until the place is sold. "Right. Back to the list, then." I nod. "You were saying something about a fowl."

"Fowl?" Frankie's face puzzles. "There are no chickens on this farm."

"But you said a fowl was on the way."

"Oh, a foal. You've got a *foal*, which is a young horse. In your case, one that hasn't been born yet. Fowl is chicken."

With my stylus, I'm scribing furiously into my tablet. "Got it."

When I look back up, Frankie is rubbing her eyes. "You really have no idea what you're doing."

"I don't," I say, desperate. "Do you think you have any time to show me? I know you have a wedding. I'm sorry."

"I gotta git all the decorations picked out and delivered to the venue now, but I'll help you first thing tomorrow." She heads back toward the castle house.

"I really appreciate that." I lick my lips, realizing they've gone bone dry. As I follow behind her, walking on the balls of my feet, I say, "So, you were close with Bo?"

She nods curtly, folding her arms. "Friends since he moved here twenty-plus years ago. I was close with his wife, too, before she passed. She had a laundry list of health problems." Frankie hesitates, then asks, "How did you know Bo?"

"I was gifted this beautiful estate, but I never met Bo or Lily." A corner of my mouth quirks up as I shrug. "I was actually hoping you could explain the connection."

"I wish I could help you. I'm sorry."

"Did Bo or Lily ever say anything to you about me?"

She stops and stares at the ground. "I really can't recall anything. I'm very sorry."

When she starts walking again, I kick up my pace to stay beside her. "Did you ever hear him mention my parents, Ed and Sharon Dawson?"

"Those names don't ring a bell either." She rubs her forehead.

I continue talking, telling her how I'm adopted, and my Pops taught me everything I know about restoring homes. "I was wondering if Bo and my adoptive father might've done some construction job together."

"Look, I get the questions. I'd want to know too, but I just don't have any information. Frankly, I was wondering why they left it to you, too."

"Right." I sidestep a mud puddle. Just to make sure, I ask, "So, Bo and his wife didn't have children?"

"No, they didn't."

Then I ask her about the memorial, and although she's seen the tree, she has no idea about the cross. When we get back to the front of the house, Frankie stops walking and holds out the notebook. "Study this. The only thing that has to be done tonight is the goat feeding. It's in the notes."

That sounds easy enough. "On it."

"Then we'll start tomorrow, five-thirty a.m. sharp."

I take the notebook from her. "Thank you, and no problem," I say, as I'm always up by five.

"You'll meet the horses."

Horses. "I'm looking forward to it." I feign a smile, but it falters. "I just have so much to figure out."

"It's a lot, I'll give you that." Frankie's face stays stern.

The bright red Ford reappears and pulls into the driveway. Mary Louise is waving her hand out the window again.

"Christ on a cracker," Frankie mutters.

Mary Louise cuts the engine before hopping out of the truck. She bustles over to me with a pie, saying, "I'm Mary Louise Smith. It's so nice to meet you…" she trails off, waiting for me to fill in the blank.

"Willow." I smile, then add, "Dawson," as she keeps staring.

"I'm your other next-door neighbor." She points down the road, in the opposite direction of Frankie's house. "I just want to welcome you to Lilac Lane, Ms. Dawson." Mary Louise hands me the pie belonging on the cover of a Southern cooking magazine, with bursting ripe apples enveloped in a crust, browned to perfection.

"Wow, thank you. This looks incredible." I take it, excited to have a small piece after dinner.

"It's my famous apple pie." Mary Louise smiles, her bright red lipstick spreading up her face. "I also wanted to let you know that me and my husband, Bill, would love to help you get up to speed in this place." Her eyes dart to Frankie as she lets out a nervous giggle. "After you graduate Frankie's training program, of course."

"That'd be great, thank you," I say, glancing at Frankie. She's giving Mary Louise the side-eye, and my gut tells me to trust Frankie's judgment.

"Wonderful." Mary Louise clasps her hands together, her bright red nails glowing against her pale skin. Then she reaches into her polka-dotted purse for something. "Here's my card," she says, handing it to me. "Call if you need anything at all."

I meet Frankie's gaze, and she shoots me a look that says, "Let me handle this," so I give her a nod. Then Frankie says, "Mary Louise, Willow's gonna need a day or two to get her bearings—I'm sure you understand."

"Of course I do. Well, I gotta git—I'm off to bake some more pies for the Brew and Chew Festival. The Fourth of July is in two days—boy, that came lickety split. Ms. Dawson, you should come and meet the folks of Violet Moon. Celebrate the Fourth."

"Sounds fun."

"Oh, it's a hoot and a half."

When Mary Louise hops in the truck and buzzes away, I exhale.

Frankie bends and plucks a weed out of the ground. "So, you going to restore this place?"

I walk toward her carefully, not wanting my pie to tip. "I'd love that, but I restore apartments, not mansions." And *certainly* not farms.

"Makes sense."

I suck in a shaky breath, managing a smile. It could help turn my business around... *if* I succeeded. If I didn't, I'd likely lose everything. I simply say, "It would be a dream creatively but a potential money pit otherwise."

She slaps her palms together, brushing off the dirt. "Too bad. This old girl could use a lift."

"I wish I could stay." I like it here, and I can't believe I just thought that. I never imagined a place would have such an instantaneous impact on me—it's so beautiful and peaceful. And the air is so fresh with a sweet vanilla smell of something, I wish I knew what. But it seems familiar.

"Things happen for a reason." Frankie folds her arms across her chest. "A fifty-acre farm falling into your lap—it's a cryin' shame not to use your skills on something so special."

"Yeah." I swallow hard, something unfamiliar tugging at my heart. "It really is."

3

House and Home

As soon as Frankie's gone, I make my way into the house, putting Mary Louise's pie in the refrigerator before beelining it to the framed eight by ten professional wedding photo of a twenty-something Bo and Lily—whom I recognize from their obituary pictures. I take it off the wall, flipping it over to see the words, "Lily and Bo Underwood. Married March 18th, 1967" scribbled on it. Lily was pretty—tiny-framed, blond-haired, blue eyes, and milk-skinned with a round face.

I study them to see if they have a familial resemblance to me. Unsure, I bring the photo to the bathroom where I hold it up next to me in the mirror.

Lily's cheekbones seem like mine. I tilt my head sideways, the way her head is. Then I smile like she's smiling, and I think we have the same nostrils.

"I have Lily's facial features." My real smile blooms across my face.

A buzz skitters across my skin, warming me as I brush a finger over the photo. In my twenty-six years, I've never met a soul who had any genetic relation to me. And now, to think I've possibly found two. It's overwhelming and amazing at the same time—the raw, hollow spaces inside me filling with crackling white light. I swallow back the scratch in my throat as I force myself to return the photo to the wall. I think it's really them—my aunt and uncle. Bo stands ramrod straight, just like I do.

I reel myself in. I vowed not to get my hopes up, although Bo didn't leave me a fifty-acre estate for nothing. But still. I need to let it go until I have the results of the DNA tests. I should be getting them anytime—it said five to seven business days, and it's been five. I need to busy my mind with other things.

It's time to feed the goats.

With Fig Newtons stuffed in my back pocket to snack on, I'm in the barn rummaging through every crevice, mumbling, "Feed, feed, feed," but only find cleaning supplies and tools. A scraping on the window makes me jump. "What was that?"

Peering out the window, I don't see anything, which is unnerving. But I've got a job to do, so I continue, stopping to study a large platform with bars beside a food bowl. Is this how I feed them? Imprison them, one by one? "Barbaric," I utter before returning to my exhaustive search until I find what I need deep in the supply closet.

The minute I heave out the feed, the goats are on me like an all-you-can-eat lobster buffet. "Hey, beasts, I can't feed you if I can't move." After wiping the sweat off my brow with a filthy hand, I check the feed's instructions. It tells me that the amount I give to them is determined by body weight. "What the actual hell?"

I glance around for something that looks like a scale, but there's nothing. Frankie didn't leave this in her notes, so I'm back on Google, looking up the average weight of a goat, which gives a range from forty-four to three-hundred and ten pounds. Not. Remotely. Helpful.

A loud pop draws my eyes from my phone. A goat has speared the food bag with his horns, and now, kibbles are gushing out like a brown waterfall. "No!"

It's a free for all—the food disappearing at a frightening pace.

Returning to my Google research, I discover that I could kill the goats if I overfeed them. Swell.

I drag my legs through the chaos and grab the bag, but when I jerk it away, one leaps up like Supergoat and knocks it from my hand, the rest of the kibble flowing through the air like a tidal wave.

The buggers eat every drop off the floor as I watch, helpless. "I dislike this game very much." I fold my arms over my chest as I study the goats for signs of distress. "Please don't die."

When something pinches my behind, I flip around. "You bit my butt!" That rascally baby goat stands there, looking perfectly innocent... holding my package of Fig Newtons in his teeth.

I go to snatch my dinner out of his mouth, but he escapes. By the time I catch him and wrestle the package away, he's got his teeth sunk into the two cookies. I pull at his mouth, trying to pry them out, but his jaw isn't budging, and let's get real—I could lose a finger. So, I let go, and he swallows everything in one gulp.

My pulse kicks up. "Are you like a dog and can't have figs? Have I just killed you?"

He looks up at me, his chin covered in crumbs.

I frantically Google, "Can goats eat Fig Newtons," discovering they're safe in small quantities. Is two considered small?

As I scold the goat, I swear he looks sad. Or is he sick? Ah, crap—I'm going to have to haul him to the vet. He lets out a burp, then perks back up. I exhale a big sigh of relief before I say, "You better not end up worm feed." I decide to name this guy Sir Fig A Lot.

His bleat tells me to chill. An unwelcome breeze on my backside draws my hand to my rear where a pocket hangs off. "Great." I twist around to see a chunk of naked cheek showing. Good thing goats are my only company tonight.

After watching Sir Fig A Lot and the rest of the goats for what feels like eons, I call it. None of them look like they're going to croak, and I'm exhausted, not to mention famished and snackless.

I could eat Mary Louise's pie whole, but not for dinner. Something scrapes the window again, and my breath freezes as my eyes dart to it. It's dark out now, but is that a man's shadowy face I see?

I scream, and then he's gone—leaving only a silhouette of a branch hitting the glass.

Phew. My backwoods-fearing mind's playing tricks on me. When I flip the lights off and open the barn door to leave, Sir Fig A Lot rushes out. "No, you don't!" Using my phone light, I wander into the dark, terror shuddering through. When I spot him halfway back to the house, I lure him into the barn with the Fig Newton wrapper, slamming the door shut behind us. After slowing my breath, I carefully open the door to leave—again.

This time, two of the big goats try to bust out. I stand my ground, backing the door closed again. A win, but I still have to leave.

Screw it.

I head toward the flapped doggie-like door for the goats and crawl out, pushing the beasts back while I go. Once I'm outside, I barely manage to put the cover over the flap.

After I let out a triumphant scream, footsteps rustling in the brush stop me cold. I swallow hard, a shiver rocketing down my spine. What *was* that? A bear? A cougar?

As I peer into the blackness, fear overwhelms me. Flashes of every eighties horror movie I've ever seen flip through my mind until I'm convinced a masked killer is about to leap out of the bramble.

4
The Note

"Willow?" It's Frankie's voice. I open my eyes to see her shadow approaching me. "You okay?"

I exhale a ragged breath before standing and wiping my hands on my jeans. "You scared the Bajesus out of me."

"I dropped off the decorations and wanted to check on things."

I lower my gaze. "I might've overfed the goats. They knocked the bag open."

"They'll be fine—they're tough." She puts her hand on my shoulder and turns me to glance at my backside. "One of them get you?"

"Just the baby. He bit my pocket." I groan. "I didn't get them into the feeding cage."

Her face twists. "Feeding cage?"

"The things with bars and a bowl."

A slow smile spreads across her face. "That 'feeding cage' is for milking." She hitches a thumb backward. "The trough out here is for feeding."

I look to see a long half-pipe thing that has a fence in front of it, probably for them to put their heads in to keep them away from one another. "Ohhh."

Frankie chuckles. "It seems like they've given you a proper initiation."

"You could say that again."

"All right." She steps away. "Good work tonight. I'll see you first thing tomorrow."

"Right." I have to do this again?

We leave the pasture together, and my type-A, hyper-driven personality is nagging me to go to the horse stables after Frankie leaves, but I can't do it. The new, wiser me realizes the damage my novice ass could cause, like a stampede. Let sleeping dogs lie—or in this case, sleeping horses stand.

I'm beyond thrilled to hop in my rental and follow the GPS to the place I'm staying—The Violet Moonlight Inn. Since I didn't know I'd be inheriting this house, I'd already paid for the stay. I might as well use it, at least for tonight.

My room's view is of downtown nestled into the mountains. The silver and lavender decor is cozy yet vogue, and I'm in love with the oversized king bed with the deep purple velvet-tufted headboard. I can't wait to dive in.

After showering, I eat my standard traveling meal—a double chicken salad from McDonald's drive-thru. Then I change into my silk pajamas before hanging my clothes in the closet, arranging them by day.

In the quietness, the cross, the tree, and the inheritance infiltrate my mind, and suddenly, curiosity trumps denial. I sit on the bed with my computer, Googling every variation of "Willow Eloise Dawson," including, "obituary," "death," "car accident," "Pineview Road accident," and so on, finding nothing. Then I do it all again for "Willow Eloise Underwood," and again for "Willow Eloise Sheffield."

Nothing. Desperate, I log in to the records website I'm now a member of, finding no obituary or death record for any of those names. My phone buzzes, and it's my best friend and manager, Natanya, telling me she's ready to FaceTime. I hope all is well at RevitaHome today. And with Tesla, my pet turtle.

Popping onto the screen, Natanya stands by a pole, sweaty, in workout gear.

My brows dive. "Where are you?"

A proud smile takes over her glistening, umber-toned face. "Pole dancing lessons, girl. It's an amazing workout, and I'm upping my game." She does a worm-like wave against the pole.

"You don't need *more* game. You can't remember the names of the guys you've got." At that thought, I ask, "And what happened to Vatican hat guy?" Natanya's latest fling is a chef, who, according to her, has a hat that looks like the Vatican's.

"We sinned." She lowers her voice when she says, "Nine times." She laughs her signature laugh, which is melodic, full-bodied, and contagious—one of the many reasons men fall at her feet. "But it's over. It was just raw, carnal desire."

"I want raw, carnal desire." I stick out my lower lip before I say, "Actually, I did meet a gorgeous guy on the side of the road."

"Did you now?"

"Yes." Then I fill her in on how I inherited the castle, the barley farm, and even Sir Fig A Lot.

Her big brown round eyes go rounder. "So. You met a hot man, and you own a castle. Did I get that right?"

"Yeah, I guess you did."

She sticks the pole between her breasts and lolls her head back. Her screen flips to the ceiling, and she says, "Whoops, dropped the phone, sorry!" After some shuffling, she's back. "Anyway, you need to knock those cobwebs off down there with a romp in the hay. It's been forever since your asshole ex."

"Ugh. Tell me about it."

"Do it." She performs another worm-like roll.

"Wow—you're good. I mean your moves, not your camerawork. Maybe I should take those lessons." I take a gulp of my complimentary crisp, buttery chardonnay—which the front desk attendant told me comes from Blue Vine, Georgia. "But let's not get ahead of ourselves. I'm probably never going to see him again."

"Whatever. I'm so glad you're getting away and having some time for yourself. You're a raging workaholic."

"Aw. There's that flattery of yours. Hold on." I get up and grab baby wipes out of my suitcase and my dirt-crusted heels off the floor. Then I return to the computer scrubbing them, determined to make them good as new. "On that note—I may need more time here." I squeeze my eyes shut, not wanting to see murder etched on her face. When everything's silent, I open one eye to see her looking at me with pride. "What's that face?"

"I'm just so excited for you. I want you to enjoy this once-in-a-lifetime experience."

Natanya's got a heart of gold. She's stood by my side during the good, the bad, and the ugly, always stepping out of the employee role to provide friendship and support.

I say, "You really are the best. So, what's today's report?"

Her eyes glaze over, and my stomach pretzels. When she doesn't move, I say, "I think your screen's frozen." When I see her blink, I gasp. "It's not the screen. It's you. Speak, Natanya. Is Tesla dead?"

"No, Tesla is alive and annoying as ever." Her shoulders drop. "It's the Klein account."

Oh, crap. Klein Homes is going to catapult our business out of the red. "What is it?"

Natanya swallows. "A materials delay put us behind schedule."

Crap. There's *nothing* we can do about that. "Behind meaning a few days?"

"More like a few weeks." She avoids my gaze. "Aston Klein was huffy and told me we should broaden our list of suppliers."

That's fair. "Tell him you'll take off five percent for delivering late." I type into my computer. "Scratch that. I'll call him."

Natanya groans.

I put on my most soothing voice when I say, "You know I love you, but we can't mess this one up, Nat."

"I know. I *know*, Worrywart Willow. Someday, you're going to have to learn to rely on others. You know the Kleins don't like doing business over the phone or email, and I don't want them to think you left town. Plus, you need this break. Please. Just take care of what you need to in Silver Moon."

"Violet Moon."

"Whatever. Let me handle things here. I got it." She bats a hand. "Now, stop arguing with me so I can finish my workout."

I know she's probably right, and although I trust her—in fact, she's the only person I trust—she needs more experience under her belt.

I swallow back the nerves exploding in my gut. If I lose this account, my business is done. "No, let's do quick status Zoom calls with the Kleins. I won't be in person, but they'll see my face. I'll also send them detailed weekly emails. Progress updates, paint selections, finishes, and lighting choices."

"Ten-four, boss." Natanya's smile is sour, but she gives me her standard salute.

There's a knock at the room door, so I say, "You rock," before disconnecting.

I jump up and check the peephole to see Pearl, the front desk attendant, standing there. When I open the door, she smiles when she says, "This came for you." She holds out an envelope.

"Thank you, Pearl." I take it and flip it over to see there's no return address. "Who left it?" I ask, not able to imagine anyone messaging me like this. Very few people know I'm here, and if it was someone local, like Roy, he would've just called.

Pearl shakes her head. "I don't know, I'm sorry. I left the front desk to walk some guests to their room, and when I returned, this was sitting on my computer."

That's odd. Big time. "Okay, thank you."

After closing the door, I turn the crisp envelope over in my hand to see my name typed on it. Sliding a fingernail under the flap, I tear it open with the glue freshly wet. I unfold the piece of plain white paper that only has two sentences typed on it.

Go back to New York. We don't want you here.

5

The New Arrival

Is this for real?

So, they don't want me here. Boo-hoo. Did they actually think this would scare me? When I lived out of my car, every parking attendant within a twenty-mile radius told me they didn't want me there.

Whatever. I don't think I've ever been more exhausted in my life, no exaggeration, and I'm maxing out on my ability to handle the life-altering things coming at me all at once. I don't have time to shut down, so I compartmentalize it while I work on all the emails for Aston Klein. I have a few hours left to finish before lights-out at eleven. I need to be rested when I wake at five, and as far back as I can remember, I've never needed more than six hours of sleep.

But when eleven p.m. hits and I'm lying in the dark, something whispers from deep within my conscience—an inkling I've spent twenty-one years tuning out. That nagging feeling about the unpleasant inconsistencies in my past—like why I have no memory of my life before five years old, when I was adopted. I was in a foster home upstate, but I don't have a single recollection of those days, despite my excellent memory. Pops says I got a head injury from a nasty fall off the monkey bars when I was four and a half, but something about that explanation has never felt quite right. Or why I could never get my original birth certificate, even though in New York, I should've been able to when I turned eighteen.

I have to find clues at Bo's house. There's a logical explanation for everything, and I'm going to figure out what it is, whether an anonymous a-hole wants me here or not. Mercifully, my brain drifts into a nonsensical realm before entering a deep, dreamless sleep.

I'm startled awake by my phone buzzing on the nightstand.

I sit straight up, wondering where I am and why everything is unfamiliar. It takes a beat to remember.

It's an unknown number flashing on my phone screen, but it says it's from Violet Moon, so I answer it with a croaky, "Hello."

"We've got a problem." Frankie's voice is terse.

"What's happening?" I glance at the nightstand clock, which says 1:03 a.m.

"The mare's in labor, and she's struggling. Heard her because I'm sleeping with my window open, thank god. I think the foal is breech."

If breech means the same thing for an animal that it does for a human, this isn't good. My breath freezes in my chest. "What do you need me to do?"

"Both animals could die. Get your skinny butt here. Now." She disconnects.

I fumble around, barely awake, as I fight to tug on my blouse, jeans, and high heeled boots that were *not* designed for farm work or delivering a baby horse. Preparing for this trip, I thought I was inheriting a small piece of land I could list for sale, so I packed for business meetings and hitting the town. I'm beyond grateful for how things turned out, but I definitely need a new wardrobe.

Out of habit, I grab my laptop bag and leave my room. When I make it to the Inn's lobby, I'm disappointed to see there's no coffee out yet. Then I remember—it's a quarter after one in the morning.

But man, I need joe like air.

Hopping into my rental car, I race through downtown with no other vehicles on the road. Then, I haul up the winding hill before tearing into the driveway of the castle. I lock the car doors with the key fob as I'm sprinting to the stables.

When I rush inside, I pass three stalls until I get to the most stunning horse I've ever seen, who's panting, pacing, and letting out neighs of anguish. Her mane is white, but her body is black, which shines under the barn's floodlight above.

She's so majestic, she's almost otherworldly. I love her immediately.

Shaking, I step over and hesitantly stroke her nose—I've never been this close to a horse's face before. Pain fills her huge soulful eyes, and it's utterly heartbreaking. No animal should suffer. I know birth is normal, but there are clear complications, and that makes this almost unbearable.

And where the hell did Frankie go?

"It's okay, girl," I say, but my voice trembles, and I've never felt so helpless. There's literally nothing I can do except Google tips.

As I'm petting the horse with one hand and tapping my screen feverishly with the other, Frankie bursts in with a man, built and beautiful... and very familiar.

"Windowless van guy," I squeak out. He's even hotter without the oil streaks on his cheeks. "What are you doing here?"

"I was just about to ask you the same thing." His face drops in shock as he jangles the bar and chains in his hands.

"Turns out I own the place." The words feel strange coming out of my mouth.

He swallows so hard his Adam's apple bobs. "You're the one who inherited this farm?"

"Owen's a vet. Willow got the farm," Frankie snaps. "Now cut the small talk—two horses' lives are on the line."

Owen rushes toward the mare. "I know, Ma."

Ma? Frankie is Owen's mother?

"Shhh... It's all right, Eclipse," Owen says with a deeper Southern accent than when I met him on the road.

He puts his hands on Eclipse's snout, his face right next to hers. He whispers something to her, and she immediately calms.

I wouldn't believe it if I hadn't seen it myself.

"What is he doing?" I say to Frankie.

Her face glows with pride. "What God put him on this earth to do."

And I've never seen anything like it. As my brain tries to compute all the pieces of information hitting me like paintball pellets, Frankie says, "Go get towels, Willow."

I'm glad to be useful as I beat feet to the house, running so fast my legs burn. When I make it into the bathroom, I plow through the cabinets until I find the stack of towels. A zing of guilt hits—I treated Owen like a B film creeper earlier today, and now, he's helping me with my horse in the middle of the night.

After rushing back to the stables, I enter to see Owen in a surgical gown, gloved up and inside Eclipse, who's standing. He keeps talking to her, calm and soothing, but his face tells a different story. Finally, he looks at Frankie and whispers, "I can't get a hold of the hindlimbs." He reaches deeper, and Eclipse jumps and neighs, stepping away.

"Dammit," Frankie mutters, and my stomach plummets.

After Owen shuffles around to whisper to Eclipse again, the horse calms down. He leads her around the stable, looking at Frankie when he says, "Movement should get the foal to shift." After a stroll around the perimeter of the stall, Owen puts his gloves back on and tells Frankie to hold the chains.

What are *those* for? I shudder.

The creak of the barn door pulls my eyes toward the entry, and I see a little girl, about nine or ten, dressed in thermal footed pajamas. Her tiny face, twisted in terror, glows in the light of a lantern she's holding.

"Hello. Who are you?" I say.

"Oh, no." Frankie scrambles over to the girl before kneeling. "I told you to stay in bed, baby." She takes the child's small hands. "I know you're scared, but your brother's the best vet around. You know that."

"I can be here—I'm not a baby, Ma. I heard you say they might die." The girl's lips quiver, and she's clearly fighting off tears, but she lifts her chin.

I struggle to hold it together.

Frankie runs a hand over the girl's light hair. "Trinity, you can't stay here." Her voice is calm, but it seems she's fighting to keep it that way.

"Take her home, Ma. Willow and I got this." Owen strokes Eclipse's mane.

We do? Is he serious? My stomach goes into free fall.

Owen's voice softens when he says, "Go get some sleep, Trin. You can come and name the foal when you wake up, okay?" His eyes dart to me. "If that's okay with you, Willow?"

"Of course. I'd love that." Through my raging emotions, I muster a smile for Trinity because I *would* love it if she named the foal.

Trinity folds her arms, defiant, but finally bows her head and nods.

Frankie looks at me, her tired eyes filled with concern. "Owen will walk you through it."

"I'll give it my all," I say, resolving myself to do anything and everything I humanly can.

Frankie gives me a curt nod before standing and ushering Trinity home.

The second they're out of earshot, Owen says, "Trinity plays tough, but she's not doing well with Bo's passing. They were tight."

"That's rough."

Eclipse's panting worsens, splitting my heart in two. Owen's tough facade crumbles as panic flashes on his face. "It's been too long. I need to get the foal delivered. Now." He nods at the chains. "Pick those up and have them ready for me when I get a hold of those hindlimbs."

I look at them and my vision fogs. "Chains?"

"Normally, foals are born forelimbs first. In breech, it's the hindlimbs first, and the foal can't come on his own. These are necessary to deliver the animal quickly and save his life." Then Owen mumbles, "*If* he's alive."

Acid rushes up my throat, but I swallow it back. I can't watch this—I can't see a dead baby horse, but I have to help. I force a steady tone when I say, "Got it." As I stand next to Owen, his entire arm disappears into the horse, and I fight back the gag that lurches.

Stay strong. Please let the foal be alive.

Owen pulls, then shifts and pulls, then shifts again. He takes a break, petting Eclipse's hair. When he reaches in again, his arms reappear holding two tiny hooves. I exhale as he takes the chains from me and puts them around the foal's ankles.

Another gag hits, but I close my eyes until it settles.

Then Owen yanks the triangles attached to the chains, slowly coaxing the hind legs out, along with some blood and other unsightly things I fight not to see.

As he works, I stand still, wishing I could say that I was as calm and collected as I appear on the outside, but I'm not. Inside, my ears ring, my vision's blurry, and I feel like I'm coming apart at the seams.

I'm not watching, but I still can't bear the thought of what these gentle animals are going through.

My skin grows cold, and I'm trying to catch my breath when Owen says, "Willow, stay with me, okay? I need you to pull while I reach in and make an adjustment." His steely eyes—which I realize he got from his mother—meet mine. "You got this."

I nod but can't find my words. I focus on my job—gripping the two triangular bars—as I try to steady my trembling knees. When he gives me the go-ahead, I pull it until he orders me to stop.

Eclipse lets out another neigh—a cry of pain, and she kneels to the ground.

Owen and I kneel along with her.

"Just keep going, Willow. Eclipse is tired—this is normal."

I don't believe him, but I keep going.

Closing my eyes, I focus on tuning out the sounds, the sights, and the smells that come with birth. If I let them in, I'm going to be sick, pass out, or both.

When the foal's hind legs are finally out, Owen gives Eclipse a hard pat to get her to stand again. "I need her up because something's stuck."

Eclipse obeys, fighting to rise.

"You got this. Good girl," I say, giving her a soft, proud pat.

Then it takes both of us to hold the foal's body, which is half out. On Owen's count, we both pull. I don't pray often, but I'm praying now. It has to work.

It doesn't.

The foal's legs start thrashing violently. "That's a good sign, right? That the baby's alive?"

"No," Owen barks, his tone panicked. "It means he's struggling. We're losing him."

"Oh, God." A fresh wave of panic buzzes through me, sweat beading on my brow as tears glisten in my eyes.

Owen's broad shoulders drop. "The forelimbs and head are stuck on the umbilical cord. Dammit." His voice is terse but calm. "I need to get them off. Fast."

"Okay." I hold on to the baby, keeping my gaze moving along the details of the stable—the beams, the heavy oak doors painted white, the troughs, which need filling.

"I'm untangling the cord," he says, more to himself. "Willow, come back to me."

I force myself to look at Owen, who's ready for me to pull again, so I take a wide stance for balance. I accidentally look at Eclipse, and her eyes are gray, drooping.

"We're doing this one more time, and we're doing this right, okay?" His jaw tenses. "Otherwise, I'm going to have to perform a Cesarean without the proper tools. Not to mention I'll be delivering a dead foal."

"Last time," I repeat. "I'll give it all I've got."

And I do. So does Owen.

6

The Search

❋

We pull in tandem, so hard my arms tremble, and I hope with everything in me I'm not killing the baby or hurting Eclipse. Finally, I see the head, and I grunt out a ragged breath.

"Almost there." Owen guides the foal the rest of the way out, and together, we lower her to the ground.

"She's blinking!" I cry out, my eyes misting. Her rib cage grows and shrinks with her gulps of breath as she lies still.

I sit in silence as Owen moves quickly, rubbing the foal with a towel before shifting her around.

When she squirms, he releases her. Then, when she fights to balance on her twiggy legs, I say, "She's trying to stand. That's a good sign, right?"

"She's a he, but yes, it is." Owen's voice crackles with emotion. "That's a good boy."

I hold back the sob that's bubbling in my chest, but a tear escapes. I furiously blink it away.

I rarely cry. Doing everything in my power to stop, I focus on what's in front of me.

A new life—who barely made it—struggles to stand, so innately beautiful and pure. And he's supremely cute with those eyes, way too big for his small face. At the same time, he's blinking as he looks at us, trying to figure out this wild new world he's entered.

Eclipse struggles, but she approaches her baby before licking him. The foal continues to fumble around until he finally stands on his wobbly legs.

I gasp, letting another tear fall off my cheek. "He did it."

"Yes, he did."

Now, all Owen and I can do is watch in awe as nature does its miracle. There's just perfect love filling the air around us.

"Amazing," I whisper, the word catching in my throat. "He's gorgeous." He's got a white mane and black hair, just like his mother.

"Yeah, he is. They're purebred Gypsy Vanner horses." Owen studies the colt. "He's got a mild case of contracted tendons in his forelimbs, but that can be fixed. I'm just glad he's alive."

"No kidding." I meet Owen's gaze, and we exchange proud glances. His expression is one of unbridled joy, a beautiful look on him, his long lashes showing in the bright lighting. He's so tall and muscular, it's hard to believe he's the one who whispers to animals, literally.

And that's outrageously cool. I'm still trying to take in everything that just happened, and my emotions are changing by the second. I can't keep away the glaze in my eyes, so I stop trying. "How do we keep finding ourselves in tight situations?" I run a clammy palm over my face. "I feel like I already know you."

"Me too. And I'm glad. Twelve hours ago, you thought I was a serial killer. Was it the white windowless van?"

"You think?"

He scrubs his chin. "Yeah, it's for my animals, but it's not a good look."

A weak laugh escapes. "Nope." I look around to see spots appearing in my glossy vision. Sweat films my face.

Owen grins, but it falls away. "You look like a ghost."

And then, as though my mind has finally relaxed enough to listen to my body, my stomach rebels, churning like I ate bad fish. "Not okay."

I dart out the stable doors, my heels clicking on the cement, and yak into a bush.

Owen's right behind me. "You gonna live, Manhattan?" he asks.

"I'm from Queens," I manage to say, squeezing my eyes shut. "I think I'm okay now." My stomach feels like it's empty, at least.

"Let's get ourselves over to the horse shower." He takes off his surgical gown.

I don't know what that is, but I say, "Fantastic."

Behind the stable is a gigantic cedar-walled roofless shower with a bench, several faucets, and a huge overhead panel that has multiple nozzles. There are side nozzles and faucets too. It's the type of system that I've seen installed by luxury outdoor pools. "Bo got this to wash the horses."

I nod, but don't have the strength for words.

Together, we use the mid-level nozzle to clean our arms and faces with one of the many liquid soaps there. It seems like it should feel like too intimate an activity to do with someone I just met, but it's not. Maybe because I'm too out of it to care.

Owen puts a hand on my back. "We should get you inside to rest. I've got it from here."

I nod, and he puts his arm around me as he walks me back to the house. By the time we arrive, I feel better. Maybe it was the cold water on my face. Maybe it was the fresh air. Maybe it's the gorgeous man holding me up. Maybe it's all the above.

We make our way inside the castle where he fetches me a glass of water as I go and brush my teeth with my fingers and use mouthwash. When I return and start to sit on the couch, I decide against it because my shirt is filthy. It reminds me of what just happened, and it's surreal.

Owen puts the glass on the end table. "Here—my shirt is clean. Why don't you take it for now?"

"That'd be great."

He unbuttons his short-sleeved pocketed flannel before slipping it off. Through the slits in my tired eyes, I take in his magnificent chest—carved, tan, so touchable. There's a scar just under his pec that runs under his arm, and my fingers itch to travel along the trail of mottled skin. I want to ask what happened, but Owen says, "Willow?"

I blink, finally noticing that he's holding out his shirt. "Oh, thank you." I take it before turning around to slide off my blouse. When I put on his flannel, I love being surrounded by his smell of cedar, soap, and warm skin.

When I'm done, Owen hands me the glass. "You've got two hours to sleep before the farmhands arrive."

"Two hours." That sounds like a dream. I take a swig of water, then lie down on the couch.

Owen carefully puts a throw blanket over me, then brushes a wisp of hair off my face. He's so *not* a B film creeper, and if I wasn't falling asleep, I'd be dying to kiss him. Which is my last thought before I drift away.

I wake to my phone alarm chirping, and I sit up straight, wondering, again, where I am. When I remember, I get up and head to the coffeemaker.

It's five a.m., and I have thirty minutes to get my brain functioning. I manage to find all the supplies for coffee, then make myself a cup before heading into Bo's office. I walk inside, inhaling the smell of old books and leather. Bo's laptop sits neatly on the desk, and I eye it nervously. That thing might give me the answers I so desperately need.

A glorious and terrifying thing.

I sit at the desk and power up the laptop, running my hand over the copper cap rivets of the arms of the leather chair. I stare at the blank screen, fear tempting me to walk away. But I know I can't do that.

I remind myself that I always push forward, even when it's hard. That's what I do.

When the welcome screen appears, a prompt for a password shows up along with it.

Ugh. Of course, it's asking for a password!

I groan as I check under the keyboard before shuffling through the drawers of Bo's desk. Office supplies sit neatly in trays—pens, pencils, Post-its, a stapler, and paper-clips, like most offices. But unlike most offices, there is no paperwork, no files, no notebooks. Only a stack of plain white paper that goes into the printer.

How did Bo get by with no filing? And why? The more I search, the more desperate I get, but I find nothing. And I don't have the first clue on how to break into a computer. Regardless, I try, "password123," Bo's birthday, then Lily's birthday. But I stop because I don't want to get locked out.

I sigh, scrubbing my head. I know I must want answers, despite my earlier hesitation, as my cheeks burn with growing frustration that I can't log in.

I stare at the password prompt as though Bo will whisper it to me from the grave.

But I don't dare another attempt, and I have only twelve minutes left before I have to meet Frankie. I grit my teeth, desperation blooming inside me. I leap up, finding myself in a frenzied search through the rows of Bo's aging books. The only thing I come across of interest is an album, placed between the other books, like it's nothing special. The first picture is that same wedding photo of Bo and Lily, so I continue to flip through the pages, seeing the couple on a tropical beach vacation, probably for their honeymoon. I keep going until I find something that makes my heart stop beating entirely.

One of the sleeves contains a ring.

Maybe the one Roy couldn't find?

With unsteady fingers, I shake it out before running my fingers over the many tiny diamonds, set in platinum—and arranged in the shape of a willow tree.

7

The Helper

The ring fits perfectly on my right-hand ring finger, and I absolutely love it. Soon, I'm going to find out if this ring belonged to my aunt. Or maybe she's a cousin?

Anyway, time's up.

With butterflies flitting around in my gut, I make my way to the pasture with my trusty tablet tucked away in the oversized pocket of Owen's shirt, my knees unsteady and my boots sinking into the ground wet from the dew—again. I *really* need a free minute to run into town for different shoes and clothes.

I see Frankie waiting for me in front of the barn, and she's got an extra pair of boots with her. She holds them up. "You a size seven?"

I smile, my cheeks warming from the kind gesture. "I am, actually."

"Then you've got a new pair of kicks."

"Thank you so much." I head over and sit on a five-gallon bucket as I put on the boots, which are nicely broken in. "And thanks so much for helping me—yesterday and today. It's been quite a ride."

"Owen said you did good in the delivery. I appreciate you."

I stand, adjusting my feet into the new boots. "I gave it my all." That's the best response I can muster, considering I yakked and almost passed out. I have a feeling Owen probably didn't tell her about those parts.

"Let's get started. I have to leave at one—I've got mother-of-the-bride dresses to try on." Frankie groans. "Lord help me."

"I'm more of a jeans and heels kind of woman myself."

Frankie grabs the shovels resting against the barn door. "I told Kayla that we're getting a durable dress. I've got a son and two other daughters, and I'm not getting another one, so it better last."

I don't believe that for a second. Frankie plays it tough, but if her children wanted her to wear something else to their weddings, I bet she would.

Frankie holds out a shovel. "Let's scoop shit."

I take it. "Sounds delightful."

After we do some basic cleanup in the barn, she walks me to the garage where the heavy equipment is parked. There, she introduces me to the farmhands—all three teenage boys doing the work as a summer job. Two manage the field work and one, Huck, Mary Louise's son, tends to the grounds and pasture.

I take detailed notes to pass on to the next caretaker, along with processes of working a grain farm, which are all new to me.

While Frankie and I feed the goats, she gives Sir Fig A Lot a head scratch when she says, "The fence has a loose board that needs fixin'. This kid keeps getting out."

"That doesn't surprise me in the least." I line the buckets of feed up against the wall. "Sir Fig A Lot's a crafty bugger."

"That he is." Frankie puts a hose in the watering tank, and the goats surround it, obviously thirsty. She says, "I reckon you shouldn't be naming the animals given you're leaving in a few weeks."

"True, but I couldn't help it. I'm sure the new owners can give him a different name if they wish."

She scowls. "That's bad luck. Make sure they know that the kid's got a name."

I take out my tablet and tap the screen with the stylus pen. "It's in my notes."

Then we make our way to the stables, and I can't wait to be near the horses—which, I realize, is a hundred-and-eighty-degree change from how I felt yesterday evening. I find the colt suckling from Eclipse, who looks tired, but well. I'm so glad to see mother and baby both thriving.

Frankie darts toward the new addition, breaking into a broad smile, something I haven't seen from her. "Well, hello, sweet boy. You're just as handsome as your papa." She looks at me before pointing to the stunningly big and beautiful black horse in the adjacent stall. "Blackjack is the daddy, and I like animals more than humans."

I chuckle. "I see that. I can also understand why."

Frankie and I get busy. She shows me where the supplies are kept. She teaches me that most horses just graze on the pasture, but ones that are ridden a lot or pregnant need alfalfa hay, which is full of nutrients and protein. The stables require elbow grease, which I'm used to in my line of work, mostly. With my job, there's a lot of dirt, and a whole lot of dust, but none of the manure.

At the end of the long morning, Frankie says, "You're a natural."

"Thank you." I feel a sense of accomplishment as I look around the place, which will soon sparkle. However, I can't help but notice the gaps in the windows, the cracks in the walls, and the water stains on the ceiling from leaks. "This stable needs repairing. The roof needs new shingles and fixing the cracks and holes will help keep the heat out in the summer and the cold out in the winter."

She nods. "That'll be good to get done before fall and the heavy rains hit, although in the summers, we still get a shower every afternoon."

I don't like the idea of the horses being cold or wet, and the materials are something I can afford, out of pocket. "I'll just make the repairs myself. We need to make sure the place is in good shape with the new colt."

Frankie's mouth curves, a glint in her eyes. "I think that's a fine idea."

Owen arrives, and my heart skitters. Which is pure ridiculousness—I need to get a hold of myself.

A difficult task given that he's smiling at me as he heads toward Eclipse and the baby. "I'm here to take the colt through his rehab and give him his shots."

Both Frankie and I watch Owen as he talks to the foal, stroking his mane. I'm glad Frankie doesn't get on me for not cleaning because I've decided I love watching Owen work.

His warmth. His gentle but stern way. The love he has for the animals, which just seems to seep from his pores. I could do this all day long.

Which I should *not* do.

It seems Frankie has the same thought because she says, "If you can lean, you can clean."

"Right." I point at her. "I'm gonna use that one." I march over to the wall where various reins sloppily hang on pegs before taking them off and re-looping each.

Trinity makes her way into the stable carrying sandwiches. "Lunch is here," she says, before handing me one and Frankie the other.

For a split-second, I wonder why Trinity isn't in school, until I remember that it's summer. "Thank you." I flash her a bright smile. This hard work really drives up my appetite.

"I hope you like turkey and cheese, because you need to eat." Trinity's sweet yet insistent voice makes her seem like an adult trapped in a kid's body.

"I love turkey and cheese." My heart feels like it's actually growing in my chest. Here I am with three people I've known less than a day, and somehow, they feel like family. They're feeding me, putting blankets over me, teaching me. I've had more familial interaction in the last twenty-four hours than in the last ten years since my parents died.

My Pops would love this family, one of dirty hands and clean consciences. Although, I haven't met them all since Owen has two more sisters, and a father, who I haven't heard anyone mention. I wonder if he's in the picture?

As soon as Frankie and I wash up and take the sandwiches, Trinity runs up to the colt and puts her arms around him. Then she stands beside him, petting him, slowly and patiently, like she could do it forever.

Clearly, this is her happy place.

When Owen's done checking Eclipse, he saunters over to Trinity, saying, "So, have you thought of a name yet?"

She nods enthusiastically. "Yup. Oreo."

I bust up with Owen. Frankie isn't laughing when she says, "Good god. Now, we've got a goat named Sir Fig A Lot and a purebred Gypsy Vanner named Oreo."

"It's clever. I love it." I wink at Trinity.

Trinity breaks into a proud grin, and I realize how completely adorable she is. The freckles sprinkled across her delicate nose accent her bright eyes and flowing strawberry blond hair. "Welcome to the family, Oreo." Trinity gives his head a good pat.

I swallow hard, getting sentimental. Somehow, I need to make sure that Trinity continues to see the horses after I sell the place. I'll do my best to get that worked out in the contract, but I don't want to say anything until it's a promise I can keep.

Concern flashes in Owen's eyes, but he blinks it away. "We should take some pictures and send them to Nia at *The Meddling Moon*. She'll want to report that there's a new colt in town."

Since I'm a decent photographer, I snap pictures, mostly of Trinity overjoyed to be holding Oreo. I get Frankie with the horse, but Owen refuses. What's up with that?

When Frankie leaves to go dress shopping, she takes Trinity with her.

With them gone, Owen says, "Do you need a hand at the farm for the rest of the afternoon? I'm around, and I'll be dead before I go dress shopping."

I hate to pass up free help, especially when the help looks as good as he does, but I don't want to put him out. "Thanks for the offer, but I'm actually going to make some repairs."

His mouth curves. "That's right. You have mechanically inclined, super handy hands. But I'd still like to help—I could learn from you. Things always need repairing."

"Maybe you could take me to the hardware store?" I raise a brow. "Show me around a bit?"

He shifts on his feet. "I'd love to do that, but I can't." He exhales out a jagged breath. "I'm actually trying to lie low in Violet Moon. Just for a few more days."

My curiosity piques. "And why is that?"

After a quick trip to the hardware store and MoonMart for some work clothes, I'm in the stable making a plan for the repairs. I told Owen that it'd be tomorrow before I needed his help, which was a lie—I could definitely use an extra set of hands today. But he's got so much going on, I felt guilty taking up his time.

As it turns out, he's in hiding as he's in negotiations to take over Violet Moon's vet hospital. Dr. Thompson is retiring, and Owen doesn't want the local rumor mill to explode until it's a done deal. Right now, Owen's living in Atlanta, but he's meeting with Dr. Thompson in three days, on Friday, to finalize the details. At that point, Owen will make an appearance because he has to—his sister's rehearsal dinner is that night. And I can't stop thinking about the fact that he's moving back to Violet Moon for good.

My brain keeps going there without my permission, and it shouldn't because it doesn't impact my life one bit.

On the roof, I replace the loose shingles, and it's sweltering with the sun beating down on the black roofing—worse than a packed subway station in August. I'm not used to this humidity, and worse, I forgot to bring up water, which I need ASAP. I'm stepping to the ladder to get some when Owen's head pops up—carrying two water bottles.

"What are you doing here?" My eyes bulge.

"You're not gonna last long in this heat. You need an extra set of hands to work quickly." He holds up the jugs. "And you definitely need water."

Owen Brooks just showed up for me—and in the best way possible. I feel a burning bright happiness, like the infernal sun above. And he's right—I'm going to end up with heat stroke.

"Thank you," I say, relief rushing around the words. I take the water bottle.

"You're very welcome."

After I show Owen what to do, it isn't long before his white shirt is see-through from sweat, and I'm definitely enjoying the view.

"So, how did the high heel wearing queen of Queens become such an impressive expert at roof shingling?" Owen jambs his cat's paw under a shingle and pops it loose.

"I've been working on houses since I was a kid. It's just something I always knew I wanted to do." I pump my shirt to try and cool off. It's useless. "And I love it, mostly. I don't particularly care for roofing."

"I don't blame you one bit there." He hesitates, cocking his head. "So, how did you know Bo?"

I groan. I already hate this question, but I'm prepared to tell people that Bo knew my father, which is my best guess. Except I don't want to give Owen just that placating answer. "Well, I'm adopted, and I have no idea who my biological parents are, so I could possibly be related to him. I'm waiting on the DNA test results now. Or Bo spent some time in New York, so he could've known my adoptive father."

Owen blinks, his face softening. "That's a lot to unpack."

"You have no idea."

"Can I help?"

I rub my thumb over the back of Lily's ring. "Do you know anything about Bo and Lily before they came to Violet Moon?"

"Not really. I know they moved from Atlanta. Bo wanted a slower pace, and he couldn't wait to design the new buildings downtown. Lily was quiet and kept to herself. She liked to read, especially after she got sick and lost her mobility. Loved the farm and the horses. Both good people."

I sigh, holding out my hand. "I found this."

Owen leans over, studying the piece of jewelry. "Oh, yeah—that's Lily's wedding ring." He looks up at me, his face paling. "And it's a willow tree."

"Yes," I whisper.

"Shit."

"Right." I bend and pick up my water bottle before taking a big swig. "I'm searching for any clues that explain how I'm tied to Bo and Lily. Let me know if you think of anything that might be useful."

"I will." As if taking a cue from me, Owen chugs his water, too. "I'll ask Ma, too. She and Lily were close."

"I'd appreciate that—but can you do me a favor and wait until after your sister's wedding? Your mom's got enough on her plate."

"All right." The corner of his mouth quirks. "But it sounds like you need to stay longer. Figure out your roots. Give this place the care it needs before listing it."

"I wish I could." I explain my situation with the Klein account and Natanya, who hopefully hasn't fired most of the field crew by now—they're a handful. Then I ask, "So, you're ready to come back to Violet Moon for good?"

He wipes his brow. "I like Atlanta. It was great for the time I was there—I got to live the big-city life. Take advantage of the museums, theaters, and all the cool bars and clubs. I got my fill of dating and hookups, but at the end of the day, my heart is here, along with my family. So, when Mr. Thompson called me, I said I'd meet with him."

"Makes sense." I love that Owen's got the experience of a city boy but is a country boy at heart.

I continue prying up the old shingle nails, and when I'm done, I stand to get replacements. My foot slides, taking my body with it. My heart leaps, but in a flash, Owen's got his arms around me.

We're both dreadfully sweaty, but I don't care. All it does is make me want to peel off our wet clothes. With my pulse still thudding in my ears, I turn and meet his gaze. "Thanks. We should be wearing spiked shoes, but I don't have any."

"I'll remind you I'm a vet. If you fall and break a leg, I'll have to shoot you."

I bust into a laugh. "Aw, we're not that high up. I know how to slide and hang before dropping. I'd just sprain an ankle or something."

He shakes his head, sighing. "You're something else."

Once we put in the new shingles and add a dab of roofing cement over each surface nail, we're done. Amen.

Then, we move into the stables where we caulk the cracks. While that dries, we put sealant around the windows to keep out the draft. Owen has a genuine interest in learning how to do these things, and I certainly don't mind being his teacher.

I find the trim and door paints stacked neatly in the closet, and I decide we should put a coat over the caulking so everything's matched and sealed. While we work, I learn that Owen hates beer, something frowned on in Violet Moon, had a pet hedgehog named Onion growing up, and enjoys fixing up old cars.

As Owen starts to paint, I get back to my list of to-dos: talk to a real estate agent. Get photos of the estate so I can get it listed. Find any other repairs that I can do easily that could increase the resale value of the place. Make sure the Kleins get daily progress reports.

When I'm done with that, I notice Owen's touching up the white barn doors with the wrong color. "Hey, Owen, you're painting those gray."

"Dammit." He stands and grabs the can. Looking at it, he says, "It says white."

I glance at the can to see that he's right. "It's mislabeled." My face puzzles. "Can't you see that it's gray?"

"No, I actually can't. I'm colorblind."

"Ohhh." I nod, thinking back.

"Yup. That's why I was wearing neon socks yesterday. I thought they were white. My sisters love to screw with me."

"Got it." I purse my lips to keep a smile away. I was wrong—he wasn't making an ironic fashion statement yesterday... and it makes me like him even more.

By the time we finish, the sun is low in the sky, and we're dirty, sweaty, and covered in splotches of paint.

"It's suppertime," Owen says. "You want to come over? Ma makes a great lamb stew."

I never interfere with people's family time, and since my folks died, I'm out of practice with close-knit gatherings and small talk.

But I like the idea of what could happen between Owen and me afterward. Maybe a walk. Maybe a star-filled visit to the lake. I think about what Natanya said, and I envision him slipping all my clothes off as we stand on the balcony with the stunning view of the water and mountains. My body pressed up against his, the moonlight reflecting off the curves of his muscles.

But I can't go there with him, can I? Our fling would last twelve days, just enough time for me to hurt and get hurt when I leave. It pains me, but I say, "Thank you for the offer, but I should go get some groceries and my stuff from The Violet Moonlight Inn. I want to stay at this house, which will save me a bunch of money. Plus, I love it here." That's not a lie. I *do* love it here, except alone, at night. But I have to get over that.

He swipes a hand over his mouth. "Right. You haven't had a second to settle in."

"It's been quite the twenty-four hours. I'd really like to brush my teeth with an actual toothbrush."

He gives me a salute before leaving. As I watch that body walk away—with a confident swagger—I wonder if I'll really make it eleven more days without touching him. Or if I should bother trying.

Natanya has a point—I haven't been with anyone since Seth and I broke up six months ago, and maybe this would be good for me. I'm on a search for the truth about my past for hell's sake—that merits a nice stress-relieving distraction.

I'm headed to the castle when I notice that the setting sun is casting shades of pinks and salmons over the horizon, so I make a detour to the lake.

Which is all mine. I mean, how does one person own a whole lake? It's small, but still. It's a *lake*.

I spot the most perfect lookout point, just up the hill, so I hike it, thrilled when I turn around. The water shimmers as the setting sun reflects on the waves, and the cattails in the marsh are swaying in the breeze. The evening air has turned crisper, perfect, and it all reminds me of the summers my Pops and I spent restoring houses along the Maine countryside. I knew from the time I was little that I wanted to help him out, and I wish we'd had more years to do that.

I take in the moment, nostalgia making me feel Pops' presence around me. He's pointing at the marsh and telling me that if I look closely, I'll probably spot some frogs. Sure enough, I'd usually find one or two, which I loved.

I'd do anything for just one more moment with him.

Sometimes, you don't get more chances. Everything can slip through your fingers in an instant—I should know that better than anyone. That's why the next time I have a chance to be with Owen, I'm going to take it.

I head inside and throw the primary bed's sheets and blankets into the laundry. I'm ready to drive to the Inn so I can collect my things and check out before grabbing groceries from MoonMart.

After finding my purse on the kitchen island, I dig through it for my keys. When I don't find them, I end up dumping out the whole thing, going through every zipper. No dice.

That's odd—I always put my keys in the same pocket of my purse, so I never misplace them. I've become a stickler about these kinds of things. At the thought, a rope of fear twines around me. I've experienced lapses in memory, and not just before I was adopted. For a short while, after my parents died, I started forgetting basic things. I'd get groceries and forget, so I'd buy them again. I'd leave items in odd places and misplace things.

I remind myself that it's been an impossibly long twenty-four hours. I end up retracing every step I made through the house—the office, the laundry room, the kitchen, the living room, and even end up back in the stables.

I can't find the keys anywhere, and I'm getting nervous. The car is a rental, and god knows what the fee is to replace them, not to mention that the car came from Atlanta. I *have* to find these keys.

For the second time, I check around the coffeemaker and find nothing. Out of utter desperation, I open the refrigerator door even though I got nothing out of there.

I blink. My keys are sitting there on the top shelf by Mary Louise's pie, which I haven't touched.

Shudders rack my entire body. What the hell?

I sink to the floor and bury my face in my hands. "This isn't happening. This can't be happening."

Maybe half asleep, making coffee, I got in the refrigerator, looking for supplies? But I don't use creamer. But maybe I was confused? Then, for some reason, set my keys in there?

I'm straining my brain to remember something, *anything*, but nothing comes to mind.

Please tell me this isn't happening to me again.

8
Cut The Cheese

◆❖◆

After returning to the castle where I cleaned and stocked the fridge and cabinets, I made my mom's Italian spaghetti and meatballs, getting it reasonably right. I'll never make the dish as good as she did. It's just not in my blood.

Now, I'm back at Bo's desk, peering out the window. The silhouette of tree branches whipping in the breeze is the only thing visible in the darkness, which is unnerving. It reminds me of the face I thought I saw outside the barn, but maybe it was nothing. Anyway, I refuse to let any of it keep me from doing what I need to do.

I open my laptop and power it up. When I see what's in my inbox, my throat goes bone dry.

There's an email with the results of Bo's, Lily's, and my DNA tests.

I sit frozen for a moment, staring at the bolded message, unopened. What is it going to mean for me? I could—no, I *will*—know who some of my family members are.

My heart thuds in my ears as I click on the results, sure of what I'm going to see. Are Bo and Lily going to be my aunt and uncle? My cousins? First, second, third? Will it be on Bo's side or Lily's? My fingers tremble as I log into my account, entering my password wrong twice because of nerves.

The page takes forever to load, or it feels like it, as jitters needle my body and bring my cheeks to a boil. When the page finally appears on the screen, I blink. I can't believe my eyes, so I blink again.

It says that Bo and I share zero percent of DNA.

Zero. Meaning we are not related, even distantly. So, I have to be related to Lily.

But when I click on the results of Lily's, it's the same. Zero percent DNA.

"No," I croak. Nausea rolls through me like a wave, and I look away from the screen, as if it'll make the truth disappear. Instead, I stare at my fingers on the keyboard, trying to figure out why I feel like I just got a swift kick in the gut. I'm not related to Bo or Lily.

This means that, again, I have no explanation for this inheritance. My missing adoption papers. Nothing.

I thought that was the main reason I wanted them to be my family, but by the ache in my heart, I know it isn't. Since my parents died, I've been okay with living my life alone, but right now is the first time I feel lonely. I'm lost, floating and untethered.

Which is silly because this is exactly how I was before I'd ever heard about Bo and Lily. But after being here and learning about who they were—*feeling* who they were—it's different.

I'm grieving the loss of strangers.

I run my hand over Lily's wedding ring, and it looks beautiful, which infuriates me.

"What's the point?" I scream, slamming my laptop shut. Suddenly, I'm frantic.

I hurry to the basement, where I plan to look for any paperwork. But I'm not hopeful—during the tour Roy Livingston gave me, I'd seen the place, and it was completely empty. But I have to do something right now. Anything.

After flying down the stairs and clicking on the light, I wander around. It's so odd—a vast space with a wine storeroom, a bar with a kitchenette, a living area, and another bedroom, all with nothing in it. There's not a knickknack or piece of furniture anywhere to be found.

I check every nook, closet, and cabinet to see if that's where Bo's records are stored.

I find nothing.

Defeated and bone-dead exhausted, I stagger upstairs to the primary bathroom. It has its original cast iron clawfoot tub with a sky view above, which, right now, is filled with stars.

I want to take a soak, but I'm too tired. Or maybe too defeated. Instead, I hop in the shower before moving on to my facial scrub and moisturizing routine. After brushing my teeth for a full minute, I wipe the counter and arrange my toiletries neatly on the bathroom sink counter. I have to try to control *something*.

I crawl into bed, and after clicking off the lamp, I stare at the ceiling, studying the slated pattern of moonlight through the shutters. I hoped this trip would bring me long-awaited answers about where I came from, and why I was placed for adoption. Maybe it would dull the permanent yearning, just beneath my lungs, to find out something, *anything*, about my biological parents.

When I was little, I'd imagine they were both undercover agents who gave me away to protect me from the bad guys, and that someday, they'd come find me when it was safe. When I grew old enough to realize that was absurd, I became infuriated at them. How could they let me go? Never wonder if I was okay? Weren't they curious about me? Like how my eyes appear hazel or blue, depending on the clothes I wear. Or how I have this addiction to spicy food and loathe scratchy sheets, being late, and excuses.

The years wore on, and my fury at them faded to an ache, thrumming in the background of my life, sometimes loudly, sometimes faintly, but always there. Guilt hits like a wrecking ball—from my earliest memories, my adoptive parents gave me every morsel of love they had. Why wasn't that enough? It should've been—it should've been everything.

I'm desperate for answers, but all I have is more questions. And, somehow, heartbreak to boot.

It's the ass crack of dawn when I complete a new purchase order report for the Kleins and email it off before making my way into the pasture. One of the farmhands is already here and getting on the combine. "Morning, Levi."

"Mornin', Ms. Dawson." He waves but doesn't meet my eyes. He's got a cigarette in his mouth and one tucked behind his ear.

He scrambles away without another word. This kid is polite but acts like he's hiding something. With that said, he seems to have a strong work ethic, staying late last night and now arriving first thing. Maybe he's just shy.

I walk into the barn to make sure Sir Fig A Lot hasn't found trouble. *Yeah, right.* But from now on, I'm here to get the place sold, period. No more digging for information on my past—I've done all my heart can handle.

I blink in surprise when I see a stunning woman, winter-wheat blond hair and porcelain skin, about my age, milking one of my goats.

"Hey, there," I say, wringing my hands. "Can I help?"

Her head darts up. "Oh, hey there. I'm sorry! I didn't mean to intrude." She stands and brushes her hands on her jeans. "I'm Dakota, your milk buyer. Since Bo passed, I've been helping Frankie with the goats. We've been waiting for somebody to take over the farm, but I didn't know you were here."

"It's okay. You were just doing your job." I smile, walking over and extending my hand. "I'm Willow."

Dakota smiles, showing off a perfect set of teeth and a dimple when she says, "It's nice to meet you."

"Nice to meet you, too. This is all new to me, so I'm happy you're here to help. I actually have no idea how to milk a goat."

Her bright smile grows. "Come on, I'll show you." She waves me over to the goat, who's on that prison platform gobbling food pellets from the tray in front of her. Dakota waves a palm, saying, "Willow, meet Darling, Darling, meet Willow."

"Hi, Darling. It's nice to learn your name." I approach the goat and give her a pet. I'm pretty sure she's Sir Fig A Lot's mother, but there's one other female goat, so I'm uncertain. "So, what do you do with the milk? I mean, after you buy it?"

"I make cheese. I own the shop, Cut the Cheese, in downtown." She sits on the stand and positions her hands on the teats.

"I saw that place! And I wanted to stop there." I stand beside her. "I figured whoever owned it had my kind of humor."

"That's me." She raises her hand, but then returns her focus to the goat, telling me how to properly clean her underbelly and do a couple of pumps to the ground first to get a clean squirt. Then, she positions her hands on the udder. "Take your thumb and pointer finger and squeeze the teat. If you don't pinch, the milk'll just go straight back into the udder. Then you use the rest of your fingers to pump." She does just that, and milk sprays into the tin can below. "Now you try."

"Oh." My eyes pop. "Sure." I reach over and grab the teats, like she said, surprised by their softness. It takes a few times, but I finally get out a small spray. "You better take over, or we'll be here all day."

She does, and as she works, she says, "I've been busy expanding my business. The breweries in town carry my cheeses, and I've even got a line in MoonMart. I'm hoping to get into some stores in Atlanta, but that's down the road."

"How exciting! And who doesn't love goat cheese?" I mean my words. I can't imagine doing that as a career, but it sounds awesome. "I have my own business, too. In restoration."

"No kidding." She looks at me. "So, you're a badass."

"I wouldn't go that far."

"I would." She stops what she's doing and grabs a spray can. "Now that I'm done milking, I spray this on each teat. It's an antibacterial solution that also closes off the milk holes. This is so when the goat rolls in the dirt, it keeps bacteria away and prevents mastitis. You do *not* want that."

"Wow, thank you. I never would've had any idea how to do any of this."

"My pleasure." She stands, taking her bucket of milk. "This is three-fourths of a gallon, which is a good amount for two goats. My deal with Bo was to pay by the gallon—I can show you the contract."

"That'd be great, thank you."

As we walk out of the barn together, she sighs. "I'm so glad you're taking over. I don't want to change my milk supplier. I love these goats. Bo fed them organic food and gave them the highest standard of care, which is what's made my cheese business."

A stab of guilt hits. "I'm actually selling the place. But I'm happy to put you in the resale contract to try and keep your same business deal going."

"That's awfully kind of you." Her shoulders sag. "But this stinks. I have a feeling we could be friends."

"Me too."

"Why don't you come with me to the store? I'll show you how to make cheese... maybe give you a free taste or two."

I groan. "That sounds so awesome, you have no idea. But I have to meet with a real estate agent today and get things rolling with selling this farm. Otherwise, I'd be there in a second."

"How about I make it so you get both?" She perks a brow. "There's only one good real estate agent in town, Sally Keller, and she's my cousin. I'll call her right now. I know she can meet you for breakfast because she just had a showing canceled."

"You'd do that?"

"Of course I would. I gotta butter you up good so you help me keep my goat milk." She laughs.

That's honesty for you, but with charm—my kind of person. "A tough offer to resist."

As we're heading to the driveway to get in Dakota's car, I look into the distance, seeing the forest surrounding the gnarly tree, and I freeze.

I'm always scared of the woods, but something about that specific view just rocked me to my core.

9

The Festival

◈◆◈

Cut the Cheese's kitchen is filled with fancy stainless-steel appliances, all things to make cheese, and a commercial latte machine. After making me one, Dakota holds out a brimming cup. "Candied maple bacon coffee. Try it."

"That's a thing?"

"It is here in Violet Moon."

I take a sip, thinking I'm going to hate it, but I don't. It's rich, for sure, but a unique blend of bursting flavors. "Dessert in the morning."

While Dakota puts the goat's milk in the double-boiler pot and adds cultures, I tell her about what I do in New York. After mentioning that Bo probably left me the farm because he was friends with my father, I'm wistful when I say, "Bo's house is beautiful. I'd love to restore it if I could."

"Bo's Château is the prettiest place in town."

"Is that its name?"

"The locals call it that." She stirs the milk as it starts to boil. "Bo did such a great job with it. He was gonna build a big ol' fancy barn on the lookout spot on the hill—for weddings, birthdays, anniversaries."

"No kidding. I know the exact spot you're talking about—right over the lake."

"That's it." Her voice goes up an octave with excitement. "With that view, I gotta say—if you finished his job, I'd get married there. Not that I have any prospects."

"I feel the same. About both." I scratch a dried milk spot on the counter.

"No man in your life?"

"My boyfriend of two years and I ended things six months ago." I don't tell her the humiliating reason why.

"I feel you. I was with Brody until a month ago. He broke up with me because he said I'd never gotten over my high school sweetheart. And he wasn't wrong."

"Eek. A month ago—that's pretty fresh."

"Yeah, but I'm ready for the next Mr. Right Now. Let's make a pact." She smiles conspiratorially as she wipes off her hands on her apron. "Before you leave Violet Moon, we go for beers and find ourselves some candidates. It wouldn't hurt you to experience a nice country boy."

"I don't know."

She laughs, light and warm. "Oh, come on, now. When are you gonna have another chance like this? A town filled with hot men whom you're never gonna see again. You can sow those wild oats and then go back to New York with higher standards, if you know what I mean."

I eye her. "I have a feeling you don't stop until you get what you want."

"Your feeling would be right. I'll be man shopping for me, too, but I have to be more careful with the rumor mill around here. I need to find myself an out-of-town visitor. Dark-haired, mysterious. Keeps his pie hole shut."

I laugh. I can't believe it, but it feels like I've made a girlfriend already, and I've been here less than two days. I've lived in New York my whole life, and I can't seem to meet anybody. Well, besides Natanya.

"Tomorrow evening, let's go to the Brew 'n Chew Festival to celebrate the Fourth." She shrugs. "I've been dying to go with another single woman. All my girlfriends are married now, most with a baby in their arms and one on the way. I rebelled against taking over my family's beer company and spent my early twenties living in Paris to learn how to make cheese, then my mid-twenties scrambling to start a business. Now, at twenty-six, I'm the only old maid left on the shelf."

Wow, things really are different in a small town. "So, you studied cheese-making in Paris? I'm so impressed." I blow out an exaggerated sigh before I say, "But, you've convinced me on the Brew 'n Chew. You've got yourself a deal."

"Yay!" She does a hip wiggle. "It's Violet Moon's event of the year. You get free samples of all the local beers. There's dancing, and fried everything, even pickles."

"Fried pickles." I am really in the South.

When Dakota finishes with the batch of milk, she puts it in the refrigerator. Then she seats me on the outdoor patio of Cut the Cheese, bringing me another latte and a charcuterie board, which I can't wait to dive into, but I'll hold off for Sally.

"You must be Willow." A woman with dark hair pulled into a ponytail and dressed in a sharp navy suit approaches me, her heels tapping on the patio. "I'm Sally Keller."

"It's nice to meet you." I stand and shake her hand.

"Nice to meet you, too, Willow." She puts down her purse and takes a seat.

"Thank you for meeting with me on such short notice."

"I was all dressed up with nowhere to go, and now I get free food and coffee."

Sally and I chit-chat while eating cheese that's smoother than butter. It's bursting with distinct flavors that pair perfectly with the crackers, grapes, strawberries, and apricot jam that Dakota's arranged on the board.

After I tell Sally that I'm planning to list Bo's Château for sale, she says, "That place has the best views in town. I sure wish I could buy it for myself."

"It is so nice." I sigh, picking up a plump grape. "I shouldn't have a problem selling it, then?"

Sally looks away, letting out a long sigh. She sets down her coffee cup and leans in. "I'd love to tell you that it's gonna be easy, but I don't wanna give you false hope. People love the place, don't get me wrong, but it's not in great shape. Most Violet Moon folks don't have the resources to restore it, including me. You might have luck with out-of-town investors, but they'll probably just pay you for the price of the land. They won't want to fix it up or run the farm."

My heart sinks like cement in water. "Oh. That makes sense." I rub my forehead. "And I was hoping to add clauses in the agreement, to honor Dakota's milk contract and the horses for the Brooks family."

"I understand why you want to do that, Willow." Her face goes stern. "But if you want it to sell, you'll have to list it 'as is.'"

I blink in thought. If I don't sell the place, what am I going to do with it? I can't manage the farmhands from New York, can I? And even if I could, I don't have any money to pay them, or at least not until I get it back to peak production. Which, hello, I have zero idea how to do.

Sally's voice is gentle when she says, "So, do you want to list it?"

I loathe the thought of letting Frankie, Trinity, and Dakota down. They love and rely on the place, as well as the animals there. But I also don't see another reasonable choice. Defeated, I utter, "Yes. I have to."

The festive streets pop in reds, whites, and blues, and the smells of rising dough, cinnamon, and baking fruits fill the air, along with cooked meats and French fries.

Dakota and I browse different tents while the band plays a mix of rock and jazz, the notes fluttering through the pleasantly warm Thursday evening air. It's everything I'd ever imagined a small-town festival would be—maybe more.

There's something magical about Violet Moon, which is the perfect thing to distract me from my worries about Bo's Château. Before we list, Sally has a punch list of things to do so the selling points of the home shine, then she'll bring in a top property photographer from Atlanta. That's a good start, but it sounds like it won't be enough.

"We can't miss this booth." Dakota grabs my arm, cutting into my thoughts. We head over to the massive corner tent, and on it is the Violet Moon beer logo—an illustration of purple clouds floating over mountains with a bright moon in the sky. Somehow, it actually reminds me of Violet Moon, and I'm amazed the artist captured that in a vector drawing.

The worker, a woman with short, gray hair and rosy cheeks, smiles brightly. "Howdy, Dakota. Nice to see you, darlin'." Then she turns to me and says, "And how are you, Ms. Willow? I'm Gertie, Dakota's aunt. A little bird told me you're taking over Bo's Château."

"That's me. Nice to meet you, Gertie." I look at Dakota. "I guess news *does* travel fast around here."

"You have no idea," Dakota mumbles.

Gertie brushes off her apron. "I also heard you have a looker of a colt who almost didn't make it, bless his heart. Word is, you and Frankie delivered him yourselves. You're already something of a hero in Violet Moon."

I inhale sharply, my mouth ready to correct her when I realize I can't. Owen is in hiding until tomorrow, and I'm starting to get a sense why. "It was mostly Frankie. Really."

"Well, I saw the pictures Nia's gonna run in *The Meddling Moon*. I can't wait to come by and meet him, pretty little bugger."

"I'd be happy to have you," I say, meaning it. "Trinity named him Oreo, and he's the cutest thing I've ever seen... well besides my little goat, Sir Fig A Lot."

"Oh, look at you—already naming the animals. You're just meant to be here, aren't you, darlin'?"

Not in the mood to get into yet *another* discussion of how I have to sell the place—although, let's get real, Gertie probably already knows that, too—I say, "I'm definitely falling for the animals. But I do miss my turtle at home, Tesla."

"Tesla's welcome here." Gertie perks a brow. "Folks find themselves coming for a visit and never leaving, I tell ya. I was living in Roswell when I met my Jimmy. Moved here to be with him and never looked back." She sighs wistfully. "Anyway, come on, now, try our latest blonde lager. It turned out amazing, if I dare toot my own horn."

She pours us beers with a nice foam top. I take a sip, and it's bursting with flavor. "It's like something German, but with the lightness of an American beer. If that makes sense?"

Gertie clasps her hands and giggles proudly. "It's amazing you caught that. Our family's barley seeds actually came from Europe."

Dakota holds up her glass. "Cheers," she says, and I clink hers with mine.

With a warmness flowing through me, I say, "I don't know if it's just me, or the fresh air, but everything seems better here."

"That's because it is, silly," Dakota says. "We take our food and our fun seriously."

"That's for sure." I turn to Gertie. "I never would've thought you had so much barley growing in Georgia."

"No one does. They think cotton or peaches. It's always a surprise to visitors, but we're definitely earning a name for ourselves."

"I can see why."

Dakota and I grab a beer to-go as we continue down the bricked streets of downtown. I window browse all the charming shops, which include a bakery, a diner, and a cafe called The Sweet Bean. I can only imagine how good their coffee must be. Apparently, Bo designed this charming row of buildings, which are bricked and classic with Roman arched windows and entrances.

In the town square, everybody's dancing like nobody's watching, just the way it should be. Even kids and toddlers are going for it. Dakota grabs my hand and says, "It's time to whip out your New York moves and land yourself a cutie. Let's get you hooked up."

"Oh, man, you're serious about this."

"Hell, yeah. I need to live vicariously."

Once we're shaking our stuff, I have a pretty good buzz going as I end up getting linked up with Wyatt, another cousin of Dakota's. Definitely sexy with his blond locks and nice build, he gives me a lesson on country swinging, which is kind of adorable.

No complaints, although I can't help but wish it were Owen. Wyatt gets pulled away by another woman, and I'm back in the mix, dancing with anyone and everyone, including kids. When the fresh mountain breeze hits my face, I decide it doesn't get much better than this.

Dakota flies up to me, her jaw hanging when she says, "I can't believe this."

"What?"

"My wish might be coming true." She nods to a man standing at the Violet Moon beer tent. "I don't know that guy, which means he's a stranger. And he's dark-haired and mysterious."

"Sounds like we need to get another beer."

We make our way over, and I'm ready to help Dakota talk to this guy when I realize she doesn't need me. She tromps straight up to him and says, "I don't know you, and I know everyone in this town."

He chuckles, then says something to her, which I can't hear over the music. That's when I see Trinity with a woman in her early twenties, probably one of Owen's other sisters, Bailey or Kayla. I'm guessing it's Bailey since Kayla is getting ready for her wedding.

"Willow!" Trinity cries out, running over and throwing her arms around my waist.

"Hi, Trinity." I return the hug, my heart bursting.

"I'm Bailey," the young woman says, and she has Owen's eyes. "Looks like you've made yourself a friend."

"Willow saved Oreo's life, Bailey." Trinity's toothy grin grows ear to ear.

"If that's the case, then you're a hero." Bailey flashes a stunning smile, her chestnut hair flowing in the wind. She's got the same good looks as her brother.

Mary Louise bustles over, her strong lilac perfume wafting in the air when she says, "Well, how are y'all tonight?" Her tone's as sweet as her pies, and her red lipstick almost glows in the evening light.

"We're good," I say.

"How's graduate school, Ms. Bailey?" Mary Louise tips her head. "You home for the summer?"

"It's coming along—I'm actually in Atlanta right now, interning, but I'm here for Kayla's wedding," Bailey replies politely, but her pep from earlier is gone. Trinity says nothing as she moves closer to her sister.

"Well, it sure is nice to see you." Mary Louise puts a hand on my arm. "And how are you doing with the farm, Ms. Willow?"

"So far, so good. I've made a few repairs to the stable, and I hope to make some on the house before I list it for sale."

"Trinity, why don't you go and get us both a cream puff," Bailey cuts in, her words rushed.

Trinity scowls. "Get your own cream puff, Bailey."

Mary Louise's eyes stay trained on me. "I can save you the cost of listing the house and hiring a real estate agent. Bill and I'd love the chance to sit down and make you an offer you can't refuse."

I blink, thinking about what Sally Keller said. I don't know how many other offers I'm going to have, if any, and I don't have much time. I should be absolutely thrilled about this, but for some reason, I have to force some enthusiasm when I say, "Oh. That's great."

That *is* great, right? I'll have this place sold, and I'll be back in New York in no time. Except, why is my stomach knotting?

Bailey smiles again, nervously this time. "I reckon Willow will have other offers on the place to consider."

"I highly doubt that," Mary Louise says, indignant. Then she looks at me. "How does tomorrow sound?"

I hesitate, finally managing a weak smile. "That works."

Trinity's small, delicate face twists in anguish. "Can I talk to you, Willow? Please?" Desperation flickers in her sky-blue eyes.

Bailey grabs Trinity's hand. "Come on, little sis, let's move along. I promised to win you a stuffed horse at the basket toss."

"Stuffed animals are for babies," Trinity snaps, but she backs away with Bailey. With quivering lips, she turns to me and mouths, "Don't do it." Then she's pulled away by her sister's tug.

"What was that about?" I say, more shaken than I probably should be.

Mary Louise barks out a laugh. "Oh, that sweet little girl. She's just got her heart set on things staying just as they are."

I understand that. I wasn't one for a change either until my parents were gone in a flash. Then, I had to alter anything and everything about my life in an instant. It was soul-crushing, and I wouldn't wish it on anyone. I remind myself that change is a part of life, and logically, I know it's something Trinity should learn to cope with, but, hopefully, only a little at a time.

Anyway, I have no choice but to sell the estate, and Mary Louise seems motivated, which is always a good thing in a negotiation. "So, I'll see you tomorrow?"

"Wonderful. I'll have Bill put a proposal together tonight, and we can meet you at the house first thing in the morning. Say nine a.m.?"

"Works for me."

Dakota appears, giving Mary Louise a tentative smile and hello before turning to me. "So, Willow, how about we git ourselves to those fried pickles? You can't leave town without trying those."

"Sure." I'm glad for the save, and I'm not sure why. I just got an offer on the house—I should be doing cartwheels.

Mary Louise waves. "You two have fun. See you tomorrow, Willow."

As Dakota and I walk away, I tell her what just went down as we make our way to the pickle stand.

"Well, an offer is good news." Dakota smiles hesitantly. "Just make sure you have Mr. Livingston check it over, okay?"

"I thought he was a probate attorney."

"He is. And a property attorney. And a defense attorney. And a divorce attorney. I think he even worked as an immigration attorney once."

"Impressive." I chuckle, thinking about what a powerhouse that gentle, unassuming man is. "Well, with my restoration company, I have my own lawyers, but Mr. Livingston knows this area, so I'll definitely bring him in too."

While we're digging into our samples of fried pickles—and surprise, surprise, they're delicious—Dakota catches me up on the guy she met. "That was a flop. He was *so* mysterious, he disappeared."

"Oh, no!"

After we both laugh, she groans. "His name's Bennett, and he's from Atlanta. He's here checking out the local breweries for work. He and I were totally hitting it off, but then he got a call and had to leave."

"You didn't get a phone number?"

"Nope. He flew off like a chipmunk in a tailwind."

I grin, but then the fireworks kick off, and everyone turns their gaze to the river, where they're being launched.

After a few colorful explosions in the sky, Bailey runs up to us, all the blood drained from her face. "Have you seen Trinity?" she chokes out between labored breaths.

"What? No." My eyes immediately scan the place, not seeing Trinity anywhere, although it's dark and there are people everywhere.

Bailey scrubs her forehead, frantic. "I turned my back on her, for just a second, while Gertie was yammering on about her new brew kettle. When I turned back, Trinity was just... gone." Her lips quiver and her eyes well with tears. "I lost her."

10

The Runaway

We all presume Trinity's headed to my horse stables, as she was destroyed when she heard I was going to sell the place. Also, come on—that's where she loves to be.

Bailey and I exchange numbers, and we make a plan for me to return to Bo's Château while she and Dakota stay and look for Trinity downtown. Bailey doesn't want to call the police until I check the stables, which seems fair.

After racing to my rental, I look for her alongside the road as I drive home. When I don't see her, my nerves ratchet up as I roll into the circular driveway and jump out of the car, locking it with my key fob on the run. It hits me that this is becoming a habit, and one I'm not particularly fond of.

I sprint to the stables, calling for Trinity as I run. No answer.

When I get inside, there's no Trinity. My stomach plummets.

But there's also no Eclipse or Oreo, either. My head flips to the wall, and Eclipse's reins are missing.

That kid took the horses. How in the hell did she have time to run home and do that?

I call Owen and tell him what's going on, and he says he'll be here in two minutes. He tells me that Frankie's with Kayla right now, getting everything ready for tomorrow's rehearsal dinner.

Then, I shoot a text to Bailey, telling her that my horses are missing, and that Owen and I are going to search my property for Trinity.

Bailey responds, saying she and Dakota will go search the river, as sometimes Trinity likes to take the horses there.

When Owen walks in, he's wearing a pair of worn cowboy boots and a red plaid fleece. "Thanks for racing over here, Queens."

"Of course."

He holds out another long-sleeved fleece. "Put this on. It should fit, it's Bailey's. You're gonna need it. That night air's a little chilly on a horse."

"I'm coming?" Butterflies thrash in my stomach. I've never ridden a horse before, but I have to help.

"You don't have to. I'm sure Trinity's fine, Willow. She knows not to ride Eclipse yet—it's too soon after she gave birth. They can't be far." His lips quirk up. "We just have to find her and tell her she's in deep this time."

"Go easy on her. She had a rough night." I realize I have to talk to her myself. "Never mind—I'm coming too."

Owen lets the other mare, Raven, out of her stall, and her tail swings as Owen gives her a quick brushing. "This will relax her, which makes for a smoother ride," Owen says. The horse stands patiently while Owen places a pad and two-person saddle on her back, then releases its straps, all in a fluid motion. There's a rhythm to it that the two of them clearly perfected long ago.

And I hate that this constantly crosses my mind, but Owen's... ridiculously hot. And not because he's suddenly a cowboy per se, but more because this is like breathing for him.

After I slip on Bailey's shirt, Owen says, "Let me help you up."

"Thanks."

"You're gonna want to keep your back straight and hold on." Owen guides my foot in the stirrups, then hoists me up so I can fling my leg over the saddle.

Then he climbs on behind me. When he wraps his solid arms around my waist, it makes me feel way too much for someone I've known for three days. Maybe I prefer country to city boys?

He whispers into my ear, "You ready?" My skin breaks into goose bumps.

"Ready," I squeak. My heart's pounding a mile a minute and not just because we're sitting on top of a very tall, very proud, stud horse.

"I can tell you're not breathing, Queens." He rubs my arm. "Inhale. Exhale. Then do it all over again." His hand lands on my back, tracing circles, clearly hoping it jump-starts my stalled lungs. "I've got you, don't worry."

I know he does. In our brief time together, I've learned that.

As he whistles and tugs the reins, Raven trots forward. The wind hits my face as I get a view of the bright full moon in the lavender night sky. The cool mountain air fills my lungs, and it's so euphoric, I want to breathe it forever. There's not another soul out here, and it's so different from the world I know, it's almost surreal.

Owen says, "Hang on," before he gives the reins a whip. Raven breaks into a run, and I pull Owen's arms tighter around me. A rush of adrenaline floods my veins, like I'm on a roller coaster. I suspect that if it was just me, the ride wouldn't be anything close to smooth. But Owen's gentle command of Raven and their mutual respect make it appear easy.

When I lift my head to the sky, something deep inside me breaks free. Although I can't place what it is, there's a sense of weightlessness now that it's gone.

Admittedly, I'm starting to miss New York—the sights, the sounds, getting any kind of food delivered to your doorstep twenty-four hours a day. But here, you can have *this*.

In the distance, on the other side of the lake, I see a shadow of two horses, one big and one small. There's a fire roaring beside a pup tent.

When Owen tugs the reins and Raven halts, I squeeze my thighs to hold on. The trapped breath escapes my chest when Owen says, "We've found her."

At the campsite, Trinity strokes Oreo's mane, refusing to make eye contact with Owen and me.

After he and I climb off Raven, Owen says, "Trinity, your sister's beside herself looking for you. Ma would tan your hide if she knew."

"I know, I'm sorry." Trinity's tiny voice cracks around her words. "I shouldn't of run away, but I had to. And I didn't ride Eclipse. I know she's not ready yet."

"How did you get here so fast?" Owen asks.

She stares at the ground. "I jumped in the back of Mary Louise's truck when I saw she was leaving." She looks at Owen with fiery eyes. "And don't yell at her. She didn't know I was there with all the cotton bales."

A howl echoes through the trees, and I jump. Was that a wolf? A coyote? I shake off the willies when I say, "Aren't you scared out here, all alone?" Because I am.

She shakes her head with vigor. "I belong out here with the animals."

Okay, this kid is beyond adorable, and I pinch my lips shut to stave off a chuckle.

Trinity looks at Owen. "Willow's gonna sell the place. This is my last chance to be with Oreo." She pulls him tight again, stroking his snout with her small fingers.

I make my way over to her, putting a hand on her shoulder. "I haven't made a deal with Mary Louise yet. And even if I do, I'm sure she'll let you come see the horses."

"But you don't understand. Mary Louise is going to tear everything down. She's going to sell the animals. They'll be gone forever."

After swallowing hard, Owen asks, "Trin, how do you know that?"

She wipes away her tears before she sits on her backpack and rests her head on her knees. Finally, she looks up and says, "I was in the barn, just after Mr. Bo died. I wasn't supposed to be there, so when I heard people talking, I hid in the loft."

Owen's voice is tense when he says, "What did Mary Louise say?"

"She was talking to Bill." Trinity turns to me. "That's her husband. Anyway, she was saying that they're gonna need to tear everything down to put in a building. Something for the cotton they grow."

I stand statue still, my heart thrashing in my ears, as I process Trinity's words. Mary Louise wants to tear all this down and put a *plant* here? The thought punches my gut, and I remind myself that Trinity *is* a child. I hope with everything in me that she's wrong.

Except I know in my heart she's not. Sally Keller told me that no one in Violet Moon would have the resources to restore this place. But Mary Louise *would* have the funds to tear it down and invest in her business. I don't know what to say, so I approach Trinity and sit beside her, wrapping my arm around her and holding her tight. She puts her face in the crook of my neck, and I stroke her soft hair. "I'm so sorry," I say, although I know that's not enough. With an idea, I ask, "Could your mom take the horses and put them on your farm?"

"No," Owen cuts in. "Unfortunately, we don't have room for a pasture. That's why we don't have animals."

"That makes sense," I whisper, my heart sinking.

"What's going to happen with a building here?" Trinity starts sobbing again. "I just want Bo back."

"Okay, okay. Shhh." I rub her hair. "I'm sorry, sweetie. We'll figure something out." I don't know how to keep the promise I just made, but I'll do everything in my power to try.

Clearly, I'm not signing a deal with Mary Louise nor an investor unless they put it in writing that they're keeping the horses.

"Everyone in town loves this place, Willow. It won't be the same without it," Trinity whispers.

"I know. I love this place too, and I just got here." I pull away to look at her.

For the first time today, she cracks a smile. "Are you gonna stay?"

Her question shreds my heartstrings, and I want so much to say yes. But I have to be honest, so I answer, "Definitely a while longer." I glance at Owen, and he's watching us with a glint in his eyes.

My mind spins through its Rolodex of solutions. Maybe I can figure out a way to get more lending credit? Or maybe I can try to list the farm for sale with the clause that once it's sold, it can't be torn down? Although, I know that won't work. There's nothing to stop owners from tearing down their own property.

Unless it's a historic landmark.

Which this is.

They can still tear it down with a special permit, but, actually, that doesn't matter.

I have another idea.

11

Starry Night

When I bring Eclipse into her stall, I stroke her nose, getting lost in those reflecting-pool eyes. Yeah, this big city girl is getting swept off her feet by a horse.

Trinity agreed to move back home since I promised not to sell my farm to Mary Louise unless she can find a way to let Trinity keep the horses, but, mostly, I think it was because she was out of snacks. Since Bailey's putting Trinity to bed, Owen and I walk the horses back to the stables, and just in time because Oreo must be ready to nurse. Right now, the sky is magnificent, filled with stars, and Eclipse's white mane almost glows with the moonlight hitting it. Fireflies flicker in the sky above the marsh beside the lake.

After getting Raven settled, Owen steps into Eclipse's stall with me and pets her mane. "You okay, sweet girl?" Her ears perk and tail flips.

"She's breathtaking."

"She is." Owen gives Oreo a pet as he starts to nurse. Once we leave the stall, he says, "So, what are you going to do? I mean, about this farm?"

I wander over and pluck the broom off the wall and sweep away the hoof tracks, needing something to keep my hands busy. "I've maxed out my credit limit with the latest job I took in New York, but taking out a loan for a historic landmark is not under the same umbrella."

"And this place is a historic landmark."

"Exactly."

He raises a brow. "So, you can get a loan. But what about Natanya? And the Klein account?"

"Impressive memory." I put the broom back. "That still needs to be figured out. But Bo's Château would provide income on top of the Klein account."

Together, we walk outside and toward the outdoor shower. Turning on the hand hose, Owen says, "Fair enough. How long will it take to restore this place?"

"It depends on the contractors I find. Good ones could turn this around in six weeks." I squirt soap on my hands and suds them. And now that I'm here longer, I'll have more time to try and figure out if this place holds any clues to my past. I can investigate who wrote that note—the one about me not being wanted here. I wonder if Mary Louise left it to scare me away so she could have this property?

Well, I won't let her do that.

"Six weeks." Owen's lips split into a grin as he washes up too. "So, that's how much time I have with you?"

My heart trips over its next beat as I rinse my hands. "If I find good contractors. And if you want."

"Oh, I want."

My stomach is tossing like a pizzaiolo with a pizza crust, and I'm reminded that I shouldn't miss the chance to get Owen's lips on mine. And elsewhere. Especially since, apparently, he feels the same.

But before I can respond, he blurts, "You know, I've been dying to watch the stars from that lookout point. Above your lake."

"How odd. Me too." I dry my hands on the towel and hand it to him.

He takes it. "I was hoping you'd join me. If you want."

"Oh, I want."

"Good." His mouth quirks as he replaces the towel on the peg. "But knowing our luck, we'll end up in an intense situation. Hanging off the mountainside by the hair of our chin."

"True. But I don't have chin hair, or I certainly hope not. And we can make a promise that neither of us will go near the edge. That should cover it. Unless we're struck by a meteorite."

A teasing spark flickers in his eyes. "I'll take my chances."

"Wow, when you're not in tense situations, you're kinda flirty."

"With you, yes." He hitches a thumb over his shoulder. "How about I get us drinks?"

"How about that. Whiskey. Neat."

His mouth curves. "Bailey's got cinnamon whiskey. Which, truth be told, I don't mind."

"So, you like it sweet."

"To start."

Damn.

"I'll be back," he says before walking away.

Once he fetches the cinnamon whiskey, shot glasses, and a blanket, we meet back at the stables before making our way to the lookout point and sitting down.

We take in the star-filled sky, the smell of freshly cut grass, and the chirping of the crickets in symphony with the rustling of the branches. All things you don't get in Queens.

The full moon glows, and the cloud cover gives it a violet hue. I nod up. "I see where this town gets its name." The sky is magical, and I love being this close to Owen, breathing his scent, feeling his warmth. My body heats up instantly, and I haven't even had a drink yet. I hold out my empty shot glass, saying, "I could get used to this."

"Get used to what, exactly?" Owen pours me a nip.

"This view. The fireflies. The stars. The peacefulness. And that moon."

The breeze flicks a strand of my hair on my face. Owen brushes it away, saying, "There's something about this place. And the simple life."

"There is."

He sighs, looking away. "Just think—you could stay here and eat fried pickles, fried everything, for the rest of your life."

"Fried pickles are nothing. I put cayenne pepper in my smoothies. And everything else."

"So, you like it hot."

I lick my tingling lips. "Touché." Man, now that Owen Brooks has dialed up his flirt, I might as well skip the small talk and get naked.

But then I hear a rustle in the bramble, and I grab my pepper spray.

Owen looks at me, then follows my gaze. "It's okay. That's just Demon." He cranes his neck and calls out, "Demon! Git home. Now!"

After a bark of protest, the rustling fades as Demon appears to do what he's told. Impressed, I say, "Wow, you're really getting him trained."

"Sort of." He groans before looking at me, his brows furrowing. "You're pretty jumpy and suspicious."

"Yeah, maybe." I put the spray back in my pocket.

His face turns serious, his tone quiet when he says, "What happened to you? If you don't mind me asking."

I look away, listening to the chirping birds as I think about my response. Then, I say, "I could just be a jumpy person. By nature. How do you know something happened to me?"

"You have that way about you. That you've been broken apart. Had to put yourself back together again, and you're stronger for it."

"You're good."

He looks down, tapping his fingers together. "I'm not that good. I've just been there."

I want to ask him how, but I realized he asked me first. Instead, I say, "I don't like talking about it."

"You don't have to if you don't want to."

I chew my lip, deciding I'm comfortable enough with Owen to let him in... a little. I take a deep breath, deciding to start at the beginning. "In high school, I was just a normal teenager. A roof over my head, loving parents, a lot of friends. Then, one night when I was sixteen, my parents took a drive to Long Island for a party. They were so excited—it was all bougie, at an investment banker's house. My mom got the invite as one of his administrative assistants." I stop to steady my voice. "My parents' car hydroplaned, and they crashed on the way home." Releasing the clench in my jaw that happens whenever I tell this story, I say, "I never even got to hear if they had fun. I hope to god they did."

"Jesus. I'm sorry."

"Me too."

Owen takes my hand and rubs his thumb across my palm, featherlight. "So what did you do?"

"My parents had no life insurance. I couldn't afford the rent for their apartment. They weren't irresponsible, but they had no savings or retirement after the housing market crash of 2008. I was penniless. So, suddenly, there was a crevasse between me and my friends. They were worried about designer clothes and proms, and I was grieving the loss of my parents and my life as I knew it, not to mention I had to figure out how I was going to eat. When you become an orphan at sixteen, you don't have to go into foster care, but maybe I should have. I ended up living in my car for a while."

"Oh, shit."

"I started working any and every job I could get. I wasn't quite an adult, but I had to become one overnight. I took my dad's place as the super at our old apartment, and as soon as I had enough cash, I started RevitaHome and threw myself into work, one renovation at a time. It's a predominantly male-run industry, so most of the people I work with either want to date me or be professionals—there's no middle ground."

"Makes sense." Owen scoots closer and moves his hand to my back, which is warm, comforting.

I take a swig of the shot, and the cinnamon bursts in my mouth along with the burn of the whiskey. After I bark out a cough, I say, "This is quite a combo." I squeeze my eyes shut as I exhale, feeling like a cinnamon-and-fire-blowing dragon.

"You gonna live?" He gives me a gentle pat.

"Barely." I open my eyes to see Owen sitting there, patiently, like he's waiting for me to finish. So, I say, "I think I got so used to living alone, I forgot what it was like to have family around." I pluck a blade of grass before tossing it. "Here I am, rambling on about me. What about you?"

He looks down, his voice quiet when he says, "I feel like I've had it easy compared to you."

"It's not a competition."

He nods slowly, staring into the distance. "My dad died ten years ago, when I was sixteen, too. Strange coincidence."

"I'm so sorry, Owen."

"Yeah. But I had my mom and younger sisters, and they're all amazing—'tough as boiled owl,' as my Nana Lottie would say."

"I noticed."

"But Ma was left with her hands full. Trinity was a newborn, so I had to step in. I did my best to help my sisters, packed their lunches, picked them up from school, braided their hair, not well, I might add. I felt like I could never do enough. I actually considered delaying college, but Ma wouldn't let me." When he swallows, his Adam's apple bobs. "So, I stayed close by and went to UC Georgia—go Dawgs. By the time I graduated from vet school, everyone was grown and didn't need my help anymore. And that includes Trinity, who was eight." He chuckles. "Anyway, I just... I had to get away. I moved to Atlanta and joined a vet practice there. But I don't know if my leaving was just about that. I didn't want to be one of those people who never ventured from their small town."

"Makes sense."

He cracks a grin, his eyes brightening. "But, man, do I love my girls. Bailey's all about her friends and getting dolled up. Kayla and Trinity, they're like Ma. Tough on the outside, soft on the inside. Kayla's always been the strongest. When she came out as a freshman in high school, she didn't care what people thought. She is who she is, and she makes no apologies. She was my hero then. Still is. Her fiancée, Margaret, is great, too."

"How does the town feel about her wedding this weekend?"

"Most people are supportive and excited. Mary Louise is *not* one of those people, which is just as well. Kayla doesn't want her there."

"Mary Louise." I groan. "Good riddance. I'm happy Kayla's got so much support."

"Oh, speaking of that." He reaches into his pocket and pulls out a fancy postcard-sized parchment paper. "Kayla wanted me to give this to you. She knows you two haven't met, but you helped save Oreo, and now, Trinity, too."

I take it to see that it's a wedding reception invitation for Kayla and Margaret on Saturday night. "I'm honored."

"Good. Happy you'll be there. Happy I'll be there. Happy to be back."

"I can see why." I inhale. "It's gorgeous here, with history and beautiful architecture. Man, what I could do to some of the downtown buildings. Fresh paint and awnings. New windows and signage. Being here has been healing, in a way."

"And why is that?"

"I feel at peace, beyond the moment. If that makes sense?"

"It does." He turns and meets my gaze, his dark piercing eyes heating my skin as if he's staring into my soul. "It's like you belong here. And I can't really explain that, either."

His words kick up my pulse as I point down the hill. "The lake is literally shimmering in the moonlight. I mean, no joke, this place is storybook."

"The lake's also a great spot for a swim. Especially in July—the water's perfect." Owen downs his shot, then shakes his head like a dog.

"So, what are we waiting for?" I can't believe I just said that. Who *am* I right now? But my body is thrumming and making me feel wild.

In New York, I'm the responsible boss. Since I was sixteen, I had to project maturity and strength everywhere I went, just to land jobs and pay the bills. I was never like this with my ex, Seth. But here, at this moment, I'm none of those things.

"What?" Owen's voice hitches. "We can go tomorrow—when there's sunlight."

I stand, ready to escape this heavy conversation for now. "We don't need sunlight with this amazing moon."

"You're serious."

"It's the Fourth. We're doing this." I whip off my shirt, glad I'm wearing my prettiest black lace bra.

12
The Plunge

I catch his eye snagging on my bra for a split second before landing on my face. When he stands, he doesn't budge forward. "So, right. No swimming suits?"

"Birthday suits will do just fine."

"'Will do just fine?' Listen to you talking like a local already." He chuckles. "You're just trying to see me naked."

"Damn right. You get to see me naked too." Keeping up the show, I whip off my bra, tossing it on the ground.

Owen gasps, like I knocked the air straight out of his chest. This time, his eyes stick like glue to my breasts.

I give his hand a tug, and I don't have to pull to get him to move.

We get to the dock, the water sloshing against it, and I focus on that sound to ease the nerves bubbling inside me. I may be playing it cool on the outside, but it's a facade. Inside, my nervousness is intensifying by the second.

But I'm committed to it, so I slide my jeans and underwear off in one swift motion before leaping into the lake.

The cold water hitting my skin freezes my breath as I break into shivers. Popping above the surface, I cry out, "Holy shit!" I can see Owen's face in the moonlight, but I can't read his expression.

His tone is croaky when he says, "I can't believe you just did that."

"You're right—the water *is* just fine. Don't be a chicken."

"A chicken? I've never understood that expression. You know, chickens are ballsy."

I laugh. "Nice try with a topic shift. Stop procrastinating."

He whips off his shirt, and I don't blink so I can study him with all the intensity my vision will allow in the darkness. He looks like a statue, a chiseled centerpiece of a fountain in Rome, reflecting in the moonlight.

He flips around before sliding off his jeans.

"I'm closing my eyes," I say, which isn't a lie. They're closed, just not all the way. There's not a chance I'm missing this.

And although it's just a glimpse, it's everything. Not only is his ass round and muscular, but I think there's a large beauty mark, just left of his tail-bone, which makes it perfectly imperfect.

In a flash, he turns, then hesitates.

There he stands before me, in all his glory, and it's magnificent. I can't gather a breath as I take in every inch of his chest, his long, muscular legs, and the rest of him.

My chest and thighs tingle in response.

Then he jumps.

When his head pops up, he gasps, "Shit!" His dark hair is wet, slick, and it takes everything in me not to swim over and run my fingers through it before letting my hand roam down his chest.

But I don't. My boldness is waning, but now, Owen's seems to take off because through chattering teeth, he says, "So, what now, sport?" He swims over. "What are you gonna do with me?"

I want to say, "everything" because he really is the total package. But this is too fast, so I laugh before I say, "I can't believe you've never done this. You're the one *from* here." I paddle deeper, into a pocket of cool water. "But, okay, my doe-eyed apprentice. Now, we dip."

I'm speaking as if this is always so easy for me, but it's only so easy at this moment. Here, in Violet Moon. With Owen. Away from my carefully constructed real world.

Owen follows behind, showing off with some fancy stroke he has, which shouldn't surprise me. I'm sure swimming is part of his exercise regimen to keep his well-oiled machine running pristinely.

As he floats, I catch his eyes roaming toward my chest. I take my fingers and point upward as to direct his view back up.

"Hey, that's not fair," he says. "I know you cheated."

"Maybe a tiny peek." I tread water.

"A peek for a peek."

"You already got one." But I can't blame a man for trying to get another.

He blinks. "Kayla would be proud of me."

"She would."

He paddles closer, a glint in his eyes when he splashes me.

I splash back.

I realize we're acting like teenagers. As though he's reading my mind, he says, "I feel twelve years old."

"I think that's a good thing." I kick my legs to stay afloat. "So, Mr. Responsible Owen Brooks. Have you ever gotten yourself into trouble?"

"Hmm. When I was ten, Sheriff Baxter caught me trying to steal a piece of candy from The Sweetie Treat. Hauled me straight to the station. Even made me sit in the cell for an hour or two until my pa came and bailed me out."

I laugh so hard my head lolls back. "I bet you never stole again."

"That I did not."

After we paddle to where we can touch the sandy bottom, he says, "So what are you gonna do when you get back to New York?"

"Finish up the apartments for Klein Homes. Reinvest the money that I make from selling Bo's Château to bring my business to the next level." With my own words, sadness ripples through me. I knew this before today, but it hits much harder now—my life is work.

Owen sighs. "Ah, big cities. There, people live to work. Here, they work to live."

"Truth."

"I know it's cliché, but there's something about enjoying each moment. Getting off the hamster wheel for a while."

"Yeah. Mostly, I'm just trying to make it through the day." I can't believe I just admitted that to Owen. Or myself.

"It is good here. But it's better here with you." He smiles, shyly. His eyes drift into the distance again, and when his gaze returns, it's got a spark to it. He sighs before he says, "I don't know how."

"You don't know how, what?"

"I don't know how you got me to do this, but I'm glad."

My skin tingles, and this time, it isn't from the cold water. It's Owen's words, the way his voice shifts lower as his eyes lock with mine.

My pulse kicks up, and I step closer. "I'm glad too. And you're blushing."

"You can't see me well enough to know if I'm blushing."

"I can hear it in your voice."

"Possibly."

He moves in. So close, I can feel the heat emanating off his body and wrapping around me. So close, I can smell the tea tree oil in his shampoo.

For a moment, both of us are still, as though we're trying to figure out if we're going to make the next move—the one where everything changes.

I go for it. I'm aching to feel his skin so much, I rest a hand on his pec before moving to his scar where I run a finger over it. "You gonna tell me about this?"

"I will. I promise. But not now."

"Fair enough."

After a deep sigh escapes him, he takes my hand in his. When his thumb rubs a circle around my palm, it's comforting yet wildly sensual, and I shouldn't be surprised that he has this kind of effect on me.

"You're really something," he whispers, taking his hands and slipping them over my shoulders. Painfully slow, he closes the distance between us, and his mouth touching mine, kissing me sweetly, gently, just in the way he lives and breathes. Considerate and caring.

And it's everything. The feel of his fingers as they thread through my hair. The taste of his skin, his lips, his body. As he moves his tongue around mine, all I can do is kiss him back with everything I have.

He pulls me in, closing the gap between our bodies. Being skin on skin is a blissful torture—the zing of touch mixed with the throb for more.

His hands roam, first, caressing my spine, then over to my nipples, stroking them, taking any remainder of my self-control with it.

He pulls away, his face bright in the moonlight. "I hope you know that this is more than me just being a horndog."

"I know," I say because I *do* know. There's something between us.

I bring my lips to his, and this time, the heat between us is like this Georgia summer air, except hotter, and the sweet pressure of his tongue against mine is bringing it to a broil. I'm riding on desire, and it's making me reckless. I straddle him, my legs sliding along the sides of his waist. "Is this okay?" I ask, my breathing jagged as my heart pounds in my rib cage.

"More than okay." His hands travel up my side, and my pulse jumps with his touch. His palms are rough and warm as they inch higher, his fingertips grazing the top of my breasts again, goose bumps following in their wake.

It's electric, like the fireflies shooting off in the distance.

As our kiss deepens, his hands move down my back, and he grips my bottom and hitches me higher, until his hips meet my inner thighs. I thread my fingers through his hair and moan, the sound carrying on the breeze as it circles the two of us.

He lets out a low rumble before uttering, "Good call on the birthday suits. Yours is incredible."

"Ditto," I utter, as I no longer have access to much vocabulary.

He's hard against me, scorching my skin where it touches. His teeth nip at my bottom lip, his breath shallow, frantic. I'm officially ready to be undone.

"God, your body's amazing," he rasps. He kisses his way down my neck, and I arch my spine as he takes my nipple into his mouth, his hardness shifting against me.

My nails dig into his back, and his lips drag up my throat, hungrily. His growing need has become palpable, which only adds to mine.

A cacophony of howls echo, and I jump away, reality reverberating through me. "What was that?"

He chuckles between labored breaths. "Just coyotes."

"*Just.*"

"It adds to the ambiance, no?"

I gasp. "Um, no." I playfully push him back, and he laughs as he falls into the water.

A tap of paws on the dock followed by a splash makes both our heads whip around. My skin turns to ice as I envision the next moments of us getting attacked by a coyote.

Before I can see what's happening, Owen yells, "Demon! You got out again?"

My fear evaporating, I bust into laughter of relief. Then it turns into a genuine chuckle as I watch that bulldog swim frantically toward Owen with his tongue hanging out. "Aw, he missed you," I say.

Owen gives him a shove, and together, they swim back to the dock. "Come on, boy, you're not going to make it long at that pace." The dog pants wildly as he paddles beside Owen. Once the dog is safely out of the water, he shakes himself so hard he tips over. Owen says, "I'm gonna kill Trinity. I know she keeps letting him out."

I laugh again. Now that I have my wits about me, I realize everything between him and me just rocketed from zero to sixty. That was too good, too fast. Feeling whiplashed, I let out a long sigh before I swim over and say, "I don't usually do this."

"Me neither. Nothing about this is usual."

I'm grateful for his understanding... and how he said the words I needed to hear. I crack a grin. "I don't want to be the reason you're exhausted tomorrow. It's a big day with Kayla's rehearsal dinner."

"That is true." He blows out a sigh that matches mine. "So, I guess we should get going."

"I guess we should."

13

The Reception

◈◈◈ ◆◆◆ ◈◈◈

I break the news to Mary Louise that I'm not selling Bo's Château until after I renovate, which she doesn't take well. All her saccharine sweet manners disappear when she says, "This is a decision you'll regret, no doubt in my mind," before hanging up on me.

It stings—for about a minute. Then I realize, firsthand, why she's not the town's favorite person.

Owen and his family are getting ready for Kayla's rehearsal dinner today, and I'm on a mission. Working my way around the house, I'm taking notes and making a list of what needs to be ordered—faucets, tile, fixtures, windows, cabinet hinges, and quartz for the kitchen countertops.

After putting together cost estimates of the restoration and repairs, I see that it's a good chunk of change. Some of the walls have to go just because there's mold and bad piping. On the flip side, there are many things I want to keep—the doors, the clawfoot tub, the chandeliers, the crystal door knobs, and many of the fixtures. They're old but sturdy and have a country charm that you can't buy at Home Depot. Specifically, in the primary bedroom, there's an antique iron candelabra that looks hand-crafted and medieval.

I'm excited about implementing a floor plan that would never work in New York City. It'll be a gorgeous farmhouse with stunning views, so peaceful and quiet—and I can't wait to see the finished product.

To celebrate, I'm sitting on a blanket at the lookout spot with a pint of Ben & Jerry's Strawberry Cheesecake in my hands. My laptop's here on the ground—I'm about to meet Natanya on Zoom.

When she comes on screen, she's wearing her checked pajamas and holding Tesla.

"Oh, my baby!" I cry out. "I miss you."

"He doesn't miss you," Natanya says.

"He does too! He's following me with his eyes."

"Mm-hmm."

After filling Natanya in on everything, including the possible loan for a historic landmark, she says, "You should sublet your apartment while you're gone."

I swallow a big bite of ice cream, shivering off brain-freeze. "That's not a bad idea. It'd probably go for forty-five hundred a month." Money I need to live off of right now.

"I'll get it ready; you do the listing." She notes it on her tablet.

"Really? You're the best, Nat."

"I know. And I've got everything here handled. Antonio's back from Argentina. Hallelujah."

What? I didn't even know Antonio was in Argentina! But I move on, saying, "Great. Let's keep the Zoom calls going."

"Ugh, Willow, I can tell they're getting frustrated with that. We're just gonna have to be honest with the Klein brothers and tell them you had to oversee another job in Georgia, and I'm taking over the account. We'll assure them all is taken care of, which it is."

Logically, I know she's right, but this is too important. I want to tell her to go ahead, but my mouth can't form the words. I simply can't do it—not yet. "Let's keep the calls going for now, then transition the work over to you more slowly."

"You're the boss." Natanya leans into the screen. "Just worry about getting that house sold and sold right. Then, we'll have two jobs earning us income."

"That's what I thought. Good." I flutter out a breath.

"So, what happened with Mr. Sexy Small Town?"

I look away. "We kind of kissed."

"*Kind of?*"

"I mean, it was totally amazing and incredible, and now, I'm screwed. We were kind of naked."

"This 'kind of' crap has to go. You kissed him naked."

"Yes, but that's all."

"Girl."

"Okay, there was touching. In the moonlight. We went skinny dipping."

"Stop it!" She fans herself. "Now, I'm straight up jealous. You're about to have a steaming hot love affair. I mean really, Willow. How are you screwed? I mean, besides the obvious?"

"True." I wave a hand, as if that will help me inhale. It doesn't. "This is good. It's really good. It won't hurt so bad when I leave because I know it's coming. Right?"

"There we go." Natanya does a little dance. "Just shake off those nerves, baby. This man has gotta be better than Joy." Joy is my electronic partner, if you will.

"Hey, don't knock Joy. You may be my right-hand woman, but she's my left." I bark out a laugh.

Natanya sharply perks an eyebrow. "That's just nasty."

"Miss you, too, Nat."

Her face puckers as she looks behind me. "I sincerely hope that's not your hot country man."

I flip my head to see the baby goat eating my ice cream. "Sir Fig A Lot, no! Ugh, he got out again." I really need to fix that fence, but at least I got him a collar and tag from MoonMart. After groaning, I say, "No, this is just my delinquent kid."

"Haha. Hilarious," she deadpans, then waves. "Hi, Mr. Goat."

After Sir Fig A Lot is done studying her, I say, "Anyway, since Owen doesn't start work at the veterinary hospital for another three and a half weeks, he's offered to help me with the restoration. It'll be great to have a free pair of hands."

"Mm-hmm."

I pluck a blade of grass. "I still need to find contractors here—I'm contacting companies now."

"Go, Willow—do your thing. And the wild thing. Wear a condom." She signs off.

When I look out to the pasture, Oreo is out, all by himself. "What?" I jump up. "How is he out?" Worse, for how long? It's over ninety-degrees outside, and he could be over-heated. He's just a baby! I sprint over to him, and he looks tired and thirsty. "Ohhh, sweetie." I look to see the stable door cracked open, which means he must've slipped out, then not been able to get back in. When I let him inside, he rushes to the trough and gulps water, and I'm writhing in guilt.

I walk to his stall to see that was left open too, but Eclipse stayed inside. My brain spins as I try to think of how this happened. I put all the horses back in their stalls and shut the stable door. I swear I did. Didn't I?

But I was distracted—I had so much to do today with the house's punch list. Maybe in my rush, I didn't close the doors tightly, and they drifted back open? I return to Oreo, who looks much better after some water, thank god.

A tremble racks my body. I lucked out *this* time. I take breaths, in and out, as I fight to get my nerves under control.

I don't understand what's happening to me, but if I don't get it together, someone is going to get hurt.

After driving to the neighboring town of Blue Vine, I walk into a barn adorned with twinkle lights, candles, and crystal centerpieces. Rustic. Simple. Elegant. Guests mill around with drinks at this cocktail hour before Kayla's reception dinner, and I'm glad to see I dressed appropriately. I'm wearing my red Victorian cocktail dress, the only fancy thing I packed, and my hair swept into a side up-do.

With a lit up stocked bar and a dance floor flickering with colors, the warm, inviting atmosphere helps me envision how a barn at Bo's Château could host events locally. I'd add a stone fireplace, a loft with more seating, and a wall of windows toward the lake and mountains.

Owen approaches me with a dazzling smile on his face and a tuxedo hanging on his fine body. With champagne glasses in both hands, he holds one out. "Here." His eyes roam up and down before he croaks, "You look... incredible."

"Thank you and thank you." I take it, heating up from the sight of him as our last encounter flashes through my mind. My stomach flutters remembering the way he touched me. How his body felt pressed up against mine.

He cuts into my trip down memory lane. "You're visually redesigning this, aren't you?"

I laugh. "You read my mind. Again." I lower my voice. "I hope you can't read the other thoughts I'm having."

He leans into my ear, his breath warm on my neck when he whispers, "I might—since I'm having the same ones."

Electric waves ripple through me, and I'm so glad to be at a nice event with Owen to take my mind off the million and one things waiting for me, and how absent-minded I've become. "Aren't you just in touch with thoughts and feelings."

"Ugh, believe me, I know. My sisters tease me about it all the time. Good thing I'm secure in my masculinity."

As he should be—especially in that tux and that forest green tie and cummerbund, which complement his dark hair and stormy blue-gray eyes. "Good thing." I bite my lip.

Bailey and Trinity stop by, and they look beautiful. Trinity's wearing the same forest green dress as the others, but it's puffier, and adorable. Bailey's the fanciest, having put on a matching pearl necklace and earrings, along with a sash around her waist. Conversation with them is easy as we catch up, cut off by the tapping of glasses as the signal for everyone to take their seats.

Owen reappears and touches my arm. "Sit with us."

Oh, no way—This is a family thing, and I'm more of a fade-into-the-background girl. "Thank you, but I've already put my things down." I point to my things at a table in the back. "But I'll see you right after."

After I take my seat, a burly man who could double for Grizzly Adams approaches me with his hand extended. "Hi. I'm Jeb, a high school friend of Kayla and Owen's."

I return the handshake and hope he doesn't crush my fingers. "Willow. Nice to meet you."

He sits and introduces me to his friends, along with Owen's cousin, Sissy.

She flashes me a bright, red-cheeked smile, her perfectly drawn-in eyebrows raised. "Nice to meet you, Willow. If you ever need any tattoos, including makeup work, I'm your gal. I do piercings wherever you want, if you know what I mean."

"Thank you, Sissy. I'll think about that." Hmm. Maybe a foot tattoo would be cool.

"Where's Dakota?" Sissy asks Jeb.

"I dunno, man." Jeb shakes his head. "Probably drama there."

What does *that* mean? I don't feel comfortable asking, and the moment's gone anyway because the servers bring out dishes catered by the Fine Bone, which I hear is the nicest restaurant here in Blue Vine. When I dig in, the steak literally falls apart on my fork, and I can't help but notice my table-mates throwing back one drink after another. My phone buzzes, and I check it to see a text from Dakota.

Running late. Big emergency here at the shop, but I'll be there soon.

Owen stands and taps a fork on his glass. "Hello, everyone, I'd like to make a toast. I know this hasn't always been an easy path for Kayla, but it was the right path, and I'm so glad she stood up for what she knew in her heart." He raises his glass to her. "I love you, Twinkball. I'm so proud of you."

Kayla wipes away a tear and mouths, "Love you, Bambi." She stands and gives him a hug.

Finding myself fighting off those damn tears again, I'm annoyed at how much this keeps happening. And I can't help but notice how pretty Kayla is with her waves of dark locks, perfectly long lashes, and big brown eyes. Margaret is tiny, athletic, and they are an adorable couple.

After dinner is over, Owen comes to our table, braces for impact when Jeb stands, and gives him a bear hug along with a hefty slap on the back.

"How are you, buddy?" Owen raises his drink at Jeb, then looks at me. "Jeb led our football team to win championships senior year."

"Aw, those were the good old days." Jeb stumbles away.

"Sort of," Owen mumbles. "I was the second-string kicker so... I kinda spent my life warming the bench."

"Aw." My voice softens. "You hit your peak now. Much better."

Owen flashes me a humble nod as his cheeks flush.

I raise my glass to the crowd. "Pretty awesome reception." The words feel right as they cross my lips. It isn't anything like I've ever attended before, but there's something amazing about a whole town blowing it out to celebrate a marriage. And they all seem to really care about one another—something you don't experience in NYC.

Owen flashes me his charming smile as he gestures to the crowd of townsfolk starting to line-dance to the beat of their own drum. "These are my people."

I find myself wishing they were mine, too. I'm lucky to have Natanya. Others have no one.

When Owen's pulled away for a family photo, Jeb wanders back over and hands me a Cosmo. "Here. Since you're from New York."

I laugh. "Thanks, Jeb. That's so sweet." I absolutely hate Cosmos, but the offer is so thoughtful.

Dakota floats in looking like a classic beauty, wearing a soft pink gown that brings out the natural rose in her cheeks and accentuates her milky skin. She has a soft-featured face that you can't help but trust and love. I mean, really—does she have any flaws?

"Willow!" She approaches and pulls me into a hug. "You look gorgeous. And I'm so glad you're here."

"Same." I relax a little, having someone I'm comfortable hanging out with for the night.

After I take a sip of my drink and wince, Dakota says, "Ah, don't you like Cosmos like every other woman from New York?" She rolls her eyes. "I loathe Cosmos, too. That's just one of the many reasons why we have to be friends."

I give her a one-eyebrow salute. "Cheers to that but with a different drink."

"Here." She takes the Cosmo and downs it before her face puckers, and she shivers. "Let's go get another."

"You rock."

With a gin and tonic in hand, Dakota says, "So, have you spied any guys to hook up with? I mean, it's a wedding."

Humoring Dakota, I scan the room, spotting what I deem to be a decent candidate. "What's his deal?" I lower my voice. "Four o'clock."

"Nope. Not Calvin." Her face squishes like she's swallowed a nasty bug. "He ate glue. In high school."

"Tell me you're kidding," I choke out through a cough.

Dakota purses her lips and whacks my back. "I wish." After a glance behind me, she says, "I have someone you have to meet."

She waves, and a woman in a suit approaches, her silver hair in a high bun. Dakota says, "Hello, Mayor Rosen. This is Willow Dawson, the woman restoring the Underwood estate."

The mayor smiles at me, extending her ochre hand. "It's a pleasure to meet you, Ms. Dawson. I've been wanting to talk to you about the estate—it's an important part of Violet Moon's history."

"It's an honor to meet you, Mayor Rosen." I can't believe the mayor knows about me. "What would you like to know about the estate?"

Dakota quietly slips away, and Mayor Rosen says, "Do you have any buyers for the house yet?"

"I don't." My stomach flip-flops.

Her mouth curves. "The city of Violet Moon might be interested in purchasing it. For part of our growing tourism program."

My smile has to meet my eyes. "That'd be amazing. I'd love for the town of Violet Moon to enjoy the Château."

"It would have to be designated as a landmark with new purpose for the state of Georgia, not just the town of Violet Moon. Meaning it must be approved by Georgia's Secretary of State, and there are much stricter requirements."

"Wow, okay. I'd need to know those right away." I force myself not to fidget with my hands.

"Come by my office Monday morning? I'll make sure my assistant squeezes you into the schedule."

"Sounds perfect." I'm so excited, there's an actual buzz in my ears.

"Great. It was nice meeting you, Ms. Dawson."

"Same." I realize I could be working on a dream I didn't even know I had until now—creating a landmark retreat for the entire state of Georgia.

As soon as Mayor Rosen walks away, Dakota reappears like magic. "So, how'd it go?"

"Um, thank you!" I pull her into a hug.

She gives me a squeeze before pulling away. "So, it went well, then."

"She's meeting with me Monday morning. I owe you, big time."

"Nope. This is just what we do for each other. And honestly, if the city buys it, we all win."

"True. I like the way you think."

When Owen approaches, Dakota turns to him, her eyes brightening. "Owen." Her voice goes uncharacteristically high as she goes in for a big hug.

After they pull away, Owen clears his throat. "How have you been?"

"Great." Dakota turns to me and flashes her pearly whites. "Owen and I met when we were both seven years old. I caught him eating mud pies behind the hay bales at the Graham County Fair."

Owen glances at me, shaking his head. "That was a dare. And I take my dares very seriously, you know that, Kota."

Kota? I let out a laugh that I swear sounds like a cackling hyena, and I push away the prickle of dread skittering up my spine.

After the two engage in some catch up conversation, Owen tells Dakota, "I'm taking over Violet Moon's vet hospital. Dr. Thompson is retiring."

Dakota goes wide-eyed but blinks it away. "So, you're coming back here for good?"

"I am." His tone is quiet and a bit strained, and my prickle of dread becomes more of a nasty wave.

Dakota said she never got over her high school sweetheart, and by the look in her eyes right now, it seems like she has it bad for Owen.

Oh, god, please tell me I'm wrong about this. But Jeb mentioned drama.

The band plays Adele's "Someone Like You" and Frankie comes over. She looks almost unrecognizable with her dark hair pulled up with curls, makeup, and a simple yet elegant forest green dress. She looks at Owen and Dakota when she says, "Wasn't this your prom song?"

"Indeed, it was." Dakota gently takes Owen's hand. With that classic country drawl, she says, "May I have this dance, Mr. Brooks? For old time's sake."

So, Dakota and Owen were together. I feel a painful zing.

Owen flashes me a look, his eyes filled with concern, but I say, "You kids go have fun," through a lump forming in my throat.

Owen turns to Dakota and mumbles, "Uh, sure."

Once they're dancing, Dakota cups his jaw and uses her thumb to wipe something off his cheek.

With my chest tightening and my palms clamming, I don't want to be here another second.

My brain feels like it's in a woodchipper as I try to process everything that's happening. Clearly, Dakota is still in love with Owen, and although he seems hesitant with her, he loved her for a very long time.

And I feel betrayed by Frankie even though I know, logically, I shouldn't. It hurts that she doesn't want me for her son, even though she's right. I repeat that to myself.

Frankie is right. Who am I to get in the middle of Dakota and Owen? In six weeks, I'm back in New York, a place Owen never wants to live. Dakota and Owen both love it in Violet Moon, and they have a real chance of a happy life together.

I grab my purse and slip away. I need to distance myself from Owen, starting now.

14

The Restoration

My meeting with Mayor Rosen went amazingly well. Now I have an offer on the table for the farm—as long as it passes the Georgia state inspection—which includes the clause for the animals. I also have a deadline—August 6th, which is in exactly *four* weeks!

But with the city's name behind it, I now have additional crews to work more quickly.

So far, I'm three days in, and I've managed to avoid Owen. It's helped that I've been slammed, and he was gone for a few days, returning to Atlanta to pack up all his things before moving back to Violet Moon for good.

After Mr. Livingston worked with the local banker to secure me a historical restoration loan two days ago, the mayor helped me find additional contractors who don't mind coming in from Atlanta to get Bo's Château whipped into shape in no time. Because the landmark will have new purpose, we'll have to do a renovation along with a restoration so it can be functional as a destination resort.

The contractors are highly reputable, and I'm pumped to knock things down. Today, a demo crew made up of volunteers from Violet Moon is taking out the kitchen walls, opening it up to the dining and living areas. Then they're going to take out the back wall and weathered patio so they can be replaced with sliding glass doors and brick pavers.

I flip into professional mode when I meet Owen outside, despite my pulse going into overdrive. He's offered to help me until he starts at the vet hospital in three weeks. Today's job is messy, so Owen and I are on cleanup duty while the crew takes sledgehammers to the place.

Owen says, "Wow. It's going down fast."

"It's almost scary, isn't it?" I blink away the dust from my eyes. "The rebuild, however, is much more painstaking."

"I bet."

Owen and I glove up and begin the fun job of picking up ripped-out boards. We try not to get stuck by nails as we haul them to the dumpsters that now sit in the roundabout driveway. It's also our job to sweep out drywall dust so the place is in decent shape for tomorrow's crew, who'll start framing the new back wall. I take window measurements and place a rush order for the day after tomorrow. I can't afford a delay in materials.

The back wall comes down, and Owen and I work in the blazing sun as we haul heavy boards and debris to the dumpsters. After we've unloaded our wheelbarrow, Owen flashes me a mischievous smile and puts his arm around my waist, ready to pull me in for a kiss.

Without thinking, I lean away.

His face puzzles.

I don't know what to say to him. I'm not ready to address everything that is going on with me—not in the middle of work.

With a teasing flicker in his eyes, he says, "Is this because you found out my sisters call me Bambi?"

I can't help but laugh. "No, although it didn't help." I touch his shoulder. "I'm kidding. Sort of." I shrug when I say, "Just... not around the guys."

"We can duck behind the dumpster. I've never done it before. Romantic, no?" He winks.

"Hard pass," I say, trying not to chuckle. Owen has already started chipping away at my resolve, and we've been only together for a few hours. Of course, kissing him behind the dumpster sounds exciting, but I take off my gloves and knock them together to get the dust out, avoid his gaze. "I prefer romantic interludes with a less putrid stench. But that's just me." I try to sound teasing, but I'm not really pulling it off. I can't kiss Owen, not now—not after everything I saw Saturday night.

He studies my face, like he's trying to read me. "All right."

"You're just trying to get out of work."

We head back to a pile of trim boards to pull out the old nails so we can reuse the boards as a part of the restoration. Again, it's not a particularly fun job, so Owen and I are on our hands and knees as we pull rusty nails out with the flip side of our hammers. I show Owen which boards can be salvaged, as some are too cracked, but some can be glued. After that, feeling ripped up inside, I go quiet as we work. When I wasn't with him these last few days, I was all set to stay away. But when he's here, helping me, looking at me with that smile and those eyes, my willpower crumbles like the walls around us.

Finally, Owen says, "Is everything okay?"

"Fine." I force a smile, which I'm sure Owen sees through. But there are workers around us, and this isn't the time or place to get into it all.

Owen puts down the board he's working on. "You're distant."

I take my pliers and nudge out a nail to keep my hands busy. "I'm just stressed about kicking off the house renovation. There's so much to do, and I have such a short amount of time to get it done."

"That's understandable," he says, but something in his tone tells me he doesn't believe me. And he shouldn't.

We get back to work, and when I reach into the pile for another board, something pierces my arm, right above the glove, and I jerk away. My arm's bleeding, a shard of glass sticking out of it. "Dammit." Automatically, I yank the piece away, and the cut streams blood.

"Whoa, Willow! You're not supposed to do that." Owen yanks off his shirt and rushes over, wrapping it around my arm. "Come and have a seat." He points to an overturned bucket.

"Whoops. Too late." It's hurting, but more than that, it's bleeding... a lot. "I'm fine," I say. I can't believe I was so careless. I rarely get hurt on the job, but Owen has me distracted.

He lifts his shirt to examine the cut. "It's deep—you're gonna need stitches. Do you want to go to the emergency room, or do you want me to do it?"

"You." I don't hesitate.

"Okay, hold my shirt tightly against the cut, and don't move—I'll go get my kit. We're lucky that it was glass and not a rusty nail." He sprints off.

Jeb, who does woodwork and brought his team here today to help, wanders over. "You okay there, New York?"

"I'm good. Owen's going to stitch me back up," I say, not wanting him and his team handling me instead of the renovation.

When Owen returns, he opens his medical kit out and cleans my cut. Then he takes out a vial and needle. "I'm going to give you a localized anesthetic for the pain, okay? You don't have any allergies, do you?"

"Nope. Go ahead." He takes my arm and rubs it in various places while he pokes in the needle. I don't know how he does it, but I feel nothing. He's got that magic touch.

After a beat, he says, "I'm ready to stitch you up. You might want to look away."

"Yup." I'm not going to argue—I don't want to make myself feel worse. I'm already lightheaded, probably from skipping breakfast this morning.

I turn my head and proceed to feel tiny twinges and pinches, but it's mild. I focus on the calm lake in the distance as I take gulps of fresh air. Owen's voice is gentle when he says, "All done with stitching. You only needed four. After I bandage it, you'll be good to go."

"Wow, that was quick and painless."

"You can't get these stitches wet for forty-eight hours, and you've gotta take it easy."

"Okay." Ugh. I don't have time to take it easy. "I'll just do things one-armed."

"We'll see about that."

As he wraps me up, his gentle touch sends tingles buzzing through my skin. How can I not be hot for a guy who so carefully and expertly bandages my wounds? But I can't allow myself to feel the things that I feel for him. When he finishes, I say, "Thanks, Owen. Really."

"No problem."

I stand, feeling dizzy, and I stumble. Owen rushes to my side, putting his arms around me. "Careful. You're pale—you need to lie down for a bit, doctor's order. I bet you haven't eaten yet today. I'll get you some juice to get your blood sugar back up."

"Thanks." I'm not really in a place to argue. I didn't eat breakfast, he's right about that. And I'm used to small injuries, but I haven't needed stitches for a long time. I guess it hit me harder than I expected.

Juice in one hand and holding me up in the other, Owen walks me to my room. Once I'm seated on the bed, he slides off my boots.

After I drink the orange juice he brought me, I try to take off my clothes, but can't do it one handed. Finally, I ask, "Can you help me get these off? They're filthy." I'm torn about asking him to do that, but I don't trust anyone else.

"Of course." He gently slips off my shirt, and those rough hands leave tingles in their wake. He respectfully turns his head as he slides my jeans off, leaving me in my bra and panties.

I catch him sneaking a peek, and as much as I want him to see all of me, I climb into bed and pull up the covers. "Thanks for your help."

He fluffs my pillow, leaning into my ear and whispering, "I'm here if you need anything. Anything at all."

His breath sends electricity straight down my spine, but I turn my head. "Owen, please. Don't say those things to me."

He leans back. "I'm sorry. I wasn't trying to be insensitive."

"No, no. It's not that." I touch his arm, sighing. "Have a seat. Please?"

He flashes a puzzled expression when he sits. "Sure. What's going on?"

I swallow hard—I can't keep doing this to him. It's not fair. Finally, I say, "I didn't know about Dakota."

He groans before blowing out a long breath of air, like a tire going flat. "Dakota. We were a thing for a lot of years, but that was eons ago. And we've both changed."

"But I could see it in her eyes at Kayla's reception. She still loves you."

His pleading eyes meet mine. "But I don't love Dakota. I mean, I do as a person, but not in *that* way anymore."

Something in my heart flutters, but still—I don't want to be the reason he can't explore things with her and see if they get that spark back. I stare at the beige wall, trying to tune out the booming thuds echoing from below. "With her, you get a lifetime. With me, you get six weeks."

"Give me the six weeks." His words tear the breath away from my chest, and my pulse kicks up as I lean into him. He takes my good hand in his and strokes it, something so simple yet intimate. And maybe that's just because it's Owen doing it.

He's trying to make me cave, and it's working. When I turn, we're nose to nose, and I feel his breath on my cheek when he utters, "I can't stop thinking about you. Tell me you don't feel the same."

I do—this is unlike anything I ever had before. Owen runs a finger down my face as he ever so patiently waits for an answer. I meet his pleading eyes, and I want more than anything to tell him that yes, I want that too. But I also think I might want forever with him, which is ludicrous. I hardly know him. That's just our magnetic attraction clouding my judgment.

I glance out the window to break the spell, and there is Dakota—in the pasture with Sir Fig A Lot. She milks the goats first thing in the morning and at suppertime. That means that now, she must be swinging by on her lunch break to make sure they're fed, which is so thoughtful. She knew we were kicking off construction today, so she's doing what she can to help.

Her gesture twists the pitchfork into my gut, and it reminds me of how much this farm means to her—how much Violet Moon is a part of her.

And it's not a part of me. I simply can't do this with Owen—not just for Dakota, but for myself, too. I'm starting to have real feelings for him, which means I'm going to be crushed when I leave. My voice turns croaky when I say, "If I can't play for keeps, I don't want to play. I'm sorry."

He sighs, defeated. "All right. But I'm going to stay close by so I can monitor you."

15

Twisted Tree

❀ ── ◆ ── ❀

Owen leaves my room, telling me to get some rest and that his mom offered to check in on the farmhands and the horses today. So, I lie down, drifting off almost instantly.

It's a sound, peaceful sleep.

Until it's not. The gnarly tree is back, coming at me, strangling me. As I gasp for air, I scream a word. It's what I always scream—but I don't know what it is because I'm asleep. I try to wake myself—I know I'm dreaming—but it doesn't work.

I can't get out. I'm trapped, the tree surrounding me as sirens blare.

Everything in the dream blurs, and I'm sweating and sobbing when Owen's voice finally cuts into my panic. "Willow, wake up!" I've never heard him so loud before.

My eyes flutter open to see him hovering over me, his face wracked with worry. My entire body trembles as I'm gripping my palm on Owen's shoulder. I realize I'm now saying, "Take me home," and I finally stop, breathless.

"Willow, it's okay," Owen says, pulling me into a tight hug.

I sit for a few seconds in his arms, out of breath and in hysterics. I take far too long to calm down. I *can't* calm down. I loathe these dreams, and I'd give anything to make them stop.

"Night terror," I say through a sob.

He strokes my hair. "It's okay now. Everything's okay."

I'm still gasping for air. "Oh my god. Those make me feel like I'm dying."

"Just breathe, Willow."

I sit, letting his strong arms and gentle nature soothe me. There is no place I'd rather be than right here, just like this. When I'm finally calm enough to speak, I pull away and meet his gaze. "Would you mind taking me on a drive? There's something I want you to see."

He tucks a loose strand of hair behind my ear. "Of course."

Before I stand, I check my phone to see that Natanya has texted and called a zillion times. "Oh, no. I'm late for a Zoom meeting with the Kleins. I'm *never* late." I jump up and scramble for my computer, not caring that I'm only in my bra and panties. "Can we go after this call?" I throw on my shirt.

"Of course."

We're driving down I-85, and I'm so relieved to finally have someone I feel comfortable enough to share this with. When I see the tree up ahead, I direct Owen to pull off in a safe spot on the shoulder of the road.

I point to it. "Do you know anything about the memorial cross on that tree?"

"I don't think so, no." He eyes me quizzically. I'm not surprised at his answer—no one seems to know about it.

After we've stepped out of the car, I tell him about how it's appeared in my night terrors. As we climb the hill, I shudder, but keep moving. I know I need to tell him about the parts of my life that don't add up so he can understand the significance of this. I stop and wring my hands when I say, "So, I'm going to drop something on you, and I don't want you to make a big deal out of it."

"Okay." His brows furrow. "Worse than you losing both your parents in a car accident?"

"No. It's not worse. But it is... weird. And getting weirder. It's about my adoption." I proceed to tell him that my night terrors are about this tree, that I don't have memories before five years old, and that I can't find my adoption records or birth certificate in New York. I fold my arms over my chest trying to stave off the shivers.

He takes my hand and squeezes it. "The wedding's over, so it's time I talk to my mom, okay?"

"Okay."

When we get to the top, I take Owen's hand in mine as we carefully step over the roots. Arriving at the tree, I take a deep breath before I point to the cross.

He squats down, blinking. "Oh, shit," he mutters, before looking up at me in shock.

"Right." I shake my head. "No one I've asked knows about it. And I've researched it—there are no news articles about it either." I swallow hard. "Don't you think it's weird that I have dreams about this tree and my name's on this cross?"

"Definitely weird, but it could be a coincidence."

"It could be," I say. "I couldn't find any record of another Willow in this town for the past thirty years. I also can't imagine my adoption involving anything nefarious." My adoptive parents would never do anything like that—but maybe they didn't know.

Owen's phone pings, and his lips press together as he reads it. "Dammit." He looks at me, fluttering out a breath. "I was waiting to hear from my mom before I told you this—in case she knew anything about it. She doesn't, so I'll just tell you."

I'm disappointed, even though I don't know what he's talking about yet. He ratchets up my nerves more when he hesitates, taking my hand in his. "When you had that night terror, you kept screaming, 'Sammy.'"

"Sammy?" I exhale, squeezing his hand as a crushing weight lifts off my chest. I *finally* know the word I cry out—the one I can never remember when I'm awake. "That sounds familiar."

"Really?"

"Sammy," I say, straining my brain.

"Do you know anyone with that name?"

"No. But that doesn't mean much. There's so much I don't remember."

16
The Loft

The lake glistens with the evening sun highlighting its crests, drawing in my gaze. It was an exhausting but fulfilling day. The entire town of Violet Moon has showed up for me this week so far, which is both humbling and amazing. Volunteers helped the crews with new roof shingles. Jeb's team sanded down all the bathroom cabinetry, and all of Owen's family worked on cleanup duty except Frankie, who managed the farm for me today.

For the first time in my life, I understand the phrase, "It takes a village." I'm proof that you can get by without it, but boy, everything works better and faster in a team. Best of all, those backbreaking tasks become fulfilling and actually fun.

I covered my arm in plastic and showered, and now, I'm waiting for Owen at the lookout spot with a blanket, water, napkins, mints, two sandwiches, and chips. Oh, and Sir Fig A Lot. If I didn't bring him, he'd show up, anyway. Which reminds me—I *really* need to fix that fence.

Last night, after Owen and I got home from seeing the tree, he helped me try to log in to Bo's computer. We ended up getting locked out because of too many attempts.

As soon as I can get ahold of my farmhand, Levi, I'm going to ask him for help hacking into the computer. After he alluded to being some sort of techie, I discovered that he's starting college this fall to become a computer scientist. Meanwhile, Owen told me he was going to have a sit-down with Frankie to find out anything and everything she knows about Lily, which should be happening now—before dinner. Even a place where Lily's things might be stored would help.

In exchange for his hard work today helping on the farm with pest control, I bought Owen and me gourmet sandwiches—turkey, bacon, and avocado on ciabatta. We'll have to eat them here, as I don't have a kitchen anymore.

Once I've got the picnic all set up, I feed Sir Fig A Lot an extra bite of turkey. He's feasting when Owen trudges up the hill, all showered up. "How's the arm?" he asks before sitting next to me.

"It barely hurts. I had an amazing doctor."

"Aw, thanks." He holds out his hands near my bandage. "Do you mind?"

"Not at all."

He takes out his hand sanitizer and uses it before lifting the bandage and checking it with that gentle touch I love. "Great. Healing nicely." He puts the bandage back and does another squirt of sanitizer.

"See. I'm tough."

"I can re-bandage it for you tomorrow."

"Sure. Thank you." I hand him his wrapped sandwich before turning to Sir Fig A Lot. "Now, leave his food alone. He's our guest."

"Ah, I share." Owen breaks off a piece and feeds it to the goat. "We should call him Sir Eats A Lot."

"No kidding. I named him before I knew he inhales everything but Mary Louise's apple pie."

After unwrapping his sandwich, Owen stops before taking a bite. "So Ma said we should check the barn loft. Lily spent a lot of time up there."

A kernel of hope pops inside me. "Of course. The one place I didn't look. Let's do it."

"Yup."

After a bite, he says, "Now this is a good sandwich right here. I forgot how much I missed Dough 'n Mo."

"It's the best."

Demon comes flying up the hill, and I grab my food and hang on for dear life. Owen jumps up, ready to manage the dog, but then something wild happens. Sir Fig A Lot approaches Demon, and they chase each other in a circle before running away together.

"Did that just happen?" I shoot Owen an amazed look.

"I wouldn't have believed it if I hadn't seen it myself." Owen watches on as they run and play.

"Sir Fig A Lot and Demon are BFFs." My mouth hangs open.

"Well, they *are* both little assholes." I laugh, and Owen shrugs before he says, "So, what was your ex like? You know about mine."

"Wow, you go right for the gizzard."

"I've got nothing else to do while we eat."

"It's kinda humiliating." I chew my lip.

"You don't have to tell me."

"Hmm. Thanks for the opt out." I stare at the water, wondering what it would be like in the winter, imagining it'd look like glass. "Let's see. When I met Seth, he was everything I thought I wanted—sensitive, smart, sweet. He was, or still is, a writer, so he's artsy. And witty. Clever with words, understandably. We were together on and off for three years and spent a lot of time doing New York-y things like fancy dinners and off-Broadway shows. My life outside Seth was my work, and that was enough for me, or so I thought. I was so busy; I really didn't know how to manage any more than a boyfriend and Natanya."

"So, what happened?"

"One night we were having dinner on the patio of a restaurant below his chic Manhattan apartment, and it was a great night. The food was perfect. The wine was flowing. The holidays were approaching, and he was talking about his family's annual ski trip. With a nice buzz, I didn't think twice when I said, 'I've never been skiing. I'm so excited.'" I napkin off my face, hesitating. I hate telling this part of the story. "I couldn't believe it when he replied, 'You're not coming with me, babe.'"

"Ouch."

"No kidding. It shocked me. I couldn't believe I spent most of three years with somebody who didn't even want to bring me home to meet his family. So, I ended things. For good."

"That's ugly."

"It was—at first. But then, I was relieved not to be tied down. Work hit a rough patch, and I had to do everything to keep my head above water. I have employees to take care of, and somewhere along the way, I stopped missing him. When I got some distance from the relationship, I was glad it ended." I sigh. "Being here—it's just something I've needed for so long, and I didn't even realize it." Ugh—that's enough about Seth, for now, so I look at my sandwich and say, "All right. This thing isn't going to eat itself. Your turn. What happened with Dakota?"

Owen takes an inordinate amount of time chewing, and when I scold him with my eyes, he finally swallows. "Fine. Dakota and I dated from freshman year in high school through college, and I thought we were going to get married. I actually had a ring and was ready to propose. She told me not to because she wanted to go to culinary school in Paris while I went to vet school. Like you said with Seth, I wasn't that sad. It was more like I could finally just be with myself. Then after I graduated vet school, I could live somewhere else and *be* something else for a while. I'd spent so much time taking care of my family, the last thing I wanted to do was start my own."

"That makes sense."

"Then I heard Dakota started dating Brody, and I thought they were going to get married. I was actually happy for her." His face puzzles. "But then they didn't, and I'm not really sure what happened."

I think about what Dakota said—that it was because she'd never gotten over Owen, but it's not my place to share something she'd told me in confidence. I take a mint out of its case before holding out the can. "If you want to find out, I bet Mary Louise knows."

He takes one, grinning. "Thanks. And I'll take that bet and raise you, double." His smile falls away as he studies me, like he wants to say something else. Then he lets out a long sigh. "I'm ready now. For marriage. For kids. All of it."

Those all too familiar tingles reappear, his hint not lost on me. Am I ready for all that? I think so, but I'm not prepared to verbalize it. Instead, I say, "You'll be amazing with kids. You're already so great with your sisters, especially Trinity. You know that, right?"

"Thanks. Trin's awesome."

When we finish our sandwiches and pack everything up, I take his hand and say, "Now, let's dig through the barn loft."

We step inside, and out of habit, I check on the goats, making sure they've got everything they need, and that no one looks sick or injured. All is well, but Darling seems glad to see Sir Fig A Lot.

"Hey, Ms. Dawson."

I turn to see Huck, a farmhand and Mary Louise's son, stepping inside the barn. "You're here working late."

He's tall and lanky and honestly, looks nothing like Mary Louise. Maybe he takes after Bill? He runs a hand through his brown wavy hair when he says, "Yeah, I need to tell you—we've got a few stems showing signs of leaf rust, but I know an organic fungicide that works wonders on it. I wanted to make sure you're okay with me using it."

I look at Owen. "What do you think?"

Owen takes the barley in his hands and rubs it. "Yup. That's leaf rust. Great catch, Huck."

"Thanks, Dr. Brooks."

"Do it," I say, smiling. "And thank you, Huck."

After he disappears, I shoot Owen a puzzled look. "That's really Mary Louise's son?"

"Yeah. He's a nice guy. I don't know what happened. The apple fell far from the tree."

"No kidding."

Owen and I climb the ladder to the loft, and I can see why Lily loved this space. The air smells like hay and cedar, and the sky window has a view of the trees above the barn. There's a small turquoise couch that looks like a reading nook with a bookshelf behind it. "So charming," I say.

"No wonder Trinity sneaks up here." Owen walks over to the couch and flips the cushions over.

We wander, taking in the scene. For some reason, Owen gets down on the floor. I'm buzzing with anticipation as I go through the bookshelf, and between copies of Wuthering Heights and The Grapes of Wrath, I find a decorated box and take it. "Owen." I look to see that he's lying stomach down, his arms sweeping under the couch.

He glances up at me like a cobra, then pulls his arms out. "No way." He stands, brushing the dust bunnies off himself.

We rush to the couch and sit side by side. I run a finger over the gold bar that runs along the top of the box. It has the words "Lily Underwood" etched into it.

Owen has a glint of hope in his eyes. "You wanna open it?"

I wave a hand, my stomach flip-flopping. "No, you do it." I hand it to him.

He carefully lifts the lid, and I blink as I take in what's inside. Rings, bracelets, and earrings.

"Nothing much in here." He takes out a simple wedding band and eyes it.

After he hands the ring to me, I place it back in the box, disappointed. But I'm not ready to give up yet. "Let's keep looking."

Owen and I are combing the place again when I see that behind the couch are hinges on the wall boards, signaling a door. "There's an attic space here."

He rushes over and helps me move the couch. When I put my hand in the space between the boards, there's a cutout. Sure enough, the door opens with a tug. "Nice!"

"No way! Good job, Queens."

"Thanks."

We duck through the door and step inside, knocking away cobwebs as we go. In the corner sits a dusty aging trunk, leather with straps on it, and I gasp. "That has to have something in it."

I brush off the dust, and this time, there's no hesitation when I flip the latches before opening the lid. Peering inside, I cry out, "A wedding dress!" I pull it out to see that it's definitely the one Lily was wearing in that photo, and it's definitely from the sixties with the collared neckline, lace explosion, and poofy sleeves. "It's so adorably hideous."

Owen winces. "I'm not sure about the adorable part." He shuffles through the trunk, pulling out memorabilia, more photos of Lily and Bo, and other old photos that look like them with their families.

But that's not what makes my heart stop beating in my chest.

With unsteady hands, I reach in and take out a photo that's stuck to the bottom. It's a picture of a young woman who has a frightening resemblance to me—long auburn hair, freckled skin, and the same thin lips. But bigger than that, she has my bright green eyes.

Owen studies the picture. "Wow, she looks like you."

"She does," I whisper, flipping over the photo. Scribbled on the back, it says, "Annie, 1996." I stare at it, uttering, "She has the rare combination of red hair and green eyes like me. Could this be my mother?"

"Sure looks like it."

"And her photo is here—in Bo and Lily's house." My words barely eke out as my eyes stay glued to the photo. "Annie," I whisper, still processing the name of a woman who looks just like me. Maybe I finally know a piece of my lost history. Adrenaline's pumping through me as I stare at the photo. I can feel it in my gut: *This is my mom.*

Giddy, I spin around, so thankful for Owen, I grab him and kiss him. Pulling away, I utter, "Thank you. For talking to your mom. But also, for being here."

"You're very welcome."

Owen keeps showing up for me, something I didn't know just how much I needed until now. I move my hand down to Owen's and take it. His skin is warm, and I feel the roughness of his palm against mine. His fingers are long, but his grip is gentle.

I pull Owen in for another kiss, our mouths moving in synchrony. I'm trying to stay away—to protect my heart and his—but it feels almost impossible when I get lost in those eyes of his, part ocean, part storm cloud. I'm starting to think we're two magnets incapable of getting close without drawing together.

We stand, just holding each other. The sun shining through the sky window warms my face, and I close my eyes, taking in the moment. When I open them, Owen has an expression that I've never seen before. His lips are slightly parted, his eyes almost mesmerized as he looks at me, like I'm the only one he sees.

He moves his hands up my arms and to my shoulders, bringing his lips up to my ear. His breath tickles as he whispers, "You deserve to know your roots. You deserve everything."

His words fill a hole deep within me, and I turn and face him, just a breath away. When our mouths catch, his lips move slowly, gently, and calmness washes over me. I forget who I am, or who I might be, and how I don't belong. How Owen lives here, and how I live somewhere else entirely.

His kiss deepens with more intensity and intention, and I take in every morsel of it. The mint on his breath, the silk of his lips, the scent of the air when he's nearby. My grip tightens around him when I realize that *this* is where I belong.

Our bodies mold together, and it's beyond attraction. We're just holding each other, and it's everything as he fills my hollow spaces. He pulls away, brushing a wisp of hair off my forehead. "Let's go see what we can find out about Annie."

His words overwhelm me, and I'm terrified of what we might discover. After what happened with Bo and Lily, I'm not sure I can handle more disappointment. "I think I need another day." I rest my head on his chest. "I'm not quite ready yet."

"Of course."

And here we are again, like grooved magnets, drawn together and fitting perfectly.

17

The Ride

⊰⊱ · ⊰◆⊱ · ⊰⊱

I wake Thursday morning to everything sopping wet after it rained half the night. It's barely dawn when I meet Dakota in the barn to help her milk the goats.

"So, what happened last night?" I ask, sitting on the platform next to her. She'd written to me yesterday evening and asked if I'd wanted to join her for a beer, but I was too tired.

"You'll never believe it." She smiles, expertly tugging at Darling's utters. "That mysterious stranger I met at the Brew and Chew Festival was at The Malted Moon last night."

"No way." I'm genuinely happy for her. And, honestly, relieved. I know I should want Owen and Dakota back together because that would make my leaving easier, but I don't. And I loathe betraying my new friend. "Tell me everything."

"We just talked. Like the whole night—until close. Bennett is gorgeous and awesome. He's so smart and worldly, Willow. He also lived abroad like me—in Madrid."

"That's amazing." Sir Fig A Lot rests his nose on my leg as I pet it. "So, how did you leave things?"

"Well, he was a gentleman and just got my number, which I appreciated... I guess. I mean, it's been so long, I was also kinda hoping for a romp in the hay." She breaks into a laugh. "But I'll settle for a gentleman."

"So, he's going to call."

"He *better* call." She sighs. "Right now, he lives in Atlanta... but he's thinking of moving here because of his job distributing Violet Moon beer."

"That's promising."

And just like that, Owen is out of the picture with Dakota? Right? So, now's a good time to tell her everything. "Listen. We need to talk—"

I stop petting Sir Fig A Lot so he nudges me with his nose. Giving him a scratch, I say, "Yes, I'll give you more love, my cute brat."

"You are that, aren't you, Mr. Sir Fig A Lot?" She reaches over and gives his head a scrub. "So, Willow," she says, her tone turning nervous. "I have more news."

"What's up?" I'll listen to her news, then tell her.

She turns and faces me, her eyes sparkling. "A few farmer's markets in Atlanta may want to carry my cheeses."

"That's huge!" I give her a hug.

She pulls away and shoots me a look. "I know, right? But I'm going to be gone the entire coming week. Which means I can't milk the goats."

I bat a hand. "I've got it—this is a huge opportunity for you. And you'll get to see Bennett?"

She squeals. "Yes!" But then her face goes serious. "Are you sure?"

I'm nervous because I'm already overloaded, but I'm not about to tell her that. This could change her whole business, not to mention her romantic situation. Ugh, I don't want to bring up Owen now and ruin her happy moment. And, maybe when she gets back, she'll be in a relationship with Bennett, so telling her will be even easier. I simply say, "Absolutely no problem."

"You're the best."

The sun hangs above the mountains, hidden behind a dark cloud as I walk to the stables, the smell of rain thick in the air. It was another long day of framing and electrical rewiring, and I'm behind on my farm chores. I have to milk the goats and feed the horses. Plus, there's several updates I need to prepare for the Kleins. Right now, I need to fill the horses' water tanks, and since Owen's coming over to do Oreo's rehab soon, I want to make sure the colt is ready to go. After Friday, when he got out, I've been checking on him to make sure he's safely inside the stables.

When I find a package of Fig Newtons in my purse, my stomach flutters. Owen keeps leaving those for me there because I always forget to eat. Why is he so amazing?

Stepping into the stables, I see Trinity with her arms wrapped around Oreo, petting his mane.

The sweetest sight—the two of them. And boy, does that little girl love that horse. I'm going to miss the hell out of them both when I leave. "Hey, Trin. How's it going?" I ask as I turn on the hose and put it in the trough.

She doesn't tear her gaze away from the horse. "Good. I'm taking Oreo on a walk before Owen gets here. I want to make sure he does real well on his test today."

"That's thoughtful of you. Does your ma know you're here?" And there it is—I just said Ma instead of Mom.

Trinity finally meets my gaze with pleading eyes. "No. Please don't tell her. She thinks I'm feeding the chickens, but I got that all done."

I walk over and give Eclipse a pet on the snout, which she loves. "Okay, but you can only stay a little while. It'll be dark soon."

"I want to ride Raven. Real bad."

"You and me both." I sigh, stepping over to give Oreo a pet. "I wish I knew how to ride. It's awesome, and a great way to get to know all the areas of my property."

Trinity stands, wiping her palms on her jeans. Then she walks over to the wall and grabs the two-person saddle hanging on it before returning to me. "So, let's go for your first lesson."

I check out the stable doors to see that more clouds have moved in, but it's not raining. "Really? We'd have to ask your ma."

"Okay."

I text Frankie and ask if Trinity can take me for a ride, as she's finished feeding the chickens.

She responds.

Go ahead, she won't give up anyhow. Be back at rainfall or dark, whichever comes first.

I smile at Trinity. "Your ma said yes."

Trinity jumps up and down, saying, "She had to. Today's my birthday."

"Your birthday!" I cry out. "Happy birthday! So, you're ten? Why aren't you celebrating?"

"I'm having a sleepover party on Saturday. And, yup, I'm ten now."

"Well, then." I throw my hands in the air. "Let's go have a birthday ride."

"Okay." She brushes Raven's mane. "This relaxes the horse and builds trust." She shows me how to place the pad, then, step-by-step, how to strap the saddle on the horse.

When I repeat her steps, I'm mesmerized brushing Raven. Horses really are mystical creatures.

Trinity puts a hand on her hip. "Glad to see you're careful, like me. You don't want to miss steps."

"I hate things being out of order."

"Me too. Owen is a big fat messy pig."

I nod, my lips splitting into a grin. "Is he now?"

Well—this is a handy way to get the information about Owen that he's not going to tell me himself. "What else is wrong with your brother?"

Trinity taps her finger on her chin. "He burps real loud, but that's actually kind of funny. I've been steaming mad at him for moving to Atlanta." She mounts the horse, showing me. Then she gets off, saying, "Now you try."

"Okay." I repeat what she did, struggling a lot more as I mount and dismount. When I'm finished, I brush off my pants. "I'm sure you missed Owen a lot."

"Not just me. Ma and Bailey too. I know Kayla missed him, but she wouldn't say it."

"Are you glad Owen's back?"

"Yes." She folds her arms. "I know what you're doing."

Uh-oh. Busted. "You do?"

"You're trying to put off riding on the horse 'cause you're scared."

Phew. "You might be right about that. Let me just turn the hose off and get going." I definitely don't want to forget and find the stable flooded when we get back. Once I'm done, I return to find Trinity already on the horse.

I take two deep breaths before putting my foot in the stirrup and swinging myself over this massive creature. I manage to mount behind Trinity and once we're both ready, she says, "I can feel you shivering, but don't worry. I know what I'm doing."

"Okay, I trust you." I can't believe it, but I *do* trust her—this tiny, nine... ten-year-old firecracker. Well, as much as I'd trust anyone riding a beast of an animal. I flutter out a breath.

Trinity takes the reins and whistles, then Raven trots off—and I have to hang on for dear life! I manage to get my balance and a solid grip around Trinity as we enter the pasture. Trinity talks me through the ins and outs of pulling the reins to order a turn, or how to get the horse to speed up and slow down.

I don't have much luck though, as when I put my hands around Trinity to take the reins, Raven simply halts. I end up having to hand the control back to Trinity so she can show me, again, how to make a direction change.

We head through the trees, riding onto a path along the creek that leads away from the lake. It's so peaceful, the smell of dew and pine in the air, the only sounds the clicking of horseshoes and babbling water. With more dark clouds moving in, we weave through a thick patch of trees, a honey-dew breeze wrapping around us. It's like we've entered a secret garden with birdsong, and I know why Trinity loves this so much. We pass wildflowers she identifies, and she points out the chipmunks scurrying in the brush. This is exactly what I need, and I already can't wait to do it again.

And I love this kid.

When we're heading back, Trinity gives me pointers on how to adjust my seat position so I'm sitting comfortably as we head uphill. Once we've returned to the pasture, she hands me the reins. I loosen them, lean forward, and kick Raven in the ribs, as Trinity taught me. Raven gallops off, and I let out a scream.

"Whoa, hang on, Raven," Trinity says, taking the reins back and tugging them. "Not so fast now."

Once she's back to a trot, Trinity says, "You can't yell like that, Willow. You don't wanna spook the horse."

"Sorry." I can't believe I'm getting schooled by a kid, but honestly, it's pretty cool.

When Trinity brings us back to a fast trot, I pretend my lips are super glued shut as the evening wind rushes on my face and the nerves bundle in my stomach.

It's a bit scary but mostly exhilarating.

I bring my arms around Trinity to take the reins again, and I try another turn as it starts to rain, gently. This time, I have a little more luck getting the horse to shift directions, which smacks a big smile on my face.

"Great job." Trinity gives me a hard pat on the shoulder. "You did it."

"I did, didn't I?" I must be glowing.

When we get back to the stables, it starts to downpour—we just make it.

Owen appears, rain trickling down his face and concern in his eyes. "Trin, you git yourself home. I'll help Willow get the horse in for the night."

"Yes, sir." Trinity dismounts.

"Thanks for the lesson, Trinity," I call out as she rushes away, disappearing into the bramble that separates my property from theirs.

Owen extends his hand, dripping with rain, to help me off Raven, but I say, "No. I got this. Trinity taught me how."

"All right." He holds his palms up and backs away.

I swing my leg over, but as I go to jump down, my foot catches in the stirrup, and I tip over, doing a nice face plant in a fresh puddle.

"Shit. Are you okay?" Owen rushes over and into the mud to help me out.

"I'm fine." I laugh, wiping my face. "I landed on my good arm."

When he realizes I'm not hurt, his mouth curves, and he makes this snorting sound, which I realize is from suppressing a laugh. He says, "Sorry, but you should really get a look at yourself right now."

"Oh, really? Me?" I inch closer to him before grabbing his leg and giving it a good tug. When he tips over, mud splashes inside his open mouth.

"Christ," he utters, spewing out dirt.

I burst into laughter. So hard, tears form in my eyes. Finally, when I can speak, I say, "You should see yourself right now. There's something up your nose."

"I see how this is gonna be." He splashes mud into my hair, mouth, nose, and I think even inside my ears.

"Hey!" I grab a clump and throw it at his ear, and he returns with a toss. Before I know it, there's not an inch of our bodies that isn't wet and coated in mud.

Owen manages to put Raven back in her stall, faster than I've ever seen, and returns to me before I've even stood up. And I can't help but notice how magnificent he looks standing over me, wet, mud-streaked, and with his clothes clinging to his body.

"Come to our house for dinner this Sunday," he blurts, a vulnerable look on his face.

Oh, jeez. The family dinner thing again. I know I should go, but I'm just not there yet. I need more time, so I say, "I'll think about it. Oh, and thank you for the Fig Newtons. They were lifesavers." Then, I pull him back in the mud with me, and this time, he doesn't complain because his mouth crashes into mine. His lips are soft, his wet hands are slick and strong as they roam my body. There's no sweetness in his touch this time.

My heart galloping in my ears, I tug his shirt until it peels away. He slides his hands under mine and practically rips it off, and I melt from the liquid heat emanating from his fingers. "Owen," I murmur, pulling away to run my hands up his chest.

His chest. My god, that beautiful chest, streaked with mud, soaking wet, and heaving. My hand stops, feeling the thumping of his heartbeat that matches my own. Frenetic and wild.

Over the past weeks, I've fantasized taking Owen countless times, but it was never in the mud. And this is better than any fantasy.

I grab his belt, and it jangles as I struggle to unlatch it. He strikes his tongue over every inch of my mouth.

"I need you," he rasps.

I need him too, fast and furious, rocking over me. But all I manage to say is, "The horse shower."

Owen scoops me up and carries me inside, flipping on the water overhead. Then he sets me down before tugging his jeans off. I do mine before tossing them both outside.

Completely naked, his mouth meets mine again as we move under the lukewarm water. I'm on fire, every cell in my body quivering with anticipation.

When the water grows hot, we soap up, rushed, desperate.

"You're so beautiful," he says, his lips hot on the side of my neck as his sudsy hands move over my breasts.

My body electrifies at his touch, my bones liquefying and any semblance of composure I thought I had is a distant memory. With mud pouring off us, we scrub our hair. Our lips never stop touching as Owen soaps his way over my shoulders, my arms, and slides his hand over my hips. It seems like forever before he finally slides them between my legs. "God, you feel so good."

His mouth is hungry on mine before his tongue traces over my neck. With wet, slippery hands, he toys with my nipples as I run my fingers down his body. I'm caught between nervousness and excitement as I stroke him, but there's something nagging at me from the back of my conscience. He closes his eyes and exhales, saying, "Slow down, baby."

I stop, looking into his eyes clouding with desire. With the air filled with steam, the two of us discover how to drive one another close to the edge and back. I'm not going to be able to keep this up much longer, that's for sure. But it's more than that—I don't want to go all the way with Owen when something is needling me.

Gazing up at the night sky above and inhaling, the fresh, sweet vanilla scent is thick in the air, and it triggers a clear memory in my mind. "Stop, Owen."

He pulls his lips away from my neck, a concerned look on his face. "What is it?"

"That smell in the air. Those are the black-eyed Susans that grow between my property and yours. They bloom late, which is why they smell so strong right now."

How in the world do I know that? I look at him, my eyes wide. "I remember something. I *finally* remember something." I'm bursting with joy when I say, "I've been here before."

18

The Trip

Last night was intense... and incredible. But I'm glad we stopped when we did because it all happened so fast. I need time to process—I can't believe the feelings I've developed for Owen in this short amount of time. I mean, I've had colds last longer than our relationship.

After our amazing tryst in the shower, we showed Annie's picture to Owen's family, but no one recognized her. Then, this morning, I went to downtown Violet Moon, store to store, asking anyone and everyone. No one knew her.

After my hazy memory about the black-eyed Susans, I'm even more desperate to get onto Bo's computer. So here I am, Saturday morning, standing over Levi as he sits at the desk and turns on Bo's laptop. My stomach tumbles as I watch him work.

Levi continues to click away on the computer, saying nothing, until I can't take it anymore. "Anything?" I say.

"This isn't good." He stares at the screen intensely.

My heart sinks. "What's not good?"

Levi swings the chair around to face me. "Bo put massive security on this thing. It's password protected and encrypted. I can't crack it, no way."

"What?" I rub my eyes. "Why would a farmer require encryption?" My face heats with growing frustration that there are no answers in this house. Why are there no records? No albums except one of Bo and Lily's honeymoon? Why was the one photo I found of the woman who may or may not be my mother the only thing left? Hidden attic space in the barn? And now, why did Bo put massive security on his computer?

And then there's that threatening note.

"No reason I can think of." Levi points to the screen. "He used IronLock, the system that security companies use."

Good god. "How well did you know Bo, Levi?" I'm desperate, looking for anything.

"Not well. He was a nice boss. Friendly. Paid me on time. I never would've guessed he'd have this kind of system." Levi stands. "Sorry I couldn't help."

"No, don't be sorry. I'm so happy you tried." I wring my hands. "One more thing before you go. I found an old photo of someone, but all it lists is a first name. Do you know any facial recognition software I can use to find out who she is?"

Without hesitation, he says, "Sure. There are tons out there. I can get you set up with a good one."

"Thank you." Air whooshes from my lips. "I'm adopted, and this might be my biological mother." I hand him my laptop.

He sits, and excitement courses through me as Levi's fingers tap rapid fire on the keyboard. When the site appears, I stop breathing.

"Just create your account." He turns the computer to face me. "The rest is easy."

"Thank you, Levi. This is great."

"No problem." He pulls out a pack of cigarettes to smoke as soon as he's outside. Which reminds me, I should tell him to stop leaving his butts around. Except right now, I'm grateful for his help and don't want to deal with that.

After he leaves, I set up my account, which takes forever to verify my email and phone number. Swallowing back the ball of nerves rising from my gut, I say, "Here we go." I upload Annie's photo to the website, press submit, then wait as the "Searching" wheel turns.

Finally, the wheel stops, and a red message pops up. My stomach clenches as I read, "Photo upload error. Try again."

I groan, biting my lip. My palms get clammy as I try uploading the photo again, now concerned this isn't going to work.

That damn "Searching" wheel spins for an eternity. When the message comes up this time, it's green. My pulse kicks into overdrive as I read the words, "One match."

My breath stops. "There's a match," I say, the nerves twisting tighter in my stomach. Under the picture is the name Annie Walsh, and it's linked to an article. Clicking on it, I read the headline: "Atlanta Teen Missing."

With trembling fingers, I glance at the picture of Annie that I found. Then, my eyes scan the article, which was updated to include that she'd run away and had been located.

I stare at the screen, trying to process what I'm seeing. I *know* this is my mother. I can feel it, but since feelings don't prove things, I have to keep searching. Still. I'm vibrating with excitement because it all adds up. She was young, running away from home. She probably gave me up for adoption because she couldn't take care of me.

Immediately, I go to the birth records website and type in "Willow Eloise Walsh," finding no matches. I try different variations, using the term, "Georgia" with just my first name, then just my middle name, but nothing comes up. I repeat the process in Google but find no one linked to Annie.

I try not to let defeat get to me because I still have a good feeling about this. "I just need to find her," I utter. My knee bounces as I launch into a frantic Google search of her name. Pages and pages of results come up, as it's a very common name. And after clicking on numerous links of different Annie Walshes that are not her, I retry my search with, "Annie Walsh Georgia."

Scrolling, I come across an obituary for an Annabelle Walsh. I hope this one *isn't* her.

My stomach crashes to the floor when I see the same woman in the photo, only older. It is her. Tears well in my eyes, the grief hitting hard and fast.

Why do I feel so sad about a person I've probably never met? It has to be because now, I'll never have the chance to. And that's even *if* she is my mother, which so far, I have no proof of.

I wipe the tears from my eyes and return my focus to the computer. "What happened to you, Annie Walsh?"

Owen's not here with me, as I thought this was something I needed to do alone, but now, I'm not so sure. I wish he were here. This might be my mother, whom I'll never have the chance to meet.

I wonder if I'm okay to keep going. I should probably take a break, but I know I can't. I won't be able to stand being in my own skin not knowing everything I possibly can.

Opening her obituary, I learn she died on July 20th, 2013, and my brain spins into a calculation. Annie died so young—only thirty-two years old.

Scanning the obituary, I don't find a lot more information. No cause of death, no survivors listed. It only says that Annie was taken from us far too soon and that she was loved by many. On the bottom, it asks that in lieu of flowers, donations be made to the Women's Bright Futures Foundation, a place for runaways and domestic abuse survivors. She must've gotten help there after she ran away.

Looking the place up, I see that it's in Atlanta. With that, I go back to my properties' website and find Annie Walsh's list of addresses. They're all in Atlanta, and one looks familiar. I double-check to make sure.

Yes! It's Bo and Lily's address before they moved here to Violet Moon. The place they lived at the time I was born. Pulling it up on Google maps, I see that it's dilapidated and vacant, but something about it looks familiar. I hope it hasn't been torn down since this photo was taken.

I *need* to go to that house.

I told Owen I was fine doing this trip alone, but he insisted on joining me on this drive to a rundown neighborhood, about twenty minutes from downtown Atlanta. When I start up a winding road, it's clear that Bo and Lily preferred the country life even when living in the city. The homes are fewer and farther between by the time I pull up to the white house, which is dilapidated but standing. I flash Owen a smile. "It's still here."

Owen's lips split into a grin. "Told you."

I stare at it, hoping to remember it, but nothing comes to mind other than a vague familiarity that I can't quite put my finger on.

"Anything?" Owen says, squeezing my hand.

"Not yet."

"How are you feeling?"

I hesitate as I struggle to put my feelings into words. "I'm terrified of getting answers. I'm terrified of *not* getting answers."

"It is a double-edged sword." He stares out the window, contemplative. "Once you know something, you can't unknow it. There's no turning back."

"Exactly." I like that Owen gets me. He's been tight-lipped about his past, but whatever he's been through has definitely shaped him.

Before I go inside, I check my phone. It's Friday, and there are workers at Bo's Château, so I have to make sure I'm available if they have questions or run into problems. I told Natanya I'd write her the second the Kleins' selection of fixtures arrive at the warehouse today—they're meeting to make their decisions.

I have no messages or emails, so I'm all caught up for now.

We get out of my rental car and approach the place; the driveway is cracked and the porch is sinking but sturdy. The windows are boarded up, and, unfortunately, there's a padlock on the door. "Let's try around back." We go through the gate of the sagging chain-link fence and enter the backyard. It's full of weeds, overgrown shrubs, and a rusted fire pit near the back of the property. We wander around to see if we can find any place to get in, or at least look inside. Unfortunately, the blinds are all closed. "Dammit," I say.

Owen puts his face up to a window and moves his head at different angles, clearly trying to see if he can get any view through the blinds. "They've got this place locked up tight, probably to keep squatters away."

"Yeah." Something flashes into my mind, but it's not a memory. It's a piece of knowledge. "There's a key to the back door hidden in the birdhouse." I don't know how I know that.

Owen gives me a wide-eyed look before I put my hand through the round hole of the birdhouse and pull out a key. When I hold it up, he says, "You're remembering."

After we return to the back door, I slide the key into the deadbolt and, sure enough, it clicks.

Hope blooms in my chest as I open the squeaky door. The smell of dirt and must hit like a blow. Cobwebs fill the place, and a few cockroaches scatter.

All the furniture has been taken out, but I know the layout. I point straight in front of me. "My bedroom is down that hall." Almost in a trance, I walk through the kitchen into the living room and then down the hall, my body taking me through a familiar route. Automatically, I turn to the left and into my room. I continue on, moving straight into the walk-in closet. When Owen joins me, I put my hand on the knob of the small door that leads to a big attic space. I utter, "There's a mural of a farm and farm animals on the wall in there. It was my favorite."

When I open the attic door, there's exactly what I said, but it's much smaller than I remember. "Mom painted that. She was a good artist. I used to play in here for hours."

After we've both ducked through the door, he stands back to give me space. "Keep going. You've got this."

"Okay." But as I turn a circle, taking in the splintered door, the green drapes, the red crayon on the windowsill, one memory after another rushes into my mind. Not all of them are good.

I leave the space and run out of the bedroom. I'm racing through the house, frantically studying every nook and cranny to see what memories will come. "I lived here with Nana and Papa. I must've thought Bo and Lily were my grandparents."

I'm trembling, and I'm not sure why. "I remember happiness, but fear, too." I look at a door, the one that I know leads to the basement. My voice is just above a whisper when I say, "Behind that are cement steps that lead downstairs. That's where the laundry room is."

"Slow down." Owen takes my hand, stopping me. "Take a breath. Tell me what's going on."

My body quakes and sweat films my skin. I shake my head, almost frozen in fear. "I have a gross feeling. I think—no, I *know*—something bad happened down there."

Owen rubs his thumb over my palm. "Let's call it quits for today. We can get a room. Come back tomorrow."

Up until this moment, I've been so glad Owen insisted he come with me. But right now, I want him gone, and I can't explain why. Finally, I say, "I know what you're trying to do, and I appreciate it, but I have to do this now, and by myself."

"Are you sure?"

"Yes."

Owen's eyes fill with worry. "I'll be right here, okay?"

I'm in a fugue-like state as I walk down the steep, narrow stairs. When I get to the bottom, I reach through the darkness and flip on the switch, but the light doesn't come on. I used to have to jump to turn it on, which I did as fast as possible because it's always pitch black down here with no windows.

I turn on my phone light, which does a decent job of lighting up the space. It smells like earth, and dampness hangs thick in the air.

I shudder.

I find the door to the storm shelter, remembering it used to be beside the washer and dryer, which are now gone. There also used to be wire shelves, laundry baskets, and curtains. "I had to hide in there," I utter to myself. I open the door and step down the creaky ladder, moving the light of my phone through the cement-blocked space. My pulse skyrockets as I take in gulps of dank air, which aren't enough.

My shoulders shake as my fear reaches fever pitch, my heart hammering in my ears. There's a dirty jar, and I pick it up. Seeing my old toy princess figurines inside, I drop it. Hitting the cement floor, it smashes into pieces. The scream that's been trapped inside of me for as long as I can remember finally escapes.

Footsteps thump across the floor then tumble down the ladder. When I swing around, for a split second, I see another man's face. A bad man, and I let out another bloodcurdling scream.

"Willow!" Owen's voice brings me back as he rushes toward me.

"It happened here." I barely recognize my own voice.

Owen touches my face. "What're you talking about?"

"I don't know. I don't know!"

He pulls me to his chest, so tight it's hard to move. "It's okay."

Right now, his hug feels claustrophobic, and I take my fists and push Owen away. "Let me out!" I dart up the ladder before sprinting away. "Let me out!" I repeat reflexively before running up the stairs, through the house, then out the front door.

I fight to take in air. "It's too damn hot!" I tug at my shirt as I jog down the street. I have to get away.

"Willow! Stop!" Owen's voice is desperate as he chases after me.

I whip around, and he's right there, and his face is twisted in confusion. "Come on. Let's get in the car."

"I can't. I need air. I need to walk a minute. Alone."

"You think I'm going to leave you alone in a strange neighborhood?"

I gasp for breaths. "Please, Owen, give me a minute."

He puts his palms up. "Fine. Take a minute, but I'm waiting here." His eyes are splintered with hurt.

I feel awful for bringing him into this, but right now, I need space.

But it turns out that's *not* what I need because I take two steps away before sliding down to my knees, no longer able to stand.

To Owen's credit, he waits a beat before kneeling in front of me and pulling me into a hug. "Can we go now?"

I stop fighting, letting him hold me. I force myself to breathe in rhythm with him—slow and deep. With tears welling my eyes, I melt into his arms out of exhaustion and defeat.

"You don't have to do this right now."

I close my eyes and take controlled breaths. I force my mind to go blank until the banging in my chest slows. I steady my voice when I say, "Sorry. The shock threw me. I swear to god, I could see it. I could smell it. I could feel it. Like it just happened yesterday."

"What is *it*? What happened?"

"I don't know, but I'm not leaving until I figure it out." I have to do this because I don't have the choice not to.

"If you're not leaving, I'm not leaving." Owen's voice is steady, unaffected. "Are we in this together?"

"Yup. Let's pull the Band-Aid off."

Once we're back in the basement, I'm shivering and chilly, wishing I had a sweater on. I know I *cannot* be cold because a minute ago, I was just too hot outside. I wave my arms, shaking the shock away.

Now, with Owen by my side, I head straight to the wall of the laundry room that's clearly been patched. Tears form in my eyes again, and my throat closes as I run my fingers over the jagged edges of the spackle. "This used to be a hole the bad man made with his fist. He swung and missed my mom." I squeeze my eyes shut.

"Who was he?"

"I don't know. I don't think I knew him. I just remember that he hit her, and she fell to the floor." I look at Owen, my lips quivering. "She was lying there, not moving. I thought she was dead."

"What else do you remember?" He pulls me close, and I try to release the tension gripping my spine. "She was trying to stop him from taking me."

Owen brushes a stray piece of hair off my forehead. "Can you see what he looks like?"

"He had blond hair. Gloves. They terrified me. He terrified me. When he grabbed me and put something over my mouth, I screamed so loud my throat was raw. I woke up in a strange place." I pull away and look at Owen as the truth rattles my bones. "He kidnapped me."

19

The Dinner

As the trees whiz by, I'm so lost in my thoughts I'm beyond words. We're on our way back to Violet Moon, but we stopped at the Women's Bright Futures home and asked about Annie's photo. Just as we suspected, they aren't allowed to divulge information about any of their residents, past or present. After that, I was so bone dead exhausted, I asked Owen to drive.

"Talk to me, Queens." Owen glances at me before returning his eyes to the road.

His command opens the floodgates, as my brain won't stop. Who was the man who kidnapped me? And what happened to my mom after that man hurt her? But all I say is, "I'm fine. Just a lot to process. I mean, who am I even?"

"Hold on." Owen drives a bit before pulling the car off the road on a large shoulder. After putting it in park, he unfastens his seat belt and leans in to cup my face. "You're Willow Dawson. The woman who can get a car out of a ditch in four-inch heels. Don't forget that."

His words ground me, comfort me, just like always. But then a fearful and thrilling realization hits. Somewhere along the way, Owen has grown from a roll in the hay to my guy. And what am I supposed to do with that? I don't know, but I take a breath and utter, "I'm Willow Dawson."

"Good. That's my girl. Now think, what should we do next?"

"I need to find my adoption papers."

"Right. They'd fill holes, some really important ones, like who your dad is."

"Yes." Getting my adoption records—a task I can focus on. "Closed adoptions in Georgia require a court order."

"That definitely sounds like a job for Mr. Livingston." Owen gives me *that* look again. "Did I mention you're a badass?"

"No. And you can keep saying it if you want." I take his hand and give it a squeeze. "I couldn't have done this without you."

"No problem." He smiles, but then it fades. He stares ahead, clearly deep in thought. Then, his face clouds over, and I feel a distinct shift of mood. Finally, he says, "Stealing from The Malted Moon wasn't the only time I got in trouble growing up." His voice is strained.

"It wasn't?" I glance at him, surprised.

"I had this habit of not listening to my father. I was kind of an asshole, actually."

"Was?" I pat his shoulder, trying to lighten the mood. But he's not having it, so I say, "I'm just kidding. That's hard to imagine."

"Back then, I thought I knew everything. I resented my dad because he was away from the family so much. His job as DA took all his time." Owen starts the ignition, as if he's said all he's going to about that.

But I want to know more this time. "Tell me how your dad died."

He swallows hard, his Adam's apple bobbing as he puts the car in drive and inches onto to the road. Staring ahead, he says, "Today was a lot for you, Willow. And a lot for me, too. Can we hold off on that story?"

"Yeah, sure," I say, automatically, because he's got a fair point. At least, logically, he does. But the illogical side of me feels a touch resentful. Owen now knows my deepest, darkest secrets—things so scarring, my own brain shielded them from me, and I *still* don't know what happened to his father.

My heart is breaking and bursting at the same time. The emotional part of me wants him to tell me so it balances the scales, but that's unfair.

It's clear Owen has intense grief over his father, and I know that pain all too well. This is the first time he's mentioned anything about it, so it has to be a big deal for him. After we drive for a stretch in comfortable silence, I squeeze his hand. "Thank you. For today."

His lips split into a sweet smile, something flickering in his eyes. "Thanks for being you. A person I feel more comfortable with than anyone else."

"I feel the same."

And with that, we go quiet, the only sound the hum of the tires on the road, and I nod off, too exhausted trying to find any answers to this mess.

It's late afternoon when we roll back into the driveway of Bo's Château. All the trucks are gone, which means we must've just missed the crew before they left for the day. Phil, the manager, was supposed to text me when they finished.

My phone dings, and it's Natanya. It says, *Where are you???!! Call me NOW.*

I realize this message was sent two hours ago, but I didn't get it. Maybe I lost cell phone service through the mountains?

Then more messages come in, one after another.

Phil: *We're done for the day.*

Natanya: *Willow, the Kleins need to pick their selections, and I don't have them.*

Natanya: *Hellooo. Please. Aston Klein's forehead vein is about to burst. You really should've let me handle the selections.*

Natanya: *They just stormed out of the meeting. Now what?*

"Oh, my god!" I cry out, dialing Natanya. When she doesn't pick up, I break into a sweat.

"What happened?" Owen's face crumples.

"I'm sorry—I need to jump on my computer. I've messed things up with the Kleins. *Again*."

"Willow." He touches my shoulder. "Take a second to grab a bite. Come to my house and have dinner with me and my family. Then you can work the rest of the night. I won't bug you."

I can't imagine having a meal with his family right now—no more discomfort for today. "Thanks for the offer, but how about I make you dinner? After I finish with this emergency." Normally, I'd need some space after today, but I don't. My whole life in New York is space, and right now, I don't want to be alone.

"Okay. Fair enough. I'll go change."

"Sure." I rush into the house, in disbelief that I completely forgot about sending the Kleins their selections today. I was relying on my phone to ring, and when it didn't, it escaped me.

But I *never* forget these things. Except lately.

I make Owen spaghetti and meatballs in my newly restored kitchen with stainless steel appliances, painted quiet-close cabinets, and marble countertops. And with a gorgeous butler's pantry, including a hammered round sink and under-cabinet lighting, it's stunning.

Earlier, I rushed to my computer where I pulled up the shipment and sent out all the selections to the Kleins with an apology note and an offer to cover the cost of some of the lighting fixtures. Normally,

I get a confirmation email back from Aston Klein right away, but it's been over an hour, and it hasn't come.

I set the table, which is a stunning refurbished oak piece, as I prepare for Owen to arrive. I can't stop my mind wandering back to the events of today. Bo and Lily helped raise me. So, how come they never came to find me? Clearly, they knew I was alive because they willed me this place. Maybe I'm remembering wrong, and they didn't take care of me. Maybe they just let my mom stay at their place.

And how did my mother die? *If* the obituary I found belongs to my actual mother, which I still don't know. None of it makes sense, and it's getting more maddening as pieces of the puzzle seem to scatter instead of fitting together.

A knock at the door is a welcome relief from my thoughts. After I usher Owen inside and get him seated, I bring out the food.

We sit to eat, and Owen says, "This looks amazing."

"Yeah, well, it's spaghetti. So, I expect a *Lady and the Tramp* moment at some point." I shoot him a wink.

"Done." He takes a second and scans the kitchen. "You've really done something here." He looks down. "Even the old hardwood floors look spanking new. The place looks incredible."

"Thanks. Wait until you see the lighting touches that were installed in every room yesterday. It changes the whole atmosphere."

"I bet." After we both sit, he tries a bite. "So, you can cook." He closes his eyes. "Seriously. This is the best spaghetti I've ever had."

"I'd take credit, but I learned out of necessity."

His eyes darken and he studies me. After he pats his face with his napkin, he reaches over and takes my hand. "You have a high-functioning adrenal medulla."

"Excuse me?"

"That's what mediates the fight-or-flight response. You're a fighter."

His words bring the butterflies, but it's hard for me to take compliments. I'm trying to be better about that, so I just say the truth. "Just like you. Animal whisperer. Mechanically inclined, super handy guy. Demon exorcist."

His lips tick up, his cheeks turning a shade of pink as he looks around. "I just can't believe how much bigger the place looks all opened up."

He hasn't seen inside the place since Wednesday, and a lot of progress was made.

"It does." I carry on about how fun it's going to be to decorate each room in its own unique style, keeping it classically Southern now that it's going to be a state landmark. And the newly refurbished library—on top of the many books Lily had, more classics have been brought in from Violet Moon's public library.

I also have to show Owen my proudest creation. After we finish eating, I grab his hand. "Come with me." I take him to the spiral staircase at the back of the house and open my palm toward the new banister.

"No way." His eyes bulge. "Is that the same horse that's on the foyer step banister?"

"Yup. I matched it."

"Same detail, same stain—everything." He runs a finger over it. "How?"

"Last week, I made a silicone mold of the other one, then used that as a template to create the shape and grooves. Then I eyeballed the details." I sigh. "I installed this yesterday, and matching the stain was a bitch."

"So. Labor intensive."

"Yup. That's why you don't see this kind of work in homes anymore. At the same time, we should."

Owen looks at me adoringly. "I love seeing your badassery."

I smile before continuing on, telling Owen about Bo's idea for a barn out by the lake, complete with outdoor seating so guests can spend summer evenings by the lake under starry skies. "That'll have to be done at a later time, though. I hope the city of Violet Moon decides to add it."

He nods enthusiastically, and I love how he seems genuinely interested in hearing me ramble on about my passion. When I finally stop talking, Owen simply says, "Come to Ma's house for dinner on Sunday."

Oh, boy. This again. "You and Demon have something in common. You're both bulldogs."

He raises a brow. "True. We also both scratch our balls. What's your point?"

I roll my eyes. "My point is that Sunday dinner's family time. I don't want to intrude."

He meets my eyes with a shy glimmer when he says, "Yes, it is family time. I want you to be around my family."

My heart flutters at his words. The offer's so simple, but so complicated. There are a million things all rolled into saying yes, and I just can't do it. Not yet. I manage a smile when I say, "Next week. Promise."

He hesitates, giving me the side-eye before he says, "You have to bring your spaghetti. It's next level."

"Deal."

We decide we don't want to miss the stars by the lake, so after doing the dinner dishes together, we head out to our spot with cinnamon whiskey and blankets. Dare I say it's becoming "our thing"?

After sitting and taking a shot, the warmth spreads through me, and there's something magical about these moments. Right here, by the lake, with Owen by my side.

On the blanket, I lean back, getting a full view of the night sky, still cloudy but with a few stars peeking through.

A bright light leaves a trail through the darkness, and I gasp before saying, "Was that a shooting star?"

"I think so. Better make a wish."

"I wish this didn't have to end." The words escape my lips before I can stop them.

Owen's arms wrap around me, and I'll never stop loving his smell. "It doesn't."

With a breath, I put my head on his chest. "So, what? We just do long distance? Hope that love conquers all?"

"I happen to believe that love does conquer all, actually," he says.

With my head on him, I feel the vibration of his words. "Really?"

"Sure. My parents loved each other so much, and they were a good balance. My dad was a risk taker, goofy, and you know my mom, the opposite. Quiet. Contemplative. A big thinker with a heart that never stops. Anyway, they just worked. Like us."

I sit up and turn to meet his gaze. "We do work, don't we?" Maybe he's right. Maybe the simmering night air will carry our wish on its featherlight breeze... and make it come true. Just maybe.

His hand moves to my cheek, and he rests his forehead against mine. Then our lips are touching. Then it's our mouths, and our tongues, everything moving lightning fast, like we need to fast track it back to where we left off.

His fingers trail up my arms, the electricity making me tremble. Suddenly, the stars seem brighter. The lightning bugs flicker their magic, and time stops for just a moment.

All that matters is Owen's kiss.

I'm not sure how we found something so beautiful, but we did, and that makes us so lucky. Even if it can't last.

His warmth radiates through me as he rolls on top of me, and I love feeling the weight of his body pressed against me. His fingers trace under my shirt and up my stomach before finding their way around to my back. I arch into him, feeling every inch of his body against mine.

Then, in a flash, both our shirts vanish. We don't speak words, but we don't need to.

Our touches are feverish and desperate, like we don't have tomorrow, because maybe we don't.

My hands run along his chest, tracing the contours of his muscles. His mouth desperately moves across mine as his fingers trace circles on my stomach. Each moment becoming more frantic with his jagged breath against my neck, our bodies touching skin on skin. Running his hands up my back, Owen tries to unlatch my bra. After he fumbles for a bit, I pull away and smile when I say, "Let me help you there."

"That would be great."

With a flick of my wrist, it falls to the ground.

He pushes my jeans down until I kick them off, then I lie naked under him, and his eyes roam my body. "You're perfect."

When he takes my nipple into his mouth, goose bumps erupt all over my skin. He moves his soft lips to my ear and nips at my lobe, sucking my breath away. He shakes his head. "I'm not going to stop this time."

"Don't."

After his jeans are off, Owen hovers over me, his hardness, his muscles, all of him, looking magnificent. Almost like a warrior as his skin reflects in the moonlight, and the growing ache for him becomes unbearable.

But he stays there, taunting me, so I sit up, my lips crashing into his. He lies down as I climb onto him, taking charge as I straddle him. My hips moving over him, he pulls me closer, and I arch my back and thread my hands into his hair.

His lips trail a path down my neck, heating my skin with every touch. He flips me back around before lowering himself onto me. I let out a moan as his hardness presses into my leg, then I tug him tighter as I need to feel every solid inch of him.

He pulls away, running a finger over my stomach before kissing his way down. He stops between my legs, and I lift my knees up. He nudges my thighs, and I spread my shaking legs.

"You okay with this?" he asks with concerned eyes.

"Oh my god, yes." Maybe I shouldn't, but I feel safe. Desire has taken over, but it's more than that. I trust him.

His tongue finds the right spot instantly. He sucks and flicks it in a way that sends electric shocks through me, and I arch my back and groan.

He flicks harder, then softer, bringing me close to the edge and back. He knows exactly what to do until I'm unaware of everything except the ache between my legs. "Please."

"Please what?" he whispers, sucking me again and forcing all my breath to escape.

"I need you inside me." My whole body trembles.

"After I'm done."

Then he uses his fingers and tongue to bring me to the edge and back. With each intentional thrust of his tongue, he's giving me everything as he increases the rhythm until I explode, pleasure rippling inside me.

He gets up and takes the condom out of his jeans pocket, then bites the wrapper off before carefully rolling it on. God, he's beautiful. Just watching him do that makes me ache more, if that's possible.

I croak, "I'll never be able to eat spaghetti without thinking of you like this again."

He laughs and says, "Spaghetti night's now forever my favorite."

When he climbs back on top of me, he pulls me in so close his body scorches my skin. He moves over me, and I love the rhythm of his breathing in my ear. I pant, "Owen, please."

"Not yet," he whispers, pressing himself against my skin and stroking me ever so gently until I feel like I might lose my mind. When I can't take another second, I say, "Do it already."

I close my eyes and take in this moment I've fantasized about so many times.

Then, he pushes into me. Slowly at first, going deeper with each stroke. "You feel amazing," he rasps.

His hips rock, slowly, smoothly. But my fingers dig into his back, begging him for more.

His eyes sear into mine, and for a moment, we share a look that expresses everything we feel about each other, which is miles past skin deep. My breath becomes jagged, and I wrap my legs around him and pull him in so tight there's nothing left between us but sweat and desire. He moves in deeper until the only thing I'm able to do is cry out.

"God, Willow." He keeps going, faster then slower, never completely satisfying me, and our moans tangle in the air.

There are none of my ever-present worries. There's only his body perfectly forming to mine, waves of pleasure building and cascading. Owen tilts my hips up and appears to know exactly the spot to hit, just like he seems to understand everything else about me.

My breath catches in my throat when he's about to drive me over the edge, but then I stop myself. I see that he's close too, with the roaring heat in his eyes and the quivers of his body. "Come. I want you to come." My voice is desperate.

That's all it takes, and the muscles of his back go taut under my palms. He lets out a groan, and I cave in, arching my back as everything explodes in waves of pleasure inside me. "Oh, god, Owen."

He heaves out breaths as he shudders, then his body goes limp. He blows out a long exhale. "Christ, Queens."

"I know," is all I say. Nothing has ever felt so good, so right, and somehow, I know he feels the same way.

He rolls off then pulls me close. I place my head on his chest and listen to the sound of his heartbeat as it slows.

20

The Old Friend

This week, the days have been long with grueling work, and the sleeping has been short with Owen in my bed. I'm tired, but completely fulfilled and happy. Owen has been invaluable with the restoration, and today is Saturday—a day he needed off but didn't say why. Maybe it's because he's been burning the candle at both ends now that he's started training at the vet hospital with Dr. Thompson.

After showering and getting dressed, I step out the sliding back doors. I see the supplies for the new patio that's going in tomorrow: pallets of brick, grout, wood, commercial saws, and buckets of tools—all ready to go.

It'll be amazing, a crisp brick patio under the arched and artful pergola. I can't wait to see it once the vines go in. It's going to be quite the showcase for the celebration we're having on August sixth, the day the appraiser officially makes the home a landmark—*if* it passes inspection. I'm equal parts nervous and excited for it all.

My phone buzzes from a text, bringing me out of my reverie.

Dakota: *I'm back. It went so well! And Bennett is so hot!*

Oh, man. Dakota's home. My stomach churns—so much has happened between Owen and me this week! I need to talk to her and tell her everything.

Me: *Come have dinner with me tonight?*

Dakota: *YESSS. You can't leave Violet Moon without stopping by The Malted Moon Brewery. And hello, it's Saturday night!*

Me: *That's where it's at, eh?*

Dakota: *Yup. The brewery where everybody knows everything about everybody. LOL.*

Me: *That sounds great. See you there.*

I hope she takes the news okay, which she should since things are going well with Bennett. Either way, Dakota is becoming a good friend, and I don't want to lie to her, even if it's by omission. I hope tonight can be a celebration for both of us. This morning, I hired Roy Livingston to help me access my adoption records, since now I now know I'm from Georgia. It's taking all my willpower to sit still and let him do his job. He's going to find out all he can about my biological parents and adoption.

After a quick makeup and hair job, I hop into my rental car dressed in jeans and a spaghetti-strapped silk tank. When I pull into the gravel parking lot of the Malted Moon Brewery, I can't help but think the place has the small-town charm you only see in movies. Approaching, I smile at the sign suction-cupped to the window that reads, "Beer is the answer, but I can't remember the question."

In the entryway, there are faded paper ads stapled to old West style pillars, which I stop to read. "Your Other Mother. If you drink, Stella drives."

"Thank god for Stella." It's Dakota's voice behind me, and I turn. She's smiling brightly when she says, "She's saved my butt a time or two."

"Hey there!" I give her a hug. "Welcome back."

"Glad to be back."

We step to the doorway where the hum of chatter and music wafts through. Inside, the place is packed. "You weren't joking—half the town must be here."

"Yup."

We take a seat at the wooden bar that opens to the back patio, which is something you never see in New York. The weather doesn't allow for a missing wall.

After Dakota orders us hamburgers and blueberry lagers, as she promises they're the best thing on the menu, I say, "So, what happened with Bennett?"

She groans. "Nothing, unfortunately."

"What? Why?"

Sissy brings us our beers, and I ask, "I thought you worked at the tattoo shop?"

"I do." She leans on the counter. "I work here too. And I do hours at MoonMart for the holidays. Cash is tight."

"I understand that."

Sissy shifts down the bar to Jeb, giving him a kiss before saying, "Anyway, remember that worm you put on Ernie's electric fence?"

Jeb's full-bodied laugh roars over the noisy bar. "That damn thing threw smoke like a rubber tire. It was so foul, I thought you were gonna toss your cookies."

"I almost did." She laughs so hard, she's in tears.

These two are really cute—I didn't realize they were together.

I take a sip of the delicious malt beer with a hint of hops and berry and turn back to Dakota. "So, about Bennett."

"Ugh. I don't know, Willow. Everything was great. But I kinda went wiggy." She takes a long drag from her beer.

"Why?"

Dakota stares ahead for a beat. "I don't know. I think I'm all messed up. I mean since Owen's moved back. He's the one who got away. You know?"

Prickles of shame rise to the surface of my skin, and I swallow hard. "I get that."

Memories of Owen and me in the shower, on the lookout point, in my bed each night, come rushing back, all in a big, steamy blur. This is why I said I was going to stay away from him, but I didn't. I let our raging attraction pickle my brain, and now I have to fess up.

Dakota sighs. "You do get it. Because of Seth."

More guilt. "Wow, you already know so much about me."

"I pay attention. So, would you want Seth back? If you had the chance?"

I think about the way Owen makes me feel, and how, in retrospect, Seth doesn't compare. "I don't think I would. But if you'd asked me that a month ago, I would've said maybe."

"What changed?"

Owen. And I have to tell her that, except I need a moment to think this through because I don't want to screw up Dakota and Owen's chance together after I leave. What if I tell her, and she can't forgive Owen? And then I'm gone? What good is that to anyone? "Maybe it's just that time away from Seth has allowed me to see that it was right to end things. We didn't have that fiery connection."

"I hear you. Owen and I used to have that. We don't at this moment, but I don't know if that's just because we've been apart for so long. And now that he's back..." She sighs. "I guess I'd like some time to see if that spark returns, you know?"

My heartstrings are in a shredder, and I'm furious at myself. "Makes perfect sense," I say, because it does, and she has every right to have that. I *have* to tell her—I can't be this two-faced person who's nice to her and then is secretly standing in the way of who she wants to be with. After I explain what's happened, I'll make sure she knows it all doesn't matter because Owen and I are temporary. I'm still leaving, and he's still never leaving. I gnaw at my lip, thinking of how to tell her when they bring out our food. "About that—"

Sissy sets both our plates down in front of us, and Dakota's eyes go round and bright. "Thank you, Sis—I'm starving."

The food looks amazing, but my appetite has vanished. Since Dakota's clearly anxious to eat, I'll tell her after.

After sprinkling everything with the cayenne I carry in my purse, I take a small bite of the burger that's overflowing with lettuce, pickles, onions, and ketchup. I'm sure in a different moment, it would be delicious. But right now, it takes all I have to swallow it down and say, "Good."

"Mmm." Is all Dakota can manage with a mouthful.

While we eat, I notice Levi sitting in the corner of the bar, all by himself, and he keeps eying me. That kid makes me uncomfortable, to put it mildly, so I turn to Dakota and say, "After we eat, you want to go outside?"

"Yes, definitely."

The second we take our last bite, I say, "Look. I really need to talk to you."

She puts a finger up. "Hold on. Let me get us another round, then we can take them outside and talk there."

"Okay." That's actually a better idea. It'll be more private. With*out* Levi.

Outside, the warm evening breeze feathers my face. I wouldn't mind coming here all the time. We take a seat at a table under an umbrella beside four large vats of beer. "Killer atmosphere," I say.

"Told you."

Wearing a cowboy shirt and a rosy-cheeked face, Jeb makes his way over to us and flashes that permanent mischievous smile of his. "Good to see you two. Willow, I heard you're gonna be here another month."

"Yup. Tore down some walls. Building new ones."

"Badass. I wanna stop in and check on your handiwork."

"Come by anytime. We always appreciate you and your team."

Dakota asks Jeb about using his monster truck to advertise Cut the Cheese for the Labor Day parade, but I don't hear the rest of their conversation. My phone buzzes, and I look to see a new text.

Owen: *Can you meet me at The Malted Moon Brewery? I could use your company.*

Wait. Owen's here? Confused, I look around, not seeing him. I stand and peer inside at the bar, but don't find him there either. Finally, I say, "Hey, Jeb. Have you seen Owen here?"

"Yup." Holding his beer, Jeb points to a patio divider covered in vines. "He's back there, alone, and he's in a mood." The crowd watching the TV inside lets out a cheer, and Jeb says, "Gotta get back. I'm missing the game."

"Thanks." I flash Dakota a look before we get up to peer around the seating divider. Owen's sitting in the corner, nursing an amber-colored drink on ice. His eyes are bloodshot, and he's not looking anything like himself.

"Oh, shit." Dakota grabs her phone and looks at it. "It's July twentieth. The anniversary of his father's death."

It hits me like a tsunami—Dakota knows everything about Owen's father's death, and I know nothing because Owen hasn't told me. I want to ask Dakota what happened, but she's now darting toward him. But he texted *me*. I should talk to him.

Together, we approach Owen, and Dakota puts her hand on his shoulder before pulling him into a hug. Then she sits next to him. The sting of envy races down my windpipe.

I want to be the one to comfort him—I'm dying to be that for him, but it's not my place. Is it?

I must think no because I stay rooted right where I am, behind him, out of view. I have no idea how to comfort Owen, as I don't even know what happened to his dad.

Dakota strokes his shoulder. "Owen, you know you can get through this day. You've gotten through so many of them."

He puts the heel of his hand over his eye. "I'm good, Kota. You can go."

"I'm not leaving you like this. And you've come so far," Dakota says. "Remember when you were seventeen? We found you at the river, and you wouldn't talk to anyone? You're talking now. That's progress."

"The river," he slurs, raking a hand through his disheveled hair.

Seeing Owen like this splits my heart in two, but I don't move. I just stand here, a third wheel, shifting on my feet as I'm desperate to find the right thing to say.

So, there was a river involved. That scar of his—was that from trying to save his dad?

Dakota pulls a chair next to Owen and sits. "You almost got yourself killed trying to get to him, Owen."

"Something like that," he says, his voice hoarse.

"That river has a nasty riptide."

So, Owen *did* try to save his dad? I can't help but question whether he and I are as close as I thought we were. I shared my parent's death. I asked Owen about the scar, and he told me none of this. I get that we haven't known each other that long, but I've told him everything.

He came with me and helped me yank my repressed memories from the darkest depths of my soul. And now I feel silly about it, which I shouldn't. But I do.

Dakota says, "Remember that time your pa kept you out fishing so long you both got sunburned?"

His mouth quirks. "Even my ass got crispy because the thigh-high current pulled my pants half down most of the day."

Pearls of laughter escape Dakota, then she says, "Of course I remember when you burned your ass. It was me that had to put aloe on it."

"Yeah. Well, you liked it."

"I sure did." She massages his shoulders.

My stomach tumbles. I want to be angry at Dakota, but how can I? She's doing nothing wrong. It's time to get out of here. I hitch a thumb over my shoulder when I look at her and mouth, "Work emergency. I gotta go."

Dakota nods, concern on her face.

Now that I've heard all this, I'm sure of what I have to do. Dakota is good for Owen, and she understands him. They have a connection we'll never have. She knows his past—I don't. He didn't even tell me where he got that scar from, or how his dad died. I need to step away and make sure that I don't interfere with these two people getting back together—the way it's clearly meant to be.

21

The Bond

Early morning, I'm back in the barn milking the goats. Dakota wrote and asked if I could take her morning shift because she was up late.

Up late because she brought Owen home with her last night? The thought makes me nauseous.

At the same time, Owen and I never said we were exclusive. In fact, I've gone out of my way to make sure he knows we're not. So it's more than fair if he went home with her.

Except why doesn't it feel that way? It feels like the worst kind of betrayal, even though logically, it's not. But I'll just have to get over it. If they're together, it's for the best. I understand that Owen said he didn't care for Dakota *that* way anymore, but I know all too well how those old feelings can reignite. That's how Seth and I kept ending up back together.

When I finish milking, I give the jugs to Huck because he's going to drive them to Cut the Cheese for me. I'm sitting and petting Sir Fig A Lot when footsteps echo from the barn door. I turn to see Trinity there. "Hey Trin, what are you up to?"

She scuffs her foot. "I finished my chores, so I came over here to check on the horses. But then I also wanted to say hi to Sir Fig A Lot." She walks over and gives his head a scratch.

This goat is a total attention hog. He's also an escape artist, which reminds me. "I have to fix the fence so Sir Fig stops getting out. Want to help me out?"

"Sure!" A bright smile takes over her face.

I just need to keep busy so I don't have time to think about Owen and Dakota. And hanging out with Trinity always makes me happy.

After heading to the toolbox and grabbing a hammer, a scrap slat of wood, and some nails, Trinity and I walk the perimeter of the pasture's fence. We tug each board until I find one that's cracked, which means it can buckle with weight—say, from a baby goat. "Here it is."

She walks over and studies it, saying, "I can't believe he found that."

"I know. Crafty, huh?"

"He sure is." She gives me a head nod that involves her whole body.

I show her how to nail the slat of wood over the crack, tugging it to make sure it's tight. "That should do it."

She nods emphatically. "Take that, Sir Fig A Lot."

"He's getting so big I'm surprised he still fits through this."

"He is getting big because he's eating like a piggie."

I watch him as he approaches us before sniffing the fence. "He loves everything but Mary Louise's pies."

"He loves popcorn."

I look at Trinity. "How do you know that?"

Trinity heads toward a bucket, then lifts it and grabs a brown lunch sack. "I made this for him to give him treats when he does tricks for me."

"No way! You're teaching him tricks?" This little girl never ceases to amaze me. "How have I not seen this?"

"I wanted to surprise you. Watch how he'll jump over the hay bale." She walks behind one and holds up the popcorn. He knows exactly what to do because he takes a running leap and jumps clean over, which is jaw-dropping. Then Trinity feeds him the popcorn as a reward.

"No way—I'm way impressed!" I head toward her and the popcorn. "I want to try."

"Do it." She has a proud smile as she hands me the bag and shows me how to get Sir Fig A Lot lined up to do the jump.

Per Trinity's instruction, I say, "Go, Sir Fig A Lot."

He takes a running leap over the hay bale again, and I reward him with a handful of popcorn. "That's a good boy. You are my good boy." Well, most of the time.

"You *are* a good, good boy," Trinity says, smiling. "See how he can catch the popcorn from anywhere?"

"He does do that, doesn't he?" I fold my arms as I watch him. "I wonder if I could do that?"

"Well, if I can train a goat to do it, I bet I can train you, too." She laughs a full-bodied laugh in the way only kids can do, and it's contagious. I find myself all smiles as I attempt to jump and catch popcorn in my mouth. After I miss a few, Sir Fig A Lot is right there, ready to pick up any pieces that fall on the ground.

"Let me try!" Trinity waves her hands in the air, and I throw pieces at her mouth as she attempts to catch them, too.

I say, "You're better at this than I am."

We're both in a fit of laughter when I hear Kayla's voice. "Trinity, you need to get home now."

Like her mother, Kayla is naturally curt, but right now, her voice has an edge to it. Her face is uncharacteristically twisted with concern when she looks at Trinity. "You didn't ask permission to come over here, and I went looking for you. Now you're grounded."

I'm taken aback by Kayla's harshness, although I understand her reaction if she was worried about her sister. It also might be the last straw—Trinity can be listening challenged. I can't stop myself from saying, "It's my fault. I got her into this by asking how she'd trained Sir Fig A Lot."

Kayla sighs. "It's not your fault. Trinity needs to mind."

Her words say one thing, but something about her intensity tells me there's more going on. Guilty and uncomfortable, I say, "I'll make sure to text you if Trinity comes over here."

Trinity seems to know better than to speak, and her head hangs low as she starts walking back. "Bye, Willow. Bye, Sir Fig A Lot."

After Trinity's gone, Kayla gives me a sharp nod before she says, "Can we talk?"

I wring my hands together, and I don't like the look on her face. Kayla doesn't seem the type to go overboard expressing happiness, but at the same time, right now, her eyes are dark and stormy. It's beyond gruffness. "Sure. What's going on?"

"It's about Owen," she says.

"Okay." My stomach tightens.

"I know my brother is a grown man and can make decisions for himself, but I'm his sister. I can't stop myself from watching out for him—it's my job. And I see the way he looks at you, Willow. What he feels for you is legit."

Inside, I know what she's saying is true, but to hear it out of Owen's sister's mouth, especially someone like Kayla, so reserved, hits hard. "I care about him, too. Deeply."

"I know you do, but you don't understand. Owen's been through hell and back, and when Pa died…" Kayla trails off, shaking her head. "It wasn't a good situation. And now Owen's finally come home. He's happy. I can't sit by and watch him get his heart ripped out again."

"I hope you don't think I want to hurt him."

She looks at me, somehow gentle but stern, and I realize her mannerisms are so much like Frankie's. "I like you, Willow, you know I do—and I don't think you'd ever hurt him intentionally, but I also know how these things go. I know what you're doing here has an expiration date. I just don't see how this ends well."

I bite my lip. "I've said the same thing."

"You may have said it, but your actions don't. If you really care for him, stop leading him on."

I hesitate, swallowing hard. She's right—I keep telling Owen no, but in every nonverbal way, I've said yes. Finally, I mutter, "You're right."

"I mean it, Willow. This applies to Trinity, too. She's fragile after Bo's death, and she gets attached. I understand that life's gonna happen. But I can see this one coming from a mile away, and she's gonna get crushed." Kayla puts a hand on my shoulder. "Now, if your situation changes, and you decide to stay, things would be different. You understand?"

"I got you, Kayla. I'll keep my distance." My heart is splintering in my chest, but it's the right thing.

This is the end of Owen and me, and Trinity and me—for good.

So much for Sunday dinner tonight.

22

Shattered Lines

❧ ・ ◆ ・ ☙

Crisp chardonnay in hand, I'm sitting in a folding chair and enjoying the new back patio that was finished just today, as the crews work Sundays because of our tight deadline. Right now, the mango and golden sky peeks through scattered rain clouds.

I've got a lot on my mind, as usual. Owen and Dakota. Trinity. How much I'm going to miss them, and the town of Violet Moon, when I go. I'm trying to push it all from my thoughts when I see it.

It's just a puddle on the ground, but it hasn't been raining today. I stand and approach it, finding another puddle, then another.

When I glance in the backyard, I gasp.

There's water spraying up from the ground. "Oh, no!" I rush over to it to find a big hole in the earth around exposed water piping. Did the crew puncture a line while they were digging today?

But I had the water and gas companies come out and mark all the lines yesterday.

Didn't I?

I know I did! I checked for the flags this morning. Except, when I look around now, there are no markings for anything. It can't be. It was early and still dark out when I checked, but I *saw* them. Didn't I?

And there were so many workers here today! Actually, Huck is still here. I look to the field to see if he's there on the combine, but he's not. He must've left.

I realize water has soaked the bottom of my calf-length jeans, and if I don't stop this fast, the basement is going to flood.

Oh, god. This could compromise the structure of the house. And it won't pass the state tourist landmark inspection if the basement's been flooded!

And the brand new bricked patio! The grout is fresh, so sitting water will ruin it.

I take off running, grateful to know exactly where the water shutoff valve is, and that Bo had the proper tools to do the job. With the fitted wrench in hand, I sprint down the road between me and Mary Louise's house, which is where the valve is. My lungs burn when I get to it, but the wrench works. *Hallelujah*.

I bend over my knees to catch my breath before walking home, formulating a plan on how to fix the pipe. I've done it before, but never by myself. Maybe I should call Owen.

No. I can figure this out, and I'm resolved not to spend another minute with him. I'm sure he's furious I was a no-show for dinner earlier this evening, and I *can't* ask him for yet another thing now that I have to end things for good.

I run to the barn to see what equipment I can find. I need a pipe cutter, extra piping, and the clips and binders that hold the replacement piece in place. I'll be lucky to find even half that. But as I scan the equipment area of the barn, there's a shelf marked "Water line replacement."

Clearly, Bo had been through this before because he has every part I need. I truly wish I could've met this man. I grab the supplies and return to the burst pipe where I lay them out. It starts to sprinkle, ever so slightly, which is no big deal. Now that the pipe has stopped spraying water, I can work quickly. Normally, I'd use an auger to dig the hole, but since the teams took it away today, I'll have to do it by hand.

I get started, alternating between a shovel and hoe. As I work, I'm grateful for the recent rain, as it made the Georgia clay soft—a prayer answered since usually, it's impossible to penetrate. If nothing else, I've learned that all too well these past weeks here.

I grunt as I jump onto the shovel to get it under the dirt, which is getting harder the deeper I go. The sprinkle turns into a shower, which is all I need right now—more water near the property. My arms ache, but the animals and farm need water, so I work through the pain.

"Willow." It's Owen, and he looks pissed.

I spin around to see him covered in mud, dripping from the rain, and a scowl on his face. "What are you doing?"

I stand up straight, brushing the sticky strands of hair off my face, which I'm sure leaves a trail of mud behind. "The workers must've hit one of the water pipes. I'm fixing it."

He puts his hands on his hips. "I see that. But our fields share a line. When you turned your water off, you turned ours off too. I've been going through the field trying to figure out why our sprinklers stopped working."

"Oh." I groan. I'm not sure this day could get much worse. "I'm sorry."

He looks at me, shaking his head. "You promised to call if you needed something."

"I know. But you've been so kind to me already—going to Atlanta and back with me on Friday."

"You mean going to hell and back with you." His tone is sharp.

Wow. He *is* pissed. "See? I know. That's why I'm sorry." An apology about missing dinner is on my lips when I check the house and drop my shovel. "Oh, shit. Water's about to seep into the basement window well that leads to the mechanical room."

His face drops. "That could short out all your electricity."

"Exactly."

We race into the mechanical room, glad to see the water heater is on a stand and all the electrical wiring is off the floor. But tucked away behind the heater is an aged cardboard box, which Owen picks up and moves to the only wire shelf in the room.

So, there's a box of memorabilia... and I'm dying to know what's inside, but that has to wait.

By the pelting against the window, we can tell that the rain shower's turned into a downpour, and I nod toward outside. "We should get back to it."

"Yup."

I hate this side of Owen—the curt, one-word answer side that makes me feel two inches tall. But after we head back to the burst pipe, he looks at it and says, "So, we need to dig a gigantic hole?"

"About four feet long and five feet deep." I have two shovels and hand one to Owen.

He takes it, and we work together, which is a million times easier than trying to do it alone. Except my stomach is churning because Owen's really steamed, and rightly so. Also, there's nothing else to think about while I shovel, so I can't help but question how I got into this situation. Did I overlook another thing?

Owen is only slightly out of breath as he continuously flips over more scoops of dirt. "Levi's cigarette butts are everywhere."

"I know—I need to talk to him."

When we finally have the hole dug, I show Owen how to cut the broken pipe and line up the new piece to fit. Then, on either side, we'll put braces on and clip them as tightly as we can.

It's getting harder to work as our hole is turning into a mud puddle.

As I place the binders, my hands quickly turn red from the wet clay. My fingers ache from the chill and holding the pieces in place for so long. But I keep going because I have no choice.

As usual, Owen and I make a great team—once I've shown him what to do, he puts his muscles into tightening the clips, something I don't think my fingers can do.

It takes a while, but we manage to get the replacement piece of pipe installed. To ensure everything fits correctly, I inspect each joint carefully before having Owen tighten it down one last time with a wrench.

When Owen runs away to turn back on the waterline, I have him on the phone so I can tell him to turn it back off if there's still a leak.

"I'm turning it on," he says.

My stomach clenches as I stare at the pipe. "Ready." After a moment passes with no spraying water, I'm hesitant when I say, "I think we did it." When I hear water rushing through with no leaks, I let out a cry of joy. "It's holding!"

"Good." There's that curt one-word answer from him again.

I swallow back my frustration with him. "You're free to go home now. Thank you for all your help," I say before I disconnect.

I glance at the bricked patio to see the puddles of water creeping dangerously close. "Shit!" I have to get a trench dug. I grab the shovel again, now wishing I hadn't sent Owen home. At the same time, I'm dead sick of his attitude.

But it all doesn't matter because that stubborn man reappears, as usual, and grabs a shovel.

I turn to him, the rain dripping in my eyes. "I've got it."

"Oh, yeah, you've really got it." His sarcastic tone carries a bite.

"I do." With no time to argue, I get busy shoveling, working as fast as my arms will allow. Owen joins me, and we dig in tense silence as we carve a trench in record time.

When it's done, my frustration has grown to anger, and it shows in my tone when I say, "Thanks for your help. But I don't need you rescuing me."

He looks at me, fire in his eyes. "It's not just about you. Ma doesn't need a cotton plant blowing toxic fumes at her house."

"But I told you I had it."

"Oh, you had it all right." Drenched and shivering, he grits, "We have two weeks left before the appraisal, and there's a ton of work to do. And, dammit, when I say I'll do something, I do it."

"Right, unlike me—I get it." He's being an ass, and now, I don't feel like explaining why I missed dinner. I toss the shovel down and storm past him toward my house.

When I rush onto my covered front porch, I make muddy puddles with every step, so I sit on the swing and take off my boots.

Caked head-to-toe in mud, just like me, Owen stomps onto the porch and approaches me with fire in his eyes. He must see the agony on my face because he says, "What the hell is going on?"

Anger simmers in my gut, and I want to run anywhere, just to get away from him. This is a conversation that I never wanted to have, not with Owen. But he deserves the truth.

A silence passes between us as I work up the courage to speak. Finally, I stand, clearing my throat before I say, "So...you and Dakota. Last night."

"This again? Yeah, she's a friend." He looks away, his jaw clenching. "We have a long history, so she knows my shit."

"I wish I had a friend who knew all my shit. There's something special about that."

"Maybe there is." His words make my heart lurch into my throat, and I dread to hear what's coming next. But then he says, "She and I are very different people than when we were in high school."

I close my eyes and quietly exhale the air that was trapped in my tightening chest. "What does that mean?"

"There's nothing between us." For the first time today, he looks at me with hurt in his eyes instead of anger. "Is she why didn't you come to dinner?"

"No." I bite my lip. "Well, yes, and no." I can't tell him about what Kayla said to me in confidence. Anyway, it's not about Kayla, so it's useless to throw her under the bus. I stare in the distance as I try to form the right response, the rain still dripping off my face. "It's more complicated than Dakota. I just... I couldn't."

His tense jaw ticks. "You're gonna have to do better than that."

I know he's right, but it's hard to give someone an answer to something when you don't have it yourself. The real reason's in my mind, swirling around—an amorphous thing haunting me. The answer finds its way to my lips, heating my cheeks as it goes. Finally, the words come out. "You know everything about me, but I don't know much about you. You won't tell me about your scar. You won't tell me about the day that changed you forever. But Dakota. She knows everything."

He swipes a muddy hand over his forehead. "Christ, Willow. I've never told anyone about that day. Despite therapy, I might add. I haven't spoken about it since it happened." He shakes his head. "The only people who know are those who were there."

My tone softens along with my heart. "There's something powerful about being with the people that were by your side during the toughest moments of your life."

"Maybe there's something to that. But Dakota doesn't know me now. I'm not the same person I was then. Neither is she, honestly. But none of that matters." He grabs my hand and pulls me in, desperation flickering in his eyes. "I want *you*."

As always, his words do things to me: a thousand tugs of my heartstrings. A sweetening of the air I breathe. A crackle of electricity humming through me, and I don't know what to do with it all. "I want you, too," I whisper. "And you're always here for me." I look down, not able to meet his gaze when I say, "But it's not enough."

"Since when are all these feelings not enough?" His voice goes hoarse with emotion.

It triggers my own, and I have to fight back tears when I utter, "What if Dakota's better for you in the long run, huh? What if I stop you from giving her a real chance?"

He lifts my chin with his finger, forcing me to meet his eyes again, which are shadowed with pain. "I won't end up with her whether you're here or not. She and I don't fit, not anymore. She's not who I think about. Dream about. Would give up anything for."

Butterflies flit in my stomach, and I can't let him have that effect on me, not now. "I just..." I trail off. Everything in my head sounds ridiculous, so I blurt out the truth. "I care too much. And I'm leaving."

He shakes his head, saying nothing as he stares into the distance. Finally, he asks, "Why? You love it here."

"I can't stay."

His lips form a hard line. "Why?"

"My business is in New York. It's my home." My words are clipped.

His eyes bulge and his tone turns incredulous when he says, "Are you listening to yourself? You're mostly alone in New York. And your business could move here." He raises his voice, impassioned. "You don't get to pick who you love. I know you want all the control, but this doesn't work like that."

"I don't want control." I fold my arms again, and they're so wet they slip apart. "That's not it." I know I'm lying, but just as much to myself as to Owen.

"Then what? Tell me. You owe me that." He shoots me a glare, his eyes matching the stormy sky.

I'm struggling to answer him because I don't know for sure, but there's something deep in me that won't let me give in. When my limbs grow cold at the thought, I realize that the something is fear. I'm absolutely terrified, so I say, "It's not just location." I wince, physically aching from the icicles flowing through my veins. "It's *who* we are."

"Who we are works amazingly together." He leans into me.

I step closer, touching his chin to bring his eyes to mine. "Listen to me." I meet his soulful, broken gaze. "You're an amazing man. But this is about me." I try to sound sure even though I'm anything but. "We can't be together because if we are, I'll fall in love with you. I'll want to marry you. And that can't happen."

"*Why* can't that happen? And why can't we just take it one day at a time?" He rakes a hand through his sopping hair.

Feeling pushed and defensive, I cry out, "Because I already know how I feel about you!"

His stormy eyes flicker. "Me too. I'm already never getting over you, so what's the point?" His face twists in anguish. "You're all I think about. You're in my dreams. I miss you when you're gone, even if it's just a few hours. I want to talk to you at the end of every day. What am I supposed to do with all that?"

My heart is bursting and breaking at the same moment. "Let it go."

"I don't want to let it go."

"We have to." I run my bare foot through the puddle my shoes made on the porch, my jaw clenched.

"Dammit, Willow. Stop trying to love with your head. You can only love with your heart, and I love you. From the moment I met you."

His words make my pulse skyrocket, but then there's that fear again, racing up my spine like an arctic blast. And that's the part that brings everything to a halt. "I don't know what to say to that."

"Say you feel the same. Say you love me too."

I might love him—and it might be more than I've ever loved anyone, but knowing for sure seems impossible. Letting myself *feel* it is impossible. I fight off tears as I stare at my trembling hands, trying to find the right words. But there aren't any. When the silence becomes too much to take, I blurt, "We've only known each other for less than three weeks."

"It's not about time. It's about the connection we have. It's unlike anything I've ever had before. More than that, I want to *keep* having it… for the rest of my life."

I know these beautiful things he's saying should mean everything to me, but I stare in the distance as I feel myself shutting down. "Not everybody who loves each other ends up together."

His eyes are wide, and his face is soft. "So, you do love me."

Yes. The word's right there, right on the tip of my tongue. But when I open my mouth, I say, "I don't know." I'm furious at myself, but it's all too much. Owen doesn't realize this, but I *never* thought I could feel this way or open myself up to someone like I have with him. I was never like this with Seth, which, looking back, was probably a big part of our problem. Owen's made me more vulnerable than I could ever imagine, and for a fleeting moment, I could almost see forever with him. But life has taught me to know better.

Owen exhales as his eyes seem to shatter. "Fine, then. I'll go."

I swallow back the sob that's prickling my throat, but I'm too angry to give in to it. God damn it! It's my dead biological mother. My biological father, who clearly doesn't care about me. It's my adoptive parents who died. Living or dead, everyone leaves me or lets me down. "I can't." I ball my hand into a fist. "I can't let myself trust you. Or anyone."

He looks up in exasperation. "And there it is." His forehead creases, and for the first time since I've known him, he clenches his jaw in bridled anguish.

"I'm sorry." My voice is firm, but my limbs are collapsing. I can almost feel my heart shattering in my chest.

"Don't be sorry," he murmurs. "You're going through so much right now, and, logically, I understand you need space. But the way I feel about you isn't logical, and I can't let myself get crushed." His eyes grow distant. His face hardens. He drops his hands to his sides. "So, I'll be here tomorrow to work. And that's it."

He doesn't look back as he walks away; the rain rapping on the porch roof, in synchrony with the breaking of my heart.

What do we do when our buried roots grow and strangle us?

23

The Discovery

After Owen leaves, I fumble to the mechanical room, glad it's dry. I pull the box down from the shelf, desperate to distract myself from what just happened. Except once I get it on the floor, all I do is sit and stare, my eyes welling with tears. How did I get here?

I just broke up with a man I love with all my heart, and I'm such a mess, I can't remember if I had the water lines marked.

But I *saw* those flag markers. I take my phone out of my pocket and scroll through my texts, checking to see if I missed any from Phil, like one saying how the utilities weren't marked. Maybe he asked if they should proceed without them. But there's no text from him other than the one he sent saying the job was finished. Maybe they aren't as careful with that in Georgia?

Whatever. It doesn't matter now. The water line's fixed.

So, I move my focus to what's inside that aging box. A single container that could've gotten overlooked if someone picked this house clean before I got here. I'm starting to wonder.

I gently tug the dusty cardboard flaps, my only remaining chance at clues until Roy can get the court order for my adoption records, which could take months. Inside, I see a photo album.

I lift it from the box and open the cover. The very first picture turns my arms to gooseflesh. It's of Annie, and she's in a hospital gown, her hair tousled, and her eyes tired, but happy. She's wearing a hospital wristband and holding a newborn baby.

Annie had clearly just given birth.

I sit for a minute, my chest rising and falling. That's me! It *has* to be me. I'm frantic as I flip through the pictures, one of Annie and a toddler who has red hair and hazel eyes... like me. The next one, this toddler is picking berries, the next, eating chocolate ice cream. The toddler grows into a girl, *me* because I recognize myself from the earliest photos my adoptive parents had. In the next one, I'm looking four or five, smiling as I ride a bike with handlebar ribbons, Annie hanging on to my seat.

These are my lost photos!

I frantically pull each picture out and flip it over, trying to see if there's anything written on the back of them.

There isn't. But Annie is my mother.

So I got adopted out, but why? Annie and I look so happy.

I keep digging, picking up a tiny hospital bracelet, bringing it to my eyes so I can read the faded print. With rapid breath, I read the inscription. *Willow Eloise Murphy, born at 4:03 a.m. on September 7th, 1997 at Southern Atlanta Medical Center.*

"That's not my birthday," I croak out, realizing that it probably is. The day I've celebrated my whole life, September 21st, is probably made up... or they made a mistake in my adoption papers.

Baby pictures of me and my hospital bracelet are sitting here. In an old box. At a farmhouse. In a tiny town in Georgia. "And my name was Willow Murphy," I whisper.

Joy and relief rush through me as a lifetime of subconscious thirst is finally quenched.

That's why I don't remember anything here—Bo and Lily moved here after I was adopted. But why do I remember the black-eyed Susans that are on the far edge of the property?

I look back into the box and put a trembling hand over my mouth.

I slowly reach for what's inside, afraid to touch it. It's a picture of that godforsaken cross in front of the tree, freshly planted with a bouquet of wildflowers and a framed picture of a black lab. "I know that dog." I flip the photo over to see the date, scribed in familiar chicken scratches. In the same handwriting that was on Bo's will and the back of his and Lily's wedding photo, it says, "October 12th, 2002."

My breath grows cold in my chest. Blood is rushing from my face, and my vision fogs. Unsteady, I pull out a newspaper clipping. As my eyes scan it, all the blood drains from my limbs.

It has a picture of me, four years old, holding a red lollipop and smiling at the camera. The paragraph reads, "Willow Murphy returned to her heavenly home on October 9th, 2002, leaving behind her mother, Annabelle Walsh and her caregivers, Bo and Lily Underwood."

Caregivers? I stop and squeeze my eyes shut. So I was right—they did help raise me. That's why they left me this estate. I fight to get my mind to recall any scattered memories, but there's nothing. A fire ignites in my gut at a realization. "They helped raise me, but then they faked my death at five and gave me away? What the hell?"

I grip the article. Everyone says Bo and Lily were good people, but it doesn't seem like it. "Was my adoption even legal?" My chest is rising and falling. Maybe I don't *have* adoption papers, which is why they can't be found. I mean, you can't adopt a dead person!

And my last name was Murphy, different from Annie's, which was Walsh. That's why I could never find an obituary or any information about myself. So is Murphy my biological father's surname? That would mean I might be able to find him.

But maybe I don't want to.

My heart thundering in my ears, I crumple to the floor and let out a cry as another realization hits—the one that might break me for good. "No, no, no. My parents didn't know. They couldn't have known." I cry out, shaking. "My adoptive parents were good people." I wrap my arms around my knees and rock back and forth. "Ed and Sharon were good people!" I repeat in a howl, barely recognizing my own voice. They were, right? But they lied and said I was adopted in New York. They must've known something, otherwise, why would they lie? Or were they just lied to?

Pieces of information pelt my mind, one by one, each more heinous than the last. I plead with my brain to stop, but it won't.

Bo had a New York address for a while, which means he could've known my father. Which means they could've arranged the adoption under the table.

"And why were Bo and Lily giving me away when they're not even my blood relatives?" I shriek, balling my fists. And why would *anyone* do that? What did it do to my poor mother? "And who the hell is my biological father?"

The rage—I think it's rage, I'm not sure—consuming me is almost unbearable. There's fire rushing through my veins, burning my skin, and making my body tremble.

I'm terrified to know anymore. I simply can't. And this is why I ended things with Owen.

It's *this*.

The part of my life where I fear whatever comes next will make me never want to live in my own skin again. The part I can never escape.

24

The Tension

~~~~~~~

It's been one week and two days since Owen and I stopped seeing each other. Although he's helped me with the house, we've mostly avoided each other because it's easier that way. I decided not to tell Dakota about him and me because now, there's nothing to tell.

The sun peeks over the mountain tops, which I see from the primary bathroom's new big, beautiful window. It was added yesterday, along with new fixtures, faucets, and a fresh coat of paint.

"Hello, Ms. Dawson." It's Mary Louise's voice echoing from the bedroom, and I fight off an eye roll.

"In the bathroom," I call out.

She comes through the door with a breeze of strong perfume carrying a basket of sandwiches. "Oh, my stars!" she cries out, looking around with a dropped jaw. "This place is pretty as a peach."

"Thanks, Mary Louise."

"I brought you and the crew Dough 'n Mo sandwiches today. I know you're all putting in long hours." She sets the basket down on the new white and gray streaked quartz countertop.

"Thank you—we love Dough 'n Mo." I stare at the sandwiches, wanting to eat one right now. "You are so thoughtful, and believe me, this is the best gift we could've received today."

"It's my pleasure." She rubs her gloved hands together. "Bill and I just wanted to express our appreciation for what you're doing for this town. He's the commissioner, as you know, and he's thrilled about all this. And... to apologize. I wasn't very nice to you on the phone when you told me you were going to restore all this. I'm sure sorry about that, and I was wrong. This was a wonderful decision."

"It's okay, Mary Louise. You were disappointed, but I'm so glad to hear you're on board now." Her apology means a lot, and I'm not exactly sure why. Maybe because it's completely unexpected—she doesn't seem like the type to apologize, and I always appreciate people who surprise me. I've met Bill once, and he seems like a decent guy. He's not nearly as divisive as his wife, but not nearly as kind as his son.

"Well, I'm off," she says. "I'm hosting a luncheon today for the city council members." And with a wave, she's gone. I can't help myself from exhaling.

After I tile the floor, this bathroom will be done, and it's going to be an exquisite white and gray bathroom. Or at least, that's the vision. I'm mixing grout when I hear, "Willow."

I swallow hard before looking up to see Owen standing there in his work clothes. I sigh before asking a question I already know the answer to. "What are you doing up here?"

"Workers said you needed me in here."

I don't want him this close, but at the same time, I really, *really* need the extra set of hands, and we have exactly one week left to finish everything for the appraisal and party. That means this bathroom needs to be done today, minus the glass for the shower that'll be put in tomorrow. And I'm really feeling the pinch—I have to make it back to New York in time before the next critical stage on the apartments for Klein Homes. After an internal battle with myself, I finally manage to say, "Thank you. Do you know how to tile?"

"Not the first thing." He saunters over and squats next to me. "So, you'll have to give me a lesson."

"All right." I launch into the steps: how to use the clips to position the tiles so they're perfectly lined up. How to measure twice and cut once. How to grout properly. Then, I walk him to the tile cutter and show how to use it. The saw is loud, so I give Owen a set of earplugs.

It isn't long before the two of us are doing what we do—making a great team—as we cut and place the tiles across the expansive bathroom floor. It's not easy work, and worse, it's July, and we have to turn off the AC. When you're cutting tile, the floating dust can destroy an entire air conditioning system.

So, yeah. It's extraordinarily hot in here.

And it's just like the day on the stable roof—Owen looks incredible with his clothes clinging to his ridiculous body. But unlike the day on the roof, the conversation between him and me is stilted. It's always flowed so easily, but right now, I don't know what to say, and I'm grateful that we have to use the saw. It gives us a reason to work without conversation.

Until my finger gets pinched. "Ouch!" I flip my hand as I sit on the floor.

"You okay?"

"Yeah. The tile got me, but I'm not bleeding." I look to see a blood blister forming. It's truly nothing, but for some reason, I'm crying.

"Willow." Owen is kneeling beside me.

"It's fine. These tears are automatic, like from an onion or pulling a nose hair."

His hand is on my shoulder. "Okay. But then why is your voice unsteady?"

I meet his gaze, my lips quivering. "I found my own obituary, Owen." The words come out before I can stop them.

"Jesus." He sits next to me, and that's all it takes.

I tell him everything. The pictures I found of my own grave. My newborn bracelet that said my birthday is September 7th, not September 21st. That Bo and Lily weren't the people he thought they were. "They faked my death and adopted me out."

His face pales. "I'm so sorry."

Then, I finally tell Owen about the note, the face in the barn, Oreo escaping the stable, the cut water line, and the other odd occurrences, like me finding my keys in the refrigerator.

"Whoa, Willow. I'll give you Mike Baxter's direct number. He's the sheriff. Call if you even feel someone watching you—tell him you know me. And you need to pack a bag and stay at the inn."

"Thanks. I'll take the sheriff's number, but I'm not letting anyone scare me away. I have to be here—I've got a job to finish and six days to do it."

"All right." Owen hesitates, seemingly taking time to find his words. He finally says, "I don't know what else to say except that I'm very sorry." As usual, his voice is calm, gentle, but there's something different about it. A coldness. A degree of distance that wasn't ever there before.

And because of that, I don't feel as comforted by him as I usually do. In fact, I might feel worse. "Anyway, thanks for listening."

"No problem." He pats my back. "Seriously, call Mike if you suspect anything. He won't hesitate to help."

His suggestion feels patronizing, even though I know it shouldn't. I guess it's because before, he would've asked more questions. He would've been more curious about my bombshell discovery, anxious to hear what I was going to do. But those days are behind us, and I made it that way. I can't be angry at him for *my* choices, so I swallow back the simmer in my gut and say, "Thanks. We better get back to work—we have to get this done."

"Sure."

We return to work, eating Mary Louise's sandwiches as we go. The hours crawl by with long drags of uncomfortable silence, and it's dinnertime when we finish the job. After cleaning up, we stop to survey our handiwork.

"This looks incredible." Owen's eyes pan the room which only yesterday morning, was covered in pink tile, houndstooth wallpaper, and a cloudy, flimsy shower wall. Now, it's looking like something out of a real estate magazine.

"It's better than I'd hoped." I put my hands on my hips as I peer around, taking in the new crystal chandeliers hanging from the high ceilings, the freshly painted gray-blue walls, and now, the shiny new flooring.

Demon comes blasting through the door, his claws tapping on the fresh tiles as he leaves muddy prints in his wake. "Demon, no!" I cry out, trying to catch him, but he's too fast. "How did he get in here?"

"Demon, halt!" Owen has his palm out and a miracle happens: Demon *actually* halts, and without protest. "Good boy," Owen says, pulling a treat from his pocket and feeding it to the little devil. "Now git home." Owen points out the door, and Demon flies away.

I flutter out a breath. "Wow. Impressive."

"Damn dog." Owen groans as he takes the mop and cleans up Demon's paw-work. When he's finished, he pans the space again. "I'm going to miss this," Owen says wistfully.

"That's right." The reminder of his deadline makes my stomach drop, which is why I've tried to push it out of my mind. "Tomorrow is your first day taking over the vet hospital." And his last day of helping me.

"Yeah. It is."

I nod, wanting to wish him well, but not ready to say those words just yet. It feels too much like goodbye.

As I bring the leftover tiles to the bedroom for pickup, I realize I stacked them too high, and it's very heavy. As I bend over to set them down, some start to slide off. Owen rushes behind me and helps me balance the stack before we place them down together.

His body against me and his arms over mine affect me, but I fight to not let it show in my voice. "I took on more than I could handle. Thank you." We both stand.

"You're welcome." Owen starts to move away but stops. Instead, he stands statue still behind me, his breath on my neck.

I missed this. So much. I miss him. I want to turn around. I want him to hold me like he's always done. I *will* turn around.

But then he steps away, and my heart sinks like it's tied to a cement block.

I wish I could take back all the things I said to him. But if life has taught me one thing, it's that there are no do-overs. People like me don't get second chances.

I catch my breath before facing him and smoothing my shirt. I want to say that I'm sorry, that I can't bear for things to be this way between us. But when I meet Owen's gaze, it's clear he's a million miles away. Then he says, "I'm gonna take off. I have to get ready for my first day on the job tomorrow."

"Oh, right." I force a chipper tone when I say, "Best of luck at the hospital. Although you don't need luck."

"Thank you." His voice is strained. "And good luck finishing the house. You know I'm still here if you need anything."

"I do know that." I manage a smile, but it falls away. I swallow back the lump in my throat when I say, "Thanks for everything, Owen Brooks."

"You're welcome."

He doesn't say my full name, like always. Then he turns and walks away from me, all over again.

This time, it cuts me to the bone, and I deserve it.

25

The Code

The summer heat drifts from July into August, and today's the day. The appraiser from the secretary of state's office said the house passed the preliminary inspection, so today, he'll tour the house again and give us the final word on whether it'll become a state tourist landmark. It's a momentous day for me and the town of Violet Moon, and I can't believe we finished all this in four weeks. It just goes to show what can happen when an entire town comes together.

I'm rushing to get all the last-minute stuff done. The polishing, the cabinet knob tightening, the cleaning of lingering construction dust, and all the other things on my extensive checklist. And that's not even mentioning my Zoom call with the Kleins in ten minutes.

This past week, Owen hasn't been around, as I'm sure he's incredibly busy with his first week at the vet hospital. I didn't call him for help—I know it was critical for him to focus on his new position.

To say I've missed him would be a gross understatement. But it's good preparation for what's coming, I guess. After I sign the papers on this house tomorrow, I've got my flight booked back to New York.

A little girl's voice echoes from Bo's office, and I freeze. Am I hearing things? It sounds like Trinity, but she wouldn't have come here without permission.

Except yes, she would have.

When I hear the squeak of Bo's office chair, I head downstairs and to the office where, indeed; I find Trinity... at Bo's computer.

"What are you doing here, sweetie?" My heart thrums in my chest.

Her eyes go huge as she makes a click of the mouse before flipping her head to look at me. "Sorry, Willow."

"Don't be sorry." I walk over and put a hand on her shoulder. "You know how to get onto Bo's computer?"

I look at the tattered laptop, and for the first time since I've been here, I'm actually seeing something on the monitor other than a lock screen. It has animated characters running around a cartoon town.

"Bo used to let me play games on here. I missed it so much... Ma won't let me play computer games."

I blink. "So, you know the password."

"Of course I know the password, silly." That sweet, insistent voice is like music to my ears. "It's Sammy seven thirteen."

My heart stops. "Sammy?"

"Bo's favorite dog. And seven thirteen is my birthday."

"I love it," I utter, speaking on autopilot. Sammy, Bo's favorite dog. The dog that died that day in the car accident when my mother hit the tree.

Wait. A tremor ripples through me at the thought of it all.

My mother hit that tree with her car. It killed Sammy, my dog. Bo's dog.

Is this really happening? More memories, more clues. And am I finally getting into this computer?

"Can I try it?" I smile at Trinity.

"Sure." She shuts down the computer and when it boots back up, I put in the password, typing it carefully. Sure enough, it grants me access.

But what I'm looking for isn't appropriate for Trinity's eyes, plus, we need to get busy for the party, so I say, "Does your Ma know you're here, Trin?"

"Please don't tell her."

"I won't, but you have to get home and changed for the party." I lower my voice. "I have a big cake coming for the celebration. Strawberry, your favorite."

"Yay!" She jumps up. "If Ma catches me here, I'll lose dessert."

"Exactly. See you soon, Trin." I give her a pat on the back as she rushes away.

Then I move my gaze to the computer, never more excited and terrified at the same moment. I spend a moment clicking in a frenzy before I see what I'm looking for. In Bo's files, I find one titled, "Willow_Murphy," and another titled, "Annie_Walsh." Another named "Annie's_Harddrive." Shaky, I click on my folder, finding more folders titled "adoption paperwork, "certificates," and "pictures." Basically, everything I ever wanted to know about myself and my mother. My stomach pretzels. Then I see it. A folder titled, "Blake_Murphy."

That's him. My father—it has to be.

I break into a cold sweat. My breathing becomes shallow, and the room closes in on me.

My phone dings, which means it's time to call the Kleins. I *cannot* be late for this Zoom.

I feverishly close all the windows because I absolutely don't have time to look at this, not now. Plus, I need to be in a good mental place for the celebration. If the past is any indicator, the information I find will shut me down. Hell, it's already shutting me down. I can't have that right now.

As soon as this celebration's over, I'll go through this computer.

26
The Party

After I get off Zoom with the Kleins, I go outside to make sure that the gigantic bow hanging across the front of the porch is ready for the ribbon-cutting ceremony. It's time for Owen and me to introduce this historic house to the town of Violet Moon.

Mayor Rosen will be here any minute, and there's a growing crowd outside. Once the mayor's speech ends, Owen and I will be giving tours of the place. Frankie will be showing off the horses. Kayla and Bailey are helping Mary Louise, who insisted on handling all the food. Dakota is here to supervise the children petting the goats. Jeb is giving boat rides, and Trinity will even be giving a horse-riding demonstration, which I'm sure will be a crowd favorite.

I rush back inside and meet Owen in the foyer. Before we officially open the doors, we take a moment to look at what we accomplished. We stand, looking at the freshly cleaned windows with the lush view. The marble fireplace, now shiny and bright. The scarred floors pristine, and the elaborate trim work looking crisp with the fresh coat of paint. The sunlight streaming in still sets the room aglow.

"We did this," I whisper, meeting Owen's gaze.

"We did, didn't we?" He flashes me that beautiful proud smile of his.

And I'm reminded of why I yearn to be with him. I miss these moments, *our* moments.

After a knock at the door, Nia, from *The Meddling Moon*, steps inside, and I finally get to meet her. She's wearing a flowing yellow summer dress with her twists piled artfully on her head. "Would you mind if I come inside so I can take photos of the place? It's just stunning."

"Please do!" I say, excited. "I can't wait to see this house in the paper."

After snapping a few shots, she approaches the wooden horse banister at the end of the spiral staircase. "This looks like the one in the foyer."

"Yes. I recreated it here."

She gasps, running a hand over it. "You did this? Tell me how."

My brain whirs to life because I love talking about this stuff. "Well, I had to create the exact shape as the other one, so I made a mold. And when I made a mistake, because it's wood, there was no undo button. So, I had to sculpt around errors."

After scribbling some notes, she says, "I'm putting that in the article. I bet this becomes our best-selling paper. This place is just magical."

"Thank you so much, Nia."

She excitedly buzzes around, taking different close-up shots of the fireplace, the chandeliers, and the kitchen island.

I head outside, greeting Gertie as she arrives with her granddaughter, Amelia, who's carrying a case of special edition Violet Moon beer. Gertie says, "Willow." Her eyes pan around as her jaw goes slack. "I can't believe it looks just as it did... way back when, but better." She pats my shoulder and flashes me a wistful smile. "I know without a doubt Bo and Lily would be so proud. You finished their dream for them. Bo obviously knew what he was doing when he left you this house."

Her words are tough to take because I can't think about Bo right now, but I better get used to it. He's surely going to come up a lot today. And it's funny—after going through all of this, I never thought about it that way. Maybe Bo gave me this house because he knew I'd restore it. He knew it, even when I didn't, and I'll just focus on that. I smile and say, "You know, Gertie. I think you may be right."

Then Roy Livingston arrives, tipping his hat at me before he says, "I'd say I'm surprised, but I'm not. I knew you'd do this place right."

I give him a hug. "Thank you, Roy."

He leans in. "Head's up, though. I just saw Mary Louise talking to the state surveyor about property lines. She's saying something about them being in dispute."

I fight off an eye roll. "So, what does this mean?"

"Probably nothing. She's just using this as a chance to see if she can weasel in some land for her plant. Word is, she's cooking up something. But don't worry—I'm on it. I'll be checking in with the surveyor when he's all done."

"You're the best, Roy." I'm so grateful I'll still be in contact with him when I return to New York. "I'm glad you're my lawyer. And my loan agent. And my friend."

"Now don't you forget that when you get back to the fast-paced city life. I'm here for you 'til my ticker stops." He pats my shoulder before wandering into the crowd.

My eyes mist, and I have a feeling that's going to happen a lot today.

When Mayor Rosen arrives, she looks around and flashes me a huge smile. "Willow. This has exceeded all my expectations." She blows out a sigh. "What a gem for Violet Moon to have. We're so blessed to have you." She pulls me into a hug, and there's that mist again.

"Thank you so much." A warm feeling rushes through me, and it's something new. I'm accustomed to restoring homes for income, but

I've never restored something that meant this much to so many people. I hope this place becomes one of the many beloved sights of Violet Moon, and now I know that there's no greater fulfillment than that. When Mayor Rosen pulls away, I smile. "I'm so glad that I could do this for the town. And I'm pretty proud of it too."

"Let's just hope the state appraiser agrees with us." She shoots me a wide-eyed look before nodding behind me.

"No kidding." I turn to see the appraiser from the Georgia's secretary of state's office, Andrew Perez, approaching us wearing a sharp suit.

He smiles at Mayor Rosen before he says, "It's good to see you, Mayor." He extends his hand. "Hello, Ms. Dawson. You ready?"

"Yes, I'm ready." My breath hitches. *Here we go*. After we exchange pleasantries, Mayor Rosen takes her position on the front porch, just in front of the ribbon. She gets her microphone ready to address the townspeople, who are spilling over the roundabout driveway onto the surrounding lawn.

Smiling faces, decorations, balloons, and running kids set the tone for this summer party. When the hum of chatter quiets, Mayor Rosen says, "We're thrilled for the opportunity to make this historic and beautiful estate a part of the city of Violet Moon. We can't wait to open it up for all you good folks and the tourists who want to experience how beer barley growing is done right."

Applause erupts and people yell, "Here, here," as they hold up their Violet Moon beers. I can't help but meet Owen's gaze in the crowd, and he's looking on with pride.

Mary Louise's husband and town commissioner, Bill Smith, hands the mayor an oversized pair of scissors. Then, she cuts the ribbon to the sound of hoots and hollers. After the formalities are done, the Mayor, Owen, and I start tours of the place, highlighting all the special design work that my team did, like the new patio, the new kitchen, and the refurbished fireplace. I talk about how some of the light and door fixtures are the originals which have been restored.

The questions hit immediately. Will the place be a wedding venue, and when can people start booking it? Will it serve as an inn for wedding and reunion parties, and how much will it cost? Will the horseback riding, goat petting, and boat riding on the lake be included? The Mayor handles these questions with grace, telling everyone that all these decisions will be made once the property is purchased.

Owen jumps in to point out all the touches I added, never failing to inform people about just how talented I am. And when he gives Gertie's granddaughter a tour on his shoulders, I can't help but watch on, my heart tripping over its next beat.

He always has a way of doing that.

As soon as her tour is over, Gertie pats her granddaughter on the back. "All right, Amelia, let's get you off to meet that baby goat. Now, remember, goats bite, so watch yourself." Gertie bustles Amelia out the back door.

It's such a joyous affair, but a sadness washes over me. I love being here, and *I* love doing all these things. I feel a knee-jerk reaction of possession—that these are *my* goats, *my* horses, and *my* lake, but I know I have to let all that go. None of these things are mine, not really, and they never were. They belong to the town of Violet Moon, and I'm honored to be the facilitator to make things how they should be.

When the appraiser finishes, we all gather around the front of the house again, anxiously awaiting his final decision. Andrew Perez takes his place at the top of the steps, holding the microphone and keeping his face even as anticipation grows. When everything is quiet but birdsong, Andrew says, "After our extensive review, I declare The Violet Moon Château an official historic site for the state of Georgia!"

Cheers roar out, and I jump up and down before pulling Owen into a hug. He spins me around, and it's *really* hard not to plant a big fat kiss on his face.

But soon, we are greeted by the many townspeople, wishing us congratulations and thanking us.

What a day!

When the celebration is over and the crowd has left, Kayla and Bailey bundle up the leftover food to take to some families in need. Dakota's helping me clean up in the kitchen when she says, "You do know I see the way he looks at you, Willow." She throws cups into the oversized garbage can that we set out.

I freeze. Then, even though I know exactly what she's referring to, I shoot her a puzzled look. "What?"

"Don't play the fool. I see it. Owen's got it bad for you, and I think you're pretty in love with him, too."

I tilt my head. "What about you and Owen?"

She bats a hand. "Put a fork in us. We're done—were years ago, just couldn't see it until we were back in the same space. That boy is all yours."

I approach her, wringing my hands. "I tried to tell you. The night at the brewery. But things went sideways, and I didn't want to ruin the chance of you two getting back together if that's what was meant to be."

"You should've told me, Willow. But I get it—our friendship is brand new."

"You're right, and I'm sorry. I just knew Owen and I were temporary since I'm heading back New York." I haphazardly clear the countertop.

She quirks an eyebrow as she brings the trash can over to me. "You don't have to be."

I release my armful into it. "I do. I got too many people counting on me." A wistful smile spreads across my face and I bring her in for a hug. "You're awesome, you know that, right?"

She pulls away, shooting me a look. "Of course I know that, duh. That's why I'm holding out for the man that does it *all* for me. For the person I am now."

"As you should."

Trinity stomps into the kitchen, her arms folded over her chest. "Ma says I have to help clean up to get dessert."

"Well, thank you for your kind offer, Ms. Trinity," I say, feigning a smile.

"Git over here, Trin." Dakota nods toward the sink. "We'll wash dishes together."

"Aw, man." Trinity hangs her head as she shuffles toward Dakota. Give it up for Frankie, who's making sure we have another set of hands.

"Ms. Dawson?" It's Andrew's voice, and I spin around to see him standing there with his clipboard.

"Yes." My heart skitters to a stop. I hope Mary Louise didn't somehow get some of the land.

"Everything looks good—the survey shows the property lines stay put. But I do need to have my electrician come out and do a check of all the wiring first thing tomorrow morning. As long as that passes inspection, you'll be all good to sign over the deed and be on your way."

"Wonderful." Relief rushes through me. "Thank you so much, Mr. Perez."

"Sure thing." He heads out, and once the kitchen's clean, so do Dakota and Trinity. Now that I'm alone, the bittersweetness of all this settles in. I step out to the patio for some fresh air, and that's when I see Owen in the yard, replacing all the divots of grass that were thrown by people's footsteps.

I wave to him. "Thank you. As always."

When he looks up and our eyes meet, an understanding passes between us. We share the feeling of this moment because we both worked ourselves to the bone for this place. Today, we gave the town something more than a building. And now, we know that deep-in-our-soul kind of joy—the kind that comes from revitalizing something truly special. To put your artistic flare and elbow grease into a place where memories will be made to last a lifetime. There's nothing better.

I grab my purse that contains my tablet and approach him—all this has given me an idea.

"Hey." I tap my stylus on the tablet.

"Hey, you," he says, quirking a brow. "You've got something up your sleeve."

"I do." I'm reminded how well he knows me. "Come with me to the lookout spot?"

"I should say no, but it's just too damn hard to say no to that."

"Don't worry. It's work related." I wink.

As we walk, I spot Levi in the barn. What is he doing? It's way past work time. I consider asking him, but when he sees Owen and me, he waves and rushes away.

That was weird. But it's Levi, so it's really not.

Once Owen and I are standing on the lookout spot, I spread my hands wide and say, "Okay, so there's one last piece missing, and I need your help for it to come to life."

"Bo's barn."

"Yup. It wouldn't be that tough. I think you could easily oversee a crew to manage it after I'm gone. It'd take two weeks, three, tops. The city would sign off on it."

"I'm listening."

"Ready?" I tick off each item with my fingers. "I'll create the architectural plans. You get a crew lined up to pour the concrete base, which will take about two days. Then the framing is one to two days. Keep the inside simple. A half bathroom, a fireplace, a counter, a loft, lots of seating, and some shelving, but the big thing will be the accordion glass doors on two sides."

He scrubs his chin. "I know, I gotta order those way in advance."

"Right." Why is he so perfect? "Because it's a barn, there's no drywalling. Just use strong PVC. So, after the windows and doors, it's just plumbing, electricity, lighting, then floors."

"Sounds like a job a novice could handle."

"I believe in you, Mr. Brooks."

"As you should." He keeps studying the spot, deep in thought. "You said Bo wanted outdoor seating. The barn should have a roof people can sit on and enjoy."

I gasp. "Yes, it should." As though the earth hears us, a light breeze brushes my face, as if to tell me, yes, a roof.

Owen stares at the sky in thought. "How would folks get up there?"

"A spiral staircase, of course." I make some notes on my tablet.

"Aren't those expensive?"

"Maybe, but not necessarily. You can find them premade." I tap a finger on my chin. "Then you'll spend more on the roofing, but that's worth it. And you'll need a railing, too."

He squints. "Do barns have spiral staircases?"

"Sure, why not?"

"All right. I trust you, Ms. Dawson."

"As you should."

He folds his arms. "You know I love being a vet and I'm doing my life's work, but this is a distant second."

"Distant, huh? I guess that's a good thing. Nothing can take you away from the animals. You have a gift. Unlike anything I've ever seen." He blushes and looks away, like he always does. I say, "You really don't like compliments, do you?"

"Nope. But it's still nice when you say them." He nods to the bare patch of the grassy knoll. "Let's dance. See what it would be like for folks who are getting married in our imaginary barn."

I cock my head, scolding him, but my pulse races.

"It's site research, Willow. Work related."

My heart does that thing it does when Owen lays on the charm, and I know I should say no, but he's making it impossible with his lopsided grin and flicker of those eyes.

I put my tablet in my purse and set it down. As we step onto the "dance floor," he appears to be at war with his wandering eyes, struggling to keep them focused on my face. At the moment, he's losing, and they've darted down to my chest.

"Owen." I smile, snapping my finger in front of his face. "Up here."

"Sorry, jeez." He exhales. "I mean, I'm really trying here. I just can't resist you."

I let out a faint laugh and shake my head. As we dance, it should be awkward because there's no music, but we're too busy laughing.

Until we're not.

We're holding each other with that magnetic pull stronger than ever. That barrier, the one *I* created, evaporates between us. Why is being close to him, touching him, and holding him almost like breathing?

I could step away. I could turn around. I could do something, *anything*, but I don't. I stand frozen as the gooseflesh appears on my shoulders where his breath hits. His smell of warm skin and tea tree oil rushes over me, and I can't believe how much I've missed it.

He leans in and whispers, "If you want me to move, just say."

I prepare my lips to tell him to go, but the words don't leave my mouth. I'm frozen as his fingers run down my side, creating electricity along their paths, and I can't bring myself to end this moment. Swallowing hard, I lean into him, hoping with everything in me that his hands continue to roam.

But they stop. Then he rasps, "Say you want more. Otherwise, I'm gone."

My lips twitch as I fight the urge to answer him. But it's useless. "More," slips from my lips.

His fingers slither up my side, slowly, intentionally, until he's finally under my shirt.

My body trembles as I wait for his next movement, his next breath, and I swear I want him more than I wanted anything ever in my life.

Why is this so bitter achingly painful?

He moves his lips to my neck, brushing them just beneath my earlobe, the place he knows makes me lose all control. Then, just like that, he pulls away. He's got a mischievous smile when he says, "Wanna catch the stars with me tonight? I'll bring the cinnamon whiskey."

"I don't know. We probably shouldn't," I manage to say, logic returning to my brain.

"Come on." He puts out his palms. "I'll keep my hands to myself, I promise."

I sigh. "It's not you. I'm not so sure I can keep *my* hands to myself."

He sucks in air through his teeth. "That's a tough one. And why is that?"

"Well, you're gorgeous, empirically, so there's that. You can also be quite charming." I jam a hand into my pocket. "From time to time."

"Fair enough. But you should experience one more starry night in Violet Moon."

How can I say no to that? "I should."

He hesitates, looking into the distance. His face goes serious, and his eyes turn dark when he says, "But first, there's some place I need you to see."

I eye him quizzically. "Okay."

27

The River

~~~~~~~~~~~

It's dusk by the time we follow a trail to the river, and the sky is putting on a show, but Owen's quiet. When I glance at him, I realize there's something about his face that isn't quite right—an intensity as he stares ahead. He squeezes his eyes tightly, his jaw clenched. I've only seen him like this once before, and it was the night Oreo was born.

So, I walk quietly as I let him have the space he needs. The frogs are croaking, and the warm evening air wraps around me like an invisible blanket. It's so peaceful.

Finally, Owen says, "It's my fault my pa's dead."

My stomach clenches, and something sharp pierces my heart. I shake my head and whisper, "What do you mean, it's your fault?"

My pulse rockets into high gear, and it feels like an eternity passes before he speaks again. He stops walking when he says, "I was sixteen, and I thought I knew everything. That I was invincible. I was sure my dad was cheating on my mom. He worked all hours being the town's district attorney, and he hadn't come home a few nights in a row. He was acting distant, and I saw Ma crying when he left one night. If he wasn't going to be the man of the family, then I'd do it. So, the next day, I followed him. I saw him in a car with a woman, and I was sure that I was finally going to catch him. Then, I could tell Ma and she'd know the truth. Pa was driving a car I didn't recognize, so I thought it belonged to the woman. Anyway, back then, I ran track and was pretty fast. Plus, I had an idea where he was probably going. That house." He points ahead.

I look to see a cabin, the ceiling caving in and rot taking over its wooden beams. I already don't like the woods, and the place gives me the major creeps.

Owen's voice is raw. "Pa used to spend a lot of time at the place, fishing, so, that day, I cut through the woods, pushing my way through the tall grass and getting scraped by branches. I got there just after they'd gone inside. I ran to the door and stopped Pa from closing it. He drew a gun, which I didn't know he had, but when he saw it was me standing there, his face turned purple with rage. 'What the hell are you doing here, Owen?'"

"Oh, no," I utter.

"And I said, 'What are *you* doing here?'" I had all this attitude. And he was so angry—angrier than he'd ever been at me when he said, 'You have to leave. Now.' When I wouldn't, and I said I knew he was cheating, he finally told me the truth. 'This is a safe house, and I'm trying to protect a witness. You're about to get yourself killed.'" Owen looks away, his eyes dark and shadowed. "I told him I wouldn't leave. Pa was fuming when he said the cops were on the way, and they were on the verge of bringing down some big criminals. Pa said he could protect himself, that he'd be fine. I'll never forget his voice. It was like acid when he said, 'For once in your damn life, Owen, do as I ask.' Then he told me to float down the river so that I wouldn't be seen leaving. I didn't want to do it. With everything in me, I didn't want to go, Willow. But I had to obey my father on something so important, so I did what he said." Owen hesitates, swallowing so hard his Adam's apple bobs. His voice cracks around his words when he says, "I was floating away when I heard the bomb explode. I wish I'd never left. It was the worst moment of my life." A single tear rolls down Owen's cheek.

"I'm so sorry." I take his hand and rub my thumb over his palm. I had absolutely no idea, from everything Owen said, that he'd gone through something like this. But it all makes sense now—his empathy toward my situation. Him being closed off about his past. The way he shuts down on the anniversary of his father's death.

He continues, "I was so completely overwhelmed with grief that I wasn't focused. The current got me and pulled me into a riptide. The last thing I remember is this overwhelming calm feeling after I inhaled the water."

"Oh my god." I want to pull Owen into a hug and comfort him like he's done for me so many times. But he's keeping his distance from me, so I don't think that's what he wants right now. And I feel so inadequate compared to him—with that soothing voice and natural calming presence that I'll never have. All I can do is continue rub his palm.

His voice is raspy when he says, "I came to when I was on the shore. Ma was doing CPR on me. She saved my life, then told me never to tell anyone that I'd been there, so I didn't. She told people I braved the river trying to get to Pa. I *wish* that were true. I've told myself over and over that it wasn't my fault. But what if I'd just argued with Pa a few minutes longer? Then he would've been outside. He would've had a chance. How am I supposed to live knowing I could've done that?" He rakes his hand through his hair. "I don't know how to live with that."

"But you were doing as you were told."

He clenches and unclenches his jaw. "Yeah."

"And if you were both standing just outside the house, you both would've died."

"I know that, logically. But there's a voice inside of me that will never let me believe it."

I put my hand on his back. "I can't entirely understand what you've been through, because what happened to my parents was very different. But I do understand what it's like to live with survivors' guilt. I know that I wasn't a part of my parent's death, but I still always wondered what I could've done differently. If I could've stopped them from going that night in the terrible rain."

His nose flares. "I'm still trying to come to terms with what happened. I thought it would help when they caught the suspect and threw the book at him, and it did some, but not nearly enough. The big criminals behind it never got caught. I've never told anyone this before, besides Ma, but I told you." He looks at me, his eyes desperate. "That's progress, right?"

"Huge progress." I manage a weak smile as I touch his face.

His voice is lighter when he says, "We both live with this impossible pain."

I blow out a long sigh. "People who say time heals all things are assholes."

"They really are." He puts his hand out, and I take it. After a squeeze, he says, "Now. You ready to watch some stars?"

"Absolutely." And I don't want this to be the last time I do it.

I'm buzzing with so many emotions, and a thought hits me so hard it almost knocks the breath from my chest.

I need to stay.

I can stay.

I *can* stay. I can open a RevitaHome office here and let Natanya run the New York office. She's clearly a rockstar, and she doesn't need me. I'll just finish with the Kleins, then move to Violet Moon. I'll have the money from the sale of Bo's Château to get myself an affordable place and open a second office.

I love it here. I love Owen. I love living on a farm and being surrounded by animals. I love taking care of animals. It's a part of my life I've always longed for, even though I didn't know it.

Now, I just have to tell Owen.

28
The Call

My phone buzzes from a text, and I look down.

Natanya: *Willow, are you in there? The Kleins want out of the deal. Call me NOW.*

I dial her instantly. "Natanya. What is going on?" My words sound choked off.

"They're pulling out." It sounds like she's been crying. Natanya never cries.

"They can't do that. We have a contract."

"They're saying we're in breech. I think they got a better price."

My vision goes hazy. "I don't understand. We're halfway through!"

"I don't know." She lets out a soft sob. "But we can't bounce back from this."

"Yes, we can. And we will." I say the words, but don't believe them. This is why I never let up, not for a second—I can't. I can't because when I do, everything falls apart. "This is my fault."

"It kind of is."

Oh, god. It *is* my fault. I wasn't in the office. I wasn't there meeting with the Kleins myself. I was late to a few meetings, and I didn't send their selections when they needed them. "If I was there, I could've matched the price or re-organized the deal."

"But you can't be everywhere. You just had to delegate, which you refused to do." Natanya's voice is sharp.

"You're right. You should've had the power to negotiate. I'm sorry." But I also should've been there for the most important deal in the company's history. My company. "I'll fix this. I'm coming home tomorrow. Hang in there."

"Okay. See you soon." She disconnects.

I *have* to fix this, or I'll be forced to file bankruptcy, and my employees will be completely and totally screwed because of me. *I'll* be screwed because of me. I put my face in my hands. "I just imploded my company."

Owen touches my back. "I don't understand how. You've been working day and night for the Kleins, giving them everything they've asked for."

"It wasn't enough."

"Maybe nothing would've been enough, Willow. Business is cutthroat. No loyalty. Companies go with the best price, or choose their friends, or work deals under the table. Shit happens in business."

I stare ahead. "Yes, shit happens all the time in business, which is why you have a contingency plan. Which is why you never put all your eggs in one basket." Why did I do this? Put *everything* into this?

"You took a risk on something that had a big payoff. And I would've done the same thing. Most people would've done the same thing." He studies me. "How would you have known that they were going to be snakes?"

"I couldn't have known, but I could've prepared for the deal falling through. I've always been prepared, but all this has distracted me."

"It has, but you've seemed so happy. What about that?"

"What does happiness matter if everything falls apart?"

"Happiness is the *only* thing that matters. You can have all the business success and money in the world, but if you're not happy, what's the point?"

"The point is that you survive." My voice is sharper than I intend. "When you have money, you survive. You have a place to live. You have food to eat."

"But you don't need this business to survive, Willow. You'll figure it out. You have a home here with people who love you. And you can still have a good life if your business goes bankrupt. It's not ideal, but maybe it's a blessing in disguise."

I stare into space, trying to process his words. Somewhere deep inside me, I know he's right, but I can't accept that. I *cannot* accept failure. I say, "When you've been fighting your whole life, you can't stop."

"When is enough enough?"

"I don't know, but not now. My employees. My clients. I have to fix this mess because I can't let them down." I should've been there.

"Oh, shit." Owen's gaze is glued up ahead, his words anguished.

My stomach knots. "What?" I look to see orange and red flickers in the sky, smoke filling the air. But I can't tell where it's coming from. "Where is it?"

"I think it's your house!"

Owen and I break into a sprint, and I can barely see as my vision blurs from stress and the gray haze filling the night air.

No, no, no. As we get to the lake, I'm forced to accept that Owen was right. It *is* my house.

As we step into the pasture, my breath stops entirely. The smell, like solder mixed with burning rubber and wood, hits like a blow.

Goats bleat in the barn, terrified. Fiery ash floats in the air, and the warm night air has turned sweltering.

I look to the house, my beautiful house. The town's beautiful house. My proudest work of art. *Our* work of art. Our blood, sweat, and tears.

It's engulfed in a blaze of deep red and amber, flames licking up the sides of the broken windows, leaving black char in its wake.

29
The Gray Night

I let out a bloodcurdling scream. "The house! It's gone!"

I can't wrap my head around it. *How did this happen?*

Did I do it? Did I forget to turn off the stove in the kitchen? I don't know. I *remember* checking everything, but these days, that doesn't mean much.

"The stables are burning too!" Owen says, turning back, before taking off.

A gag lurches in my throat, and I'm losing ground behind him, and through the smoky haze, I finally see the stables. "The horses. Oreo!" I shriek, barely recognizing my own voice.

We're running, and all I feel is the ground shifting under my feet as my legs carry me toward the billowing smoke. It's so hot it's unbearable, and the roaring sound, like a jet plane, is busting my eardrums.

Getting closer, I cough from the thick, bitter air that's sticking in my lungs.

"Stay back!" Owen orders.

Not a chance. He's faster than me, but I stick behind him. Flames engulf the stable walls, and the roof sags. The thought of what this means guts me whole. "*Please,* not the horses!"

In the distance, beyond the haze, Raven and Blackjack gallop away. I'm glad they're out, but I don't see Eclipse, and worse, I don't see Oreo. He wouldn't be fast or strong enough to make it out on his own.

I let out a wail, my eyes tearing up from emotions and the burning smoke.

I'm in a coughing fit when Owen runs directly into the flames. Choking, I fall to the ground. I can't breathe—I truly can't breathe. I stand and stagger away, and when I manage to get to fresher air, I gulp it before running back. "Owen, get out of there now!"

I blink away burning tears as sirens roar in the distance. They can still save the barn!

Seconds feel like hours as the crackle and snap of the structures breaking and crumbling has my stomach twisted into agonizing knots. My brain can't process what's happening—it's almost as if I'm floating above myself, watching a movie about my worst nightmare. No. Worse than my worst nightmare.

"Owen!" I scream again, the horses forgotten at the thought of something happening to him. "Owen, please!" I beg, my voice strangled again in the sooty air. I go to run inside, my skin burning from the heat, and a fiery beam crashes to the ground in front of me.

I halt, furiously blinking back the flood of tears from the anguish and thick smoke. The sirens stop as voices echo nearby. I can't hear what they're saying, but I yell, "Owen's in there! Help him!"

I hold my breath and sprint into the crumbling mess, beyond terrified of how I'm going to find Owen. My skin is so hot it's unbearable, but I push on.

Then, through the charcoal haze, I see him running toward the stable doors, his arms covered with black hair.

He's carrying Oreo. The foal's eyes are open, and as soon as we're safely out from under the falling debris, I run up to take the horse because Owen's clearly struggling for air.

"Where's Eclipse?" Owen squeaks out.

"I don't know." My throat is raw. "I couldn't find her anywhere."

The fire trucks now surround the stables, and firefighters run with hoses. The barn remains untouched, and I exhale. At least the goats are safe.

Kayla appears, shaking when she says, "Ma's with Trinity. Bailey's talking to the police. They're all worried sick."

"We're okay, the goats are okay, but we're still looking for the horses." I take off running again, and when I see a flash of white galloping in the distance, I gush out a breath.

Eclipse is running, frantic, and when she sees Oreo, she lets out a harrowing neigh. Oreo's clearly weak and dizzy, but Owen tells me we just need to get him fresh air and water, so we take him to the lake.

When the blaze is out with the barn spared, the firefighters surround us. Owen tells the marshal everything we know—that we came home to the house ablaze and the stables burning. All the horses made it out.

Somehow, I'm devastated, but at the same time, more grateful than I've ever been in my life that Owen is okay. That the horses are okay.

No, all that remains of the house is a pile of charred and splintered wood, shattered windows, and ashes. Owen puts a hand on my shoulder and says, "You okay?"

"I'm fine." When I look at him, I see a man covered in black soot with patches of red on his arms and legs. "You're burned."

"It's superficial."

"You should still get checked out. Burns cause infections."

"I know."

That's right—he *does* know.

The paramedics look him over and insist he go to the hospital, but he refuses to take the ambulance.

I cut in, "Come on. I'll drive you."

As we're on our way, Owen texts all his family. His sisters are beside themselves with worry, and Frankie is doing anything and everything to make sure the horses are taken care of for the night. Plus, she's got to make sure Trinity stays in the house.

"I can't believe you did that, Owen." I glance at him as I keep my hands on the wheel. "Or rather, I can't believe anyone would do that."

"I had no choice."

"The fact that you believe that says everything about you." I glance at him again, this time with adoration. But I stop myself because I can't go there—I *have* to return to New York. For good. All of this is a wake-up call, and I wasn't being logical or realistic when I thought I could stay with Owen here in Violet Moon.

I mean, what now? What in the hell am I going to do now?

Flashes of everything hit my mind like acid rain. My contract with the city of Violet Moon. All the hopes and dreams I had for the place. All our restoration work on the irreplaceable fixtures and chandeliers. The precious library of books, gone. Everything!

After Owen grabs a cloth out of the glove compartment and runs it over his face, he touches my shoulder. "Where did you go? I lost you."

"I'm here." I run a finger over a singed piece of his hair, wishing I could say I will *always* be here. But that's not true. Our lives are too different. I have a million and one problems, and I don't have a place to call home, not with a family like he does. And I never will. So, I say the one thing I can. "I've got your back." And now, with some of the soot off his face, I can see he's lost all his facial hair. "Your goatee, your eyebrows, and even your lashes. They're all gone. Your beautiful lashes."

His lips tick up. "My sisters always tell me they're jealous of them. I guess I fixed that."

I can't laugh. I can't find humor in this moment—the moment I'm watching the things we've worked so hard for slip through our fingertips. The moment I've lost everything—all over again.

Our hospital visit takes a long time, and I'm exhausted but so relieved Owen checks out fine. I do too. While we're in the exam room waiting for our discharge papers, I have Roy on the phone. He's telling me that insurance won't cover arson but will cover damages if the fire was accidental. If I did it by leaving the stove on, or something like that, at least it'll be paid for. I never thought I'd wish I did something absent-minded again, yet here I am.

The door flies open, and Bailey busts in, dressed up in a skimpy silk top, tight pants, and heels. She has tears streaming down her cheeks when she says, "I was coming home from dancing at the Moonlight Lounge. I saw who started the fire."

30
Long Way Home

Early morning, I arrive at the house, or really, the charred wreckage that remains of the house. Some partial walls remain, a few of the kitchen cabinets still standing but blackened. Random items, like a toaster and a coffee pot, are scattered about. Shattered windows lie around with broken glass and splintered wood. In a dark haze, I wander, sifting through the rubble to see if there's anything left worth keeping.

I swear I'll never get this singed metal smell out of my nose.

Tears fall from my face as I lift the charred pieces of wood and drywall. I find Bo's computer, or what's left of it, now just a shattered screen and a collection of data chips. I pick it up and hug it, not caring that I'm getting soot all over my clothes. *All* my answers were there. I saw them, neatly organized in appropriately named files, calling for me to click on them. I had them in my fingertips, and now they're all gone. My past is in shattered pieces, literally.

My eyes scan the place, looking for my personal things so I can go. But I don't have even those—the only clothes I have are the ones on my back. I don't have a suitcase, either, so why bother?

I have nothing to pack, which is somehow freeing—a silver lining in the debris. At least I have my tablet and keys, which were in my purse that I left sitting on the lookout spot yesterday evening.

I'm free to go, but I see one thing I want to take—the sapphire from the grand room chandelier. I wander over and twist it off, holding it in my hands. It's a beautiful stone to remind me of the wonderful time I had here in Violet Moon.

I shove it in my pocket, then see Owen approaching me through blurry eyes. My heart somehow breaks more, and I don't even know how that's possible. I whisper, "I can't believe it. I just can't believe it."

He rakes a hand through his burned and jagged hair. "Me neither." His face turns resolute. "We just have to keep going. We'll start over. I'll call the guys—"

"I'm going back to New York," I cut in, meeting his hollow eyes. I can't hear anything he's about to say. It's over. "Today."

For the first time since I've known him, he looks at me with utter disappointment. "What do you mean? What about finding out who did this?"

"The arson investigators are working on it. They'll figure it out whether or not I'm here."

Last night, Bailey told us what she told the fire marshal. She saw a thin-framed male, about five eight or nine, wearing a blue or black hooded sweatshirt and dark shades running across her property. She called the police and spoke to them, which is why she wasn't with us at the fire. The rest of the family was sound asleep.

Someone's been sabotaging this place since the beginning. "It could be Mary Louise. She could've had Huck do it so she could have this land for her plant. Or Levi. He acts strange and leaves his cigarette butts everywhere."

Owen's voice is desperate. "Let's talk to Mary Louise. See if we can help lead the investigators to where they need to go. This is your property."

"Not for long. My insurance won't cover it if arson caused it—and given what Bailey saw, it sounds like it. Which means I'll have no money to pay the bank back the loan, which means this will all get repossessed. Roy already advised me on everything. So, it's done. My business in New York is done. I have nothing left."

"You have me."

My heart does that thing it does when he says those things. I meet his gaze, so desperately wanting to tell him that yes, he has me too. But I can't listen to my heart—it's why I'm here in this mess, standing in a pile of rubble. It's time to go back to using my head, which I know is the only thing I can count on. Right here, right now, is proof I lose everything. "Owen, someone is out to destroy me here. If I stay, you're going to get hurt. It's not safe for you or anyone while I'm here. I have to go."

Before he can respond, Trinity runs up to me, crying.

I pull her into a hug. "It's okay. The horses are okay. The goats are okay." She shakes her head, her tears spilling onto my shoulder. Her trembling arms pull me tighter, and I try to sound confident when I say, "It's all gonna be okay, Trin." I don't say I promise because I don't know if I believe what I'm saying.

With her tiny body quivering in my arms, her croaky voice is just above a whisper when she says, "Love you."

Two words, that's all, and it's everything. "Love you too." I don't have anything more to say. I don't think there is anything left because at the end of it all, that's all that matters. I just hold her tighter, and as long as I can. When I finally pull away, I squat so I'm eye level with her. "Listen to me. I've got everything worked out. Soon, the bank will probably take this land. Roy Livingston is going to work with the city and the bank to redraw the property lines so your ma can purchase the pasture. That way, your family can continue caring for the horses and goats, okay?" I brush a stray wisp of hair off her face. I don't tell her the part about how if it was arson, I'll have to file for bankruptcy.

"Really?" She sniffles.

I manage a smile. "It's not a done deal yet, but Mr. Livingston is doing everything he can, okay?"

She nods, but then pulls me into a hug again. "But when will I see you again?"

Ugh. A question I don't have a good answer for. This is what Kayla warned me about, and she was right. But my heart is breaking too, and I know I can't go without ever seeing her again. "I'll come visit. I promise." I mean that.

"I know you will. You have to." She steps away and lifts her chin. "I'm calling you later today. I have something I have to tell you. So, bye for now."

I wonder what? "Bye for now," I say as she runs off toward the bramble that separates our properties.

I turn my gaze to Owen and hitch a thumb over my shoulder. "I better get going. I don't want to miss my flight, and I need time to drop off the rental car."

He nods curtly. "Good luck with your life, Willow Dawson, even though I know you don't need it. You're headed for big things, even if it doesn't feel like it right at this moment."

"You too." My chest collapses, but I say, "Violet Moon and animals are lucky to have you."

Right on cue, Demon scrambles up to me and licks my hands as if to wish me goodbye. I let out a bittersweet laugh before I say, "Aw, Demon, don't let anyone ever tell you that you aren't the best dog in the whole world." I scrub his tummy as he wags his tail and kicks his legs in the air in pure joy before he runs away to chew on a stick.

Owen's mouth curves. "Did I tell you that Demon's officially part of the Brooks' family?"

"No!" I act surprised, but I'm not. Of course, Owen was always going to adopt Demon. He just didn't know it. "He is, is he? Well, then. I'd tell you to change his name to something a bit nicer, but I know your mom. She won't allow it."

"Nope. It's bad luck. So. Demon it stays."

"Well, Demon. I'll definitely miss you." I flutter out a breath and meet Owen's gaze. "And I might miss you, too."

I want to say more, do more. I want to hug Owen until my arms ache, but I can't. Instead, I jam my hands in my pockets before heading to the rental car. I sit inside for a beat before I turn the engine.

Pulling away, I can't help but remember the first day I drove here. I thought Owen might be Ted Bundy. I couldn't wait to get out of this boondock town and back to New York. Funny thing. Now that I'm actually going, it's the last thing I want.

I drive the car away at a crawl, taking in my last view of the endless pine trees. And the clouds, like stretched cotton candy, hang just above the mountains with the sunlight peeking through.

And then I pass the tree. I definitely won't miss that thing.

Still. It's hard to imagine that I'm leaving this place forever. It got under my skin a lot more than I thought it would.

Owen did too.

31

The Big City

※⋙･･◆･･⋘※

Walking into the empty boardroom, I can't get over how different everything feels. The hundred-story view of the Hudson River. The building's modern design with marble floors, sharp edges, and clean yet expensive artwork and statues. It's the same as I remember it, but it feels different.

When Natanya comes through the door, I pull her into a hug. "I've missed you so much." I give her a tight squeeze, taking in her signature scent of white lilies that I missed too.

"You too, girl," she says, pulling away. "But I have to say, you've got this glow about you."

"I do?" That's shocking considering my last few days.

"Yes. Violet Moon was good for you. And you were happy there. And at peace." She looks up. "Well, except for the fire."

I close my eyes. "Yeah."

Her voice is gentle. "Do they know anything more?"

"No. And I'm trying not to think about it." Which isn't working. It's *all* I can think about—who would do something so heinous to me? And why? But I move on. "I'm sorry about the situation I left you in."

"Can I speak honestly, boss?"

"You know you will, and I want you to, so go right ahead." The air conditioner turns on and starts blowing on me, and I shiver. It hits me that I'm no longer used to the dry, cool air.

"I love you, Willow, you know that. But if you give me the tools I need to succeed, I can run the office here just fine."

"I was standing in your way, wasn't I?"

"A little bit."

I let out a long sigh. "I was so scared of letting go of my job, you couldn't do yours. But I'm going to fix this. I have a plan."

"Oh, Lord." Natanya's eyes go huge. "I don't know what it is, and I'm not sure I wanna know."

"Well, like it or not, you're about to find out very soon." I look at the door. "As soon as the Klein brothers arrive with their lawyer."

She reaches for my hand and gives it a squeeze. "Whatever it is, you deserve to be happy. I love having you in my life, but I also have you over Zoom no matter what happens. So, for once in your life, can you just let yourself be happy?"

"Maybe."

Natanya groans. "So, you think this plan of yours will work?"

"Not at all. But we're low on options. As in, no other." I'm hoping fate will save my butt on this one. I spent all day yesterday touring the Kleins' job site and talking to Roy Livingston. I can't imagine not having that brilliant man on my side.

The Klein brothers arrive with their lawyer and sit on the opposite side of Natanya and me at the long conference room table. For our end-of-contract negotiations, I get my laptop ready to have Roy to argue my case via Zoom.

To start, Roy introduces himself. "I'm RevitaHome's representation, and I've got the contract in front of me here. I just wanted to go over it with you today. Is that all right?"

The Klein brothers scowl. Their lawyer, a man with strong cologne and a slick suit, says, "Let's see what you've got, but Ms. Dawson is clearly in breech. Per contractual obligation, she was required to be present. She wasn't. There's nothing to discuss."

Roy thumbs through his papers. "Yes, I do believe it says she has to be present as the project head, but let's go, if you will, to page seven in the footnotes. It states, 'In an emergency, Willow Dawson is permitted to delegate at will.'"

The brothers' lawyer stays stone-faced. "Restoring a home hardly constitutes an emergency."

Roy perks a brow. "Per the contract, an emergency is defined as 'an urgent and serious event that necessitates immediate action to avert imminent danger to life, health, or property.' Ms. Dawson was clearly averting danger to property." Roy clears his throat, going in for the kill in his gentle, non-threatening way. "So, if you want out of the contract, you'll have to pay for all the labor and all the fees plus an additional change fee of twenty-five percent. As of now, you've only paid the third upfront, so your remaining balance would be, well... let me add it up." He slides over a large, old-school calculator. "I think we need to add a few more zeros."

Aston scowls at me. "This is a dangerous game you're playing, Ms. Dawson. If you think it's worth holding my feet to the fire, I can ensure that your business doesn't do well in New York after my highly influential review."

"I apologize for my absence." I meet his hard gaze. "Mr. Klein, in the time we've worked together, my site crew has been on site every day, putting in extra hours to yield all changes or customizations you requested. We're three weeks behind schedule, and that's because of a materials delay that the entire world is experiencing right now. I've been doing Zoom calls and emailing you daily with updates, and

Natanya has been at your service anytime you need something. And after touring your complex yesterday, I'd say it looks absolutely stunning. So please, Mr. Klein, I'd love to hear your review."

He scoffs as his face turns beet red. "You're missing the point. You said you agreed to be present during this massive project, and I have emails where you agreed to such."

Mr. Livingston cuts in with, "The terms of Ms. Dawson's contract supersede any email exchange."

The Klein brothers' lawyer lifts his chin. "We'll let a court of law decide that."

Now, it's my turn to go in for the kill. I look at Aston square in the eyes when I say, "Look, the bottom line is that you're trying to get out of this contract because you found a better price. So let's stop arguing about the legalities and cut to the chase. It's clear to anyone who's seen the apartments that both our companies have hit it out of the park. This is one of the best restorations RevitaHome's ever done, and I couldn't be prouder. And you should be, too. Honestly, Natanya's done a better job than I would have." I smile at her, and she's glowing. I turn back to Aston and say, "So, with that in mind, I have an offer for you—one where both companies continue doing the finest work of any New York builder."

The Klein brothers sit silent, glancing at each other and scribbling something down for what feels like an eternity. Finally, Aston looks at me, brows perked, when he says, "Let's hear it."

Leaving the meeting on a high, I'm walking along the crowded sidewalk of downtown Manhattan, elbow to elbow with people who don't know me and don't want to know me.

I feel a yank on my purse.

I spin around before instinctively throwing an elbow into the face of the perp, putting all my strength into pulling my purse back.

Nose bleeding, he puts a hand over his face and staggers away.

"Dammit," I cry out, shaking off the twinge in my elbow from where it hit his nose. As I look around, everyone is scattering and scurrying away, clearly not wanting to get involved.

I should expect this, I know how it goes—never get involved in a crime. That's big city 101.

But it feels all different now. Yes, I know how to take care of myself. Yes, I know how to keep my purse from getting nabbed. I know no one wants to get involved. But in this sea of people, I'm all alone.

I look down on the sidewalk to see some of the spilled contents of my purse—lipstick, a tin of mints, and a package of Fig Newtons.

My heart skitters to a stop. Fig Newtons that Owen put in my purse because he knew I always needed a snack.

Even after I broke up with him.

I pick up my things, thinking of Sir Fig A Lot, too. He's probably wondering where I am and why I left him. He's probably wondering if he did something wrong.

A memory flashes of Owen, joking on our way to the hospital with second-degree burns, missing facial hair, with sooty clothes. Suddenly, I'm never so sure in my life about how I feel.

"I love Owen," I say, looking around at the lines of backed up cars as far as the eye can see. The endless skyrises, the moving crowd, the symphony of sirens, blaring horns, and roaring engines. It's buzzing with electricity—but I don't feel a part of it anymore. "I'm madly, deeply, pathetically in love with that man."

I finally know when enough is enough.

It's now.

32

The Guest

~~~~~~~~~~~~~~~~~~

I step up to Owen's porch with a to-go plate of my spaghetti and my suitcase filled with all my clothes and Demon's favorite treat, liver-filled dog bones. Tesla's crate is strapped to the top, and yeah, I'm struggling. When I knock on the door, I shake off my case of the jitters and get my thoughts together.

When it swings open, it's Owen with shock on his face.

"I brought spaghetti," I blurt, my thoughts scattering like marbles. "For Sunday dinner. Tonight. I was wrong. About... everything." I shrug. "Violet Moon is where I'm meant to be, with you. And just so you know, you're in my dreams, too. You're all I think about, too." I bobble my head. "And... I *liked* you a whole lot from the moment I met you. I loved you from the moment you delivered Oreo and I got to see how you were with Eclipse." I meet his eyes, which are blank, unreadable, as he stands unmoving. So, I keep rambling, shifting on my feet. "You're the one I want to be with forever, even though the thought scares me. And I'm *terrified* I'm gonna lose you, but I have to try because you're worth it."

Without a word, Owen steps onto the porch and pulls me into a hug, his arms trembling as he holds me tight. We just stand in the moment, the warm, thick Georgia breeze swirling around us. Something I missed in the four days I was gone.

"I love you so much," he whispers as his fingers caress my back.

"I love you too."

When he finally pulls away, his eyes meet mine. He says, "So, you're really here to stay?"

I wring my hands. "Well, I don't have a place to live. And I don't have a job. So, yeah. I'm here, but there are some things I have to get worked out." I manage a weak smile. "But I've started from nothing before. I can do it again."

"Without question." That gorgeous smile of his takes over his face.

I take a cleansing breath, looking around. Behind the house, the sunlight reflects on the lake in the distance, the shadows of pine trees framing it. That Georgia evening sky is exploding with colors. "This view is stunning."

"You have no idea," Owen mumbles, his eyes focused on me.

The way he says those words is a jolt to the heart, and I can't wait for evenings like this for the rest of my life.

He nods to the plate in my hands and says, "So, this means another spaghetti night?"

"I sure as hell hope so."

He leans over it and my turtle carrier to bring his lips to mine. I take in his kiss, his warmth, his everything, and I know, without a doubt, this is right.

Owen takes the plate of spaghetti from my hands before he opens the front door. He stops and turns back. "Welcome to Sunday dinner. Oh, and I gotta warn you. The whole family's over tonight."

Nerves twitch under my skin, but I won't let them win. I'm here, dammit.

He lingers, saying, "Do they have any more information on the fire?"

"I got emailed the latest report. It was arson. Someone cut the electrical wires." *Which means I have no insurance coverage.*

"Shit. You think Mary Louise made Huck do it? Would she go that far to get the land?"

"Probably—what have you seen on the local news?"

Owen groans. "The only information the marshal's made public is Bailey's testimony of a small-framed man in a hooded sweatshirt. But they've interviewed everyone in town."

My heart sinks, but I nod.

We step into Owen's house, or Frankie's house, and it's so... frilly. Which, knowing Frankie, makes zero sense. But weirder than that, it's all so familiar.

Knickknacks cover every square inch of the place, and there are wooden signs that say things like, "Home is Where the Heart is," and potted plants. I'd think there were probably gnomes outside in the garden, except, again, I know Frankie.

Clearly seeing my face, Owen says, "I know. Not what you expected, right?"

I look at him, wide-eyed. "Not at all."

We both bust up.

"This place was Nana Lottie's, my father's mother," he says. "When she died and willed it to my pa, my parents moved in. I was seven, Kayla was five, and Bailey was three. They kept it the same because Pa liked it being the home he grew up in, and Ma couldn't care less about decor." Owen whisks out a chuckle. "I think she was grateful not to have to deal with any of it and just be done. So, it stayed like this. Welcome to Grandma Lottie's designs."

"I love that story." I'm speaking on autopilot because being in this place is giving me serious déjà vu, and my mind's moving a million miles a minute.

How do I know that the door in the entryway leads to an oversized closet? How do I recognize those flowered curtains that adorn every window with puffy valances? I'm breaking into a sweat, so I try to focus on the fact that dinner smells delicious, and there's something so warm and comforting about it all. This place must look like another home I've seen somewhere. Except in my heart, I know that's not true.

Owen scoots my luggage to a corner then walks me over to the brown flowery couch—the kind people haven't had in their living rooms since the eighties. It's worn and tattered, but still comfortable. "Have a seat."

Hustle and bustle echoes from the kitchen as I introduce Owen to Tesla, and, of course, he immediately befriends him until Demon blazes in and tries to eat my turtle. As Owen manages the attempted turtlecide, I look around, trying to relax and let all the memories come to me. Which they are, but I'm not saying anything until later, when Owen and I are alone.

Soon, I'm getting hugs from Bailey, Kayla, and her wife, Margaret.

We all go into the dining room, which seats ten, and it's hard for me to imagine having so many people at a dinner table. Tonight will be seven. I have vague memories of this room, too, but they're not as strong as what I felt in the living room.

Without a word, Frankie sees me and pulls me into a hug, giving me a pat when she says, "Welcome home, Willow."

"Thank you."

When Trinity sees me, I expect a big hug, but she won't even meet my gaze. I shoot Owen a puzzled look, and he shrugs.

Finally, she says, "Are you leaving again?"

I rub her shoulder. "I'll have to go back to New York to get everything finalized there and move. But after that, I'm going to live in Violet Moon."

She fidgets, looking at me with something I can't place. Mistrust?

Looking back to the day after the fire, I remember her saying she had something to tell me, and that she was going to call me, but she never did. I was so busy in New York, I'd forgotten about that. Maybe she's angry with me?

Oh, man. I can't believe how much I love this little girl, and I hate to think that leaving broke her heart so much. I put my arm around her when I say, "I'm here to stay."

She doesn't respond, but together, she and I spread the plates out around the table in silence. Looking up from the setting, I see Owen in the kitchen and meet his gaze. There's that thing between us that makes the electricity shiver up my arm and down my spine. His expression tells me he seems to know exactly what I'm thinking. I'm nervous, and he somehow comforts me with a look.

Kayla takes a pitcher out of the refrigerator, calling out, "How about some tea, Willow? You look like you could use it."

"Sure, thank you."

"Sit by me, Willow." Trinity scoots out the chair by her, so I do as I'm told.

"Thanks, Trin." I'm happy to see her warming up to me.

Bailey comes to the table and makes a good show of putting out chicken, stuffing, and mashed potatoes.

Kayla pours me a glass, saying, "I hope you like sweet tea."

"I've never tried it."

"Get ready." Margaret takes her seat. "It's really something."

Trinity's already in trouble for shoveling too many mashed potatoes on her plate.

Without a word, Bailey serves me a heaping dish of mashed potatoes and stuffing, which looks divine. I wait patiently for everyone to be seated, but it appears this rule doesn't apply here, as everyone is serving themselves and eating as they go.

"Did you get your dress all squared away, Kayla?" Bailey asks, putting serving spoons beside all the main dishes.

"I'm not wearing a dress, Bay." Kayla's tone is irritated. "I'm wearing a suit."

"Oh, well then, a suit then, jeez." Bailey rolls her eyes. "Have you got that squared away?"

"Yep. Margaret and I are wearing matching suits."

"For what?" I ask, feeling like I should contribute something to the conversation. Also, I'm curious.

Kayla comes to the table and takes her seat. "Jeb and Sissy are getting married, and Margaret and I are bridesmaids. And we're wearing suits. Bailey and the other bridesmaids are wearing dresses."

"So, can I wear a suit?" Frankie takes a sip of her water before she sits.

"Of course you can, Ma," Kayla says.

Owen sits next to me, snickering. "Yeah, Bailey, why did you tell mom she had to wear a dress?"

"Shut up, Owen, or you're gonna find your underwear over your head." Bailey scowls at him.

"Whatever, Bay. I'd love to see you try."

As the family jumps into conversation, I realize I've never seen Owen in this role—the snarky big brother. He speaks less than usual as he observes his family, and I'm surprised that he's the quiet one of the group. Although, he *is* outnumbered in spades.

"Well, Ma, ask Sissy, then." Bailey pats her napkin on her face. "If she says you can wear a suit, then wear a suit."

Kayla forks some broccoli and shoots Bailey a glare. "Ma doesn't have to ask permission. She can wear whatever she wants, good Lord." She looks at Frankie. "Sissy and all of us will support whatever your preferences are, Ma."

"Why aren't you supportive of *my* preferences?" Trinity pipes in with a milk mustache.

"Because your preferences are terrible," Owen says under his breath.

Trinity sticks her tongue out at Owen.

"Watch your mouth and your manners," Frankie says. "We've got a guest."

I chuckle along with Owen.

The table becomes a hum of laughter and overlapping conversations. My mind wanders back to this house, and I realize now why I recognized the black-eyed Susans in the back. It's because I was *here*, at *this* house, and those flowers are on the edge of this property.

I find myself eating a little of this and a little of that, and before I know it, I've had vegetable pasta, stuffing, mashed potatoes, and cherry pie, and I feel like I could pop.

Trinity points at my vegetable concoction and says, "Can I try a bite of that, Willow? I want to see if I like it before I put it on my plate and Ma makes me eat it."

I blink. I can't believe somebody just asked me to share food, and I'm flattered. Of course she can have some of my casserole. I hold up my plate, offering her a bite, and then try not to think about the fact that her fork's touching my food.

It's so hard to remember what it's like being a part of a family, and even when I was in one, it was never like this. Bickering over wedding attire and sharing food. So seemingly simple, but somehow, everything.

33

The Dock

After dinner and clean up, I invite Owen to take a walk with me to Mary Louise's house. She and I have to have a talk, long overdue.

After we step outside Owen's house, he says, "Sorry about my family. They can be a bit... much."

"You know I love your family."

"Sometimes, I like animals better." He tilts his head. "Although my family members are animals, so..."

We chuckle, but the mood turns serious as we walk toward Mary Louise's house. I step onto to her porch, steeling myself before I ring her bell.

When she opens the door, her face twists into a scowl. But she comes out to the porch, closes the door behind her, then folds her arms. "Now you two? We didn't start the damn fire."

I can't barely look at her given everything, but I force myself to when I say, "Why should I believe you?" My tone is indignant.

"I'll tell you what I've told the investigators swarming my house, interrogating Bill and me for answers. Firstly, Bill and I don't match the description that Bailey provided. And it couldn't have been Huck because the day before the fire, he left for Atlanta to start college at Emory University. He's got a whole dorm full of alibis, so he's off their list."

"Oh." It's hard to argue with that. "But you talked to the surveyor the day of the celebration."

"Yes. Because there were two maps of our property lines, and they were drawn up differently. Since there was a surveyor out, we wanted that cleared up."

"Why didn't you just tell me that?"

"I'm sorry. I should have—that was wrong." She sighs. "I didn't want to be a thorn in your side while you were working so hard to finish everything."

What she's saying makes sense, but I'm still unsure. I shoot Owen a glance, then say, "And word is, you have a plan for the cotton plant."

"Yes. I do. There are several open warehouses just outside of town since Covid took out many businesses."

"Oh." Guilt twinges at my gut.

"Yes, I wanted this land when you first arrived, but that was before I knew what you could do for Violet Moon. Since then, Bill and I have been supporting you on this project, both thrilled to have a historical place to increase tourism."

"True." In fairness, she *has* been nothing but supportive since that first argument we had after I didn't sell her the property.

"And, honestly, I don't want a plant right next to my home." Hurt shades her eyes. "I was angry with you at first, but I realized I was dead wrong and apologized. What you did was so much better for this town. And I'd support you all over again if you wanted to give it another go. And I want to find the man who did this every bit as much as you do."

"Oh." Her words hit me hard, and I approach her. "I believe you, Mary Louise. I'm sorry for everything you've had to go through for this."

"I'm sorry for you, too, Willow. I truly am." Her lips wobble. "My heart's broken, too. Please let me know how I can help."

"That means a lot, thank you." I put my hand on her shoulder. "I'll let you know if I need anything."

She fidgets with the ring on her finger. "Are you gonna rebuild?"

"I don't know, Mary Louise. Insurance doesn't cover arson."

She shakes her head. "This whole thing is just a nightmare. Absolute nightmare." She pulls me into a hug. "You take care of yourself now."

"I will. That's what I'm doing right now, actually." I nod to the water. "Watching the stars."

"Good." She turns to Owen. "Bye, Owen."

"Bye, Mary Louise."

When she clicks her way inside, Owen and I leave and head to the lake. Once we get there, I breathe in the intoxicating air while I take in the harmony of chirping crickets and endless stars. This might be the best place on earth.

I see a boat tied to the dock, and I realize it's still there from the day we had the party—only four days ago. Somehow, it feels like another lifetime. I want to get in it, but I have no idea how to paddle, and I'd probably get stuck in the middle of the lake and damage the boat. So, instead, I walk to the edge of the dock, take off my heels, roll up my pants, and dangle my feet in the water.

Right now, the lake is calm, contrasting with what's happening inside me. I squint to see the mountains in the distance, but it's too dark. So, I close my eyes and focus on the sound of the water gently lapping up against the dock. And that's enough.

After Owen sits and dangles his feet, too, I say, "Well, that leaves Levi."

"I'll wring that kid's neck."

I have to put that worry on hold for now because I have another that's more pressing. I take Owen's hand when I say, "I have something to tell you."

"Okay."

My eyes glaze over as my brain kicks into overdrive. "I've been in your house before. And being there today brought back repressed memories."

He goes wide-eyed. "No way. Are you sure?"

I describe the places of his house that I didn't see today to prove it to him. Then I say, "I had to have been there when I was five years old because it was the day that I met my adoptive parents. They met me on that brown, flowery couch. They said they'd come to take me to a really good school in New York." Owen's eyes look torn, broken as he looks at me, but I continue. "I was so sad to leave my mom and Nana and Papa, but these people were so nice. They told me they'd give me anything I needed. They'd make sure that I had everything as I started kindergarten."

He rubs his thumb over the palm of my hand. "I don't understand. My mom had to know about this. Why didn't she say anything?"

"I think maybe she doesn't know, Owen." I glance up at the starry night sky. "I remember a man being at your house with us, who was probably your father. And Grandma Lottie was his mother."

"Yeah. Dad did a lot of things without telling us or Ma."

I swirl my foot in the water. "If he was the one who faked my death certificate, which is possible because he was the Assistant DA at the time, then this might've been something he never told her. I mean, faking someone's death is pretty messed up."

"No kidding. He also didn't want to endanger our family." There's regret in Owen's tone when he talks about his father, which I understand. It's still hard to hear.

"But I remember being happy at your house. Grandma Lottie was good to me and spoiled me with candy. I'm sure she must've been hiding me after they'd said I was dead. I remember being scared to go, but relieved to get away from the man who tried to hurt me." I sit for another moment, processing my own memories as another one hits. "He left me in the woods." I look at Owen. "That just came back to me. That man who kidnapped me left me in the woods to die." So, that's why I'm so afraid of them. "Maybe here in Violet Moon—I get shivers just looking at the forest by the gnarly tree. Maybe the man who did this lives here."

"Jesus. How can I help?" is all Owen says.

"Maybe my biological father knows something." I tell him that Blake Murphy is from a ridiculously wealthy and influential family from Buckhead, the Beverly Hills of Atlanta. Son of Bradford Murphy, Georgia's State Attorney, Blake is a named partner at a law firm and is working his way up to fill his father's big shoes. I have my mother's coloring and facial features, but my father's forehead and bone structure. And, apparently, his ambition. I'm almost certain he's not the one who kidnapped me because he looks nothing like the man I remember. I close my eyes and sigh before I say, "At first, just the thought of coming face to face with my biological father made me dizzy, claustrophobic, and panicked. But after some time, and now in desperate need of answers, I think I want to meet him."

"Then maybe it's time you go see him, Willow." Owen's voice is soft. "I bet he knows something."

I stare at the stars, wishing they had some answers for me. "I don't know. I'm scared. He didn't want me."

Owen puts his arm around me. "Maybe he never even knew about you. Or, if he didn't want you then, he might now. I'll be with you. At the very least, he owes you answers."

"So many answers." Why didn't he take me instead of letting Bo and Lily place me for adoption? That is, if he knows about me. Why did my mother die at thirty-two? "I don't want to face him, but I think I have to."

"We need to find out more about him."

"I've found out all I can via Google. In search results, he seems like a wonderful man. A successful lawyer with a beautiful family."

Owen groans. "Yeah, sometimes men like that are not all they seem. He didn't take care of your mom."

"True, but maybe he regrets it." I sigh. "You're right—we need to go. I have to find answers. Someone here is after me."

"Then that answers that. Tomorrow, we head to Atlanta to meet and talk to your dad."

"Okay. I'm ready." My phone buzzes three times in succession, and I check to see that it's texts from Roy. He never texts me.

I have information for you, Willow. Call me right away.

I'm coming to your house. We have to talk immediately.

What? After I show Owen the texts, I say, "This seems bad if Roy is coming here to see me in person this late."

"It does."

A chill rattles me, but a rustle in the grass draws my eyes to the side of the lake where the cattails are. I might be losing my mind, but I swear I catch a glimpse a small-framed man in a sweatshirt scrambling away.

"Did you see what I just saw?" Owen jumps up.

"I think so," I say, my heart rate soaring.

Owen takes off running and I follow behind, both barefoot, and we end up on a frantic search through the property. In the chaos, Owen and I get separated, and the moon is our only light.

34

The Capture

I take off in the direction I hear rustling. When I get close enough, I can see I'm chasing a thin-framed man wearing a hoodie. I speed up—this has to be the person who caused the stable fire, and probably everything else.

And I have to catch him, but he's running like a rocket. As I watch him maneuver through the trees, I realize it does look kind of like Levi. It must be Levi!

I knew that kid was trouble. I push my legs till they're burning, and I can't believe I'm so close, but not close enough.

He cuts a hard left, disappearing into the foliage. When I do the same, I groan as my bare feet slip on the mud, losing further ground.

When I stand and start running again, an ache radiates from my leg, and I can't move as fast. Now, I'm a good distance behind Levi, disheartened that he's getting smaller in the distance.

I stop, bending my head over my knees to catch my breath when I see a figure burst through the trees and chase after Levi, making up ground as he runs at lightning speed.

Thank god—Owen.

Owen catches up to Levi and grabs his hood. I exhale in relief—Owen's got him.

But the kid unzips his jacket, leaving Owen holding it as he slips away from his grip. "Dammit," Owen cries out.

I'm gaining ground on them after that hiccup slowed them down, but the kid gets to the fence of the property and carefully climbs it before Owen can get there. When Levi flips to climb down the other side, he ducks his head, probably so we can't see his face.

But his deliberate moves are those of someone older than Levi. It hits me that my biological father is also small-framed and around five eleven.

Could it be?

It was an older man's face I saw in the barn window that night!

When Owen jumps on the fence, the perp loses his balance, then disappears beneath the fence before a sickening thud echoes from the other side.

Owen jumps over at whiplash speed while I lag, still fighting against the ache in my leg.

When I make it to the other side, the perp is lying on the ground, face down, and Owen is kneeling beside him. I gasp when I realize that it's *not* Levi or my biological father, as I see a dark ponytail that was hidden by the hood. And the muscular form is from a Batman suit under the hoodie. Is this he a she? Who the hell is this?

As I approach, it's clear from her slow movements that she's injured, and blood is seeping from her head.

Owen's face twists in terror as he gently flips her around. He cries out in anguish, screaming, "Ma?"

35
The Truth

Owen rips the shirt off his back to put it on her wound.

"I'm fine, Owen, stop fussing." Frankie holds his shirt to her head.

"How could you do this!" I look over toward my estate, or what used to be my estate, in utter disbelief. "How could you burn everything down? Put the horses' lives in danger? And Owen's? And mine?"

"The fire wasn't me." For the first time, Frankie's voice shakes.

"Ma." Owen rakes a hand through his hair. "What the hell is going on?"

She stands slowly and carefully. "Just hear me out. Please. If you want to press charges afterward, go ahead. But not until you hear me out."

Fire's racing through my veins and blood's rushing in my ears so loudly I can hardly hear. I've never been so tempted to storm away, but Owen's hand is on my shoulder. "Please hear her out. You may not owe her that, but I do."

I squeeze my eyes shut before opening them and avoiding her gaze. "Fine."

Owen checks Frankie's wound and lets out a sigh. "The bleeding's stopped, but you're gonna need a few stitches. I'll get the van. We'll go to the clinic."

"No." Frankie looks at me. "Not yet. We'll finish this, finish it now. And not here. At the tree where all this started. Take me there, and I'll tell you everything."

The tree. Shivers skitter up my spine. Of course, the truth lies at that damn tree.

Once Owen insists on stitching Frankie's head using the supplies from the medical bag he keeps in the van, we ride in silence; me biting my tongue as my brain attempts to put the pieces of the puzzle together until words rush from my mouth. "You did all that stuff. The note, the face in the barn, hiding my damn keys. How could you? You let Oreo out! Oh, god, the waterline—you cut it! I thought I was losing my mind."

"I'm sorry." Her voice is quiet. "I hated doing those things, but I had no choice," she says.

No choice! What the hell is wrong with this woman?

When we arrive at the creepy-ass tree, Frankie sits, and Owen and I take a seat in front of her.

"So, let's hear it," I say, my jaw tight.

Her hands fidget between her knees before she looks at me and says, "I knew your biological mother."

My blood turns to ice.

"We were close." She squeezes her eyes shut as she's getting emotional, but when she opens them, they're dry. "We met at a home for troubled teens, clicked right away. Kindred spirits. Two teens being knocked around. For me, it was my father. For her, her stepfather first, then her boyfriend. She couldn't win. Lord knows she tried, then she got knocked up with you. Lily worked at the home—one of the kindest, gentlest souls you ever want to meet." Frankie's eyes gloss. "Number one thing you need to know. Annie loved you more than anything in this world."

My mother loved me.

Something I've wanted to know my entire life, and an empty space of my being fills as the information washes over me. But as my brain continues to process everything, I can't help but think of the memorial we're sitting on.

My memorial.

I motion to the cross, tilted and weathered, the etched words glaring at me, "In loving memory of our sweet Willow." I grit, "So, how did this happen?"

"Your father, that's how." For a moment, Frankie looks off as if she's lost in painful thoughts. "Annie left him so many times and went back just as many. It's such a hard and complicated thing—that abuse cycle. She finally broke free and left him for good."

Something swells in my chest, and I meet Frankie's eyes. "She was courageous."

"As courageous as they come." Frankie's lips tick up but then flatline. "But your father wouldn't let her go. Blake—that's his name—convinced his so-called buddy, this evil piece of crap, to grab you from her. He thought this would force Annie to take him back. And the POS does it—snatched ya right from your ma's arms. Beat the crap out of your mother in the process." Frankie shudders before inhaling a deep breath. "But you, whip smart, even back then, got away from him and ran into the woods. Got yourself good and lost, though. Your mom was lucky to find you alive."

My jaw goes slack. "My own father was behind that?" So, that's why I didn't recognize him. Of course, he pawned off his dirty work.

"Yes, and that wasn't the end of it. Annie rescued you from the woods but..." Frankie sighs; her expression looks pained. "God, she must've been a panicked mess. She was driving way too fast when she veered off the road, crashing head on into this godforsaken tree. Poor Annie. Later, authorities said she'd been under the influence."

My stomach tumbles off a cliff. Somewhere, I've always known this, but I could never quite access the full memory. All I know is that I was so terrified, it stayed with me forever.

Frankie continues, "They brought you and her to the Violet Moon hospital. You both recovered, but Bo and Lily had Nick, my husband, create a fake death certificate for you and helped get you adopted out. Since your father was never caught, we felt it was our only option. We were able to get a restraining order on him. Thankfully, I haven't heard from him or seen him for a long time now."

"Oh, my god." I'm shaking my head. My throat goes bone dry. "But what about my mother? You all just took me from her?"

"No, Willow. She agreed." Frankie's voice is hoarse. "Annie made me promise to never tell you or anyone. And I'm sorry. I really am, but every single thing I did was to protect you. Your pa is out free because Annie could never prove what happened. Blake is the worst combination—well-connected and extremely dangerous. Right now, he thinks you're dead, and that's a very good thing. Willow," Frankie leans in and takes my hands, "I've never been able to prove it, but I'm certain Blake was behind the explosion that killed my husband and Annie."

I swallow back the bile rising from my gut.

Frankie's jaw tenses. A tear rolls down her cheek as she turns to Owen. "I wanted to tell you. All these years—you kept blaming yourself for your pa's death. It killed me. But there was no way you could've prevented it. I wanted to tell you everything so much, Owen, but I couldn't put our lives in danger. Please understand."

Gooseflesh covers my arms as I reach for Owen's hand. I'm not the only one who lost someone in all of this. I can't believe I didn't put it together before—how both our parents died on July twentieth. I hope now Owen can let go of his guilt.

Owen's face softens as he leans over and puts a hand on her shoulder. "You did what you had to do, Ma. I understand that."

Everyone goes quiet. The only sound is the chirping of crickets. I look up at the night sky to see a cloud cover over the stars. "I can't tell you what it means to get answers to questions I've had all my life, Frankie, but why the tricks? Why burn down my house?" I can't help but sound indignant.

"I did *not* cause that fire. I'll fess up to the other things, but I didn't do that. I was just trying to scare you away, never harm you." She kicks her foot on a bulging root. "I wanted you to go, to leave and never come back before Blake got word and figured out who you were. I didn't want him trying to get back into your life, into our lives. And well…"

Frankie looks away as I wait for her to finish.

When she doesn't, I say, "Please, Frankie, if you know something more, you need to tell me. I have to know the whole truth about my past, so I can finally be free of it."

She doesn't answer, and my lips go numb, making it hard to form words. But the anger settles in my gut again, and my tone is sharp when I say, "Who caused the fire?"

Frankie opens her mouth, but another voice answers, "I did."

It's Trinity's.

36

The Shock

⋘ ⋅ ♦ ⋅ ⋙

Seeing Trinity riding Raven, we all jump up and rush over to her.

"Trinity." Frankie groans. "What in god's name are you doing here?"

"Sorry, Ma. Roy is at our house, and he needs to talk to Willow real bad."

He wants to tell me about my father.

"I said I'd come get you guys." Trinity hops off the horse holding an iPad and approaches me. She sobs so much she struggles to speak. "Ma was just there to rescue me the night of the fire. That's who Bailey saw."

I don't respond. In shock, I can't.

"I'm so sorry, Willow." Trinity's lips quiver. "At the party, I heard the appraiser saying that if you didn't pass the electrical inspection, they wouldn't buy the house from you. I wanted you to stay, so I cut the electrical box wires. They sparked. Bad. I didn't know it would do that. I'm sorry. I never meant for a fire." She chokes out a sob. "I just wanted you to stay."

"Aw, Trinity." I pull her into a hug. She did a terrible thing, but she's too young to fully understand the consequences of her actions.

"There's more." She pulls away and hiccups. "I found something. It made me want you to stay even more. I found a video on Bo's computer that you have to see." She presses some buttons and hands me the iPad.

"But Bo's computer was destroyed." I furrow my brows.

"This was on his Google drive," she says, matter-of-factly. "There's a ton of stuff on there."

A Google drive. Of Bo's. So everything isn't lost! Relief rushes through me.

I take the iPad, and on the screen is a paused video of Annie holding a baby.

Seeing a picture of Annie is one thing. But knowing that I'm about to see her move, to hear her voice makes me crave the touch of a woman I can hardly remember.

She must be holding me, but why does she look older than in the pictures I found of her and me as a newborn?

I hit play, and Annie looks at the camera, her eyes glossy with happy tears. Her mouth presses in a half-smile, and I recognize the expression as my own.

"Hi Willow, I—" For a moment, her smile breaks and her lips tremble. She tries to talk again and has to swallow. She clears her throat and tries again. This time she's able to continue. "I wanted to send this to you so you know how much I think of you and miss you every day."

My mother's voice. It sounds so familiar, but with the rasp that comes with age. A memory of her singing to me comes back to me, and it soothes me. I realize the sound is weaved into my being.

She continues, "I don't blame you if you can't forgive me for what I've done, and lord knows, I'll never forgive myself, but I need you to know why I did what I did." She looks away, blinking away tears. When she returns her gaze, she says, "Sometimes people get trapped in relationships, and they can't get away. No matter how hard they try. It's like that with me and your father. That's not your fault; don't ever think that. It just is. And your dad is mean sometimes, Willow. Very, very mean. And he was mean to you, so I had to send you away so that he couldn't hurt you. He kidnapped you, and you could've died in those woods." She leans forward, moving her face closer to the camera. "But I miss you every single minute of every single day." She shakes her head and takes a moment to steady herself. Then she smiles wistfully. "As a little girl, you made us smile every day. Lily loved you so much—you were named after her favorite tree. You were so smart and sassy—you knew how to solve puzzles before you were even two. You'd build fancy Legos that made Bo's heart go pitter-patter. He was so proud, still is. I am too."

Puzzles. Legos. I don't remember them, but it's really nice to know something about me from my early childhood.

Annie blows out a long sigh. "I tried so hard to be a good mother to you, but every time I started getting my life on track, something happened, and sometimes I'd get a kind of sickness. It would take over my mind and prevent me from being a good mother. And you deserved a good mom, Willow. So Bo and Lily helped me. They took custody of you. They loved you so much and took such good care of you when I couldn't. Do you remember the house in Atlanta? Do you remember when I'd visit? Our walks? Our picnics? I came to see you every weekend. Every single one, until your dad found out and tried to take you again. That's when we sent you away forever." Annie purses her trembling lips, hesitating. After a moment of gathering herself, she says, "I wish I could tell you I never saw your dad again, and that I had the strength to finally get away from him, but I didn't, not until this little one came." She looks down at the baby.

And I finally realize the baby isn't me. That's why Annie looks older and this video is newer than the pictures of her with me as a newborn.

Annie smiles. "This is Trinity, Willow. She's your sister. She looks so much like you. I can't believe it."

What?

My *sister*?

I hit pause. My entire body tingles as I look at Trinity. My sister? I stare at her hazel eyes and see mine. I take in the natural strawberry highlights of Trinity's blond hair, and I shake my head. It seems so obvious now, I wonder how I could've missed it. Emotion overwhelms me, joy filling more hollow spaces of my being. I have a sister—one I may not have known but already loved. I turn to Trinity. "You're my sister?"

"Yup. Now I have three," she says so simply, smiling—like we're discussing the weather.

Owen studies Trinity, then scowls at Frankie. "Is this true?"

Frankie nods slowly, and Owen cuts in with, "So that's why you wanted us to keep Trinity's adoption a secret." He looks at me. "Ma made us promise."

Putting her hand on Trinity's shoulder, Frankie's voice is hoarse when she says, "Your ma was scared Blake was coming for her. So just after you were born and she made this video, she gave you to me to watch over you. It was just going to be for a few days." Frankie shakes her head. "But he got to her, somehow, your daddy Nick too." She looks at Owen. "We could never prove it, but when that cabin blew up, we knew it wasn't a gas leak." Frankie rubs her temple, her fingers trembling. "And I claimed Trinity as my own." She looks at Trinity. "Blake was on your birth certificate because Annie and Blake were still married. That POS refused to sign the divorce papers, so I couldn't adopt you because he'd be notified and take you. I got help from Daddy Nick's colleague to get the needed documents and I raised you as my own."

"Trinity," I whisper, looking at Frankie. "That's why you didn't want to tell me. Because you were afraid I'd take her away. Or that I'd go to my biological father, and he'd find out about her."

Frankie scowls. "I love this child like I birthed her myself, so if you're planning on either of those things, you'll have a helluva fight on your hands."

"Frankie." Tears stream down my face. "I'd never take Trinity away from her mother. And I certainly don't want that horrible man to have her. Now that I'm here, we can all be together."

"That's what I want too, Willow." Trinity says. "I love you, Ma."

Frankie pulls Trinity tight. "You're my child, you hear me?"

"I do, promise, cross my heart. But can we get back to the video?" Trinity presses play again.

A tear rolls down Annie's cheek. "Willow, I wish you were here to meet your sister. You two would be the best of friends. Anyway, Bo knew Ed, so he knew Ed and Sharon would do an amazing job raising you. I heard about their car accident a few months back." She cries harder. "All I ever wanted was for you to have a good life, and now you've lost your parents. Again. It's unbearable for me to know that you're alone at sixteen, but I can't bring you back here right now. Blake's trying to kill me, but he doesn't know about little Trinity, thank god." She leans into the computer. "Anyway, I love you. More than anything. I'm going to bring you home as soon as this is over. But I am always with you, Willow, okay? Always."

It stops playing, and I touch the screen. *She wanted to bring me home. She's always with me.*

Frankie's face is exhausted, drained. "We thought Blake's hire was going to bomb her apartment or car, which is why we took her to the safe house. But he was a step ahead of us."

So many things are hitting my brain, it's hard to process them all. "I can't believe he got away with it all."

"Me too." Frankie is calmer when she says, "Willow, Bo wanted to leave you his property, hoping maybe you'd find the peace and comfort that it brought him. He hoped to give you back something after not being able to be there for you as a kid. He really loved you, and he protected his computer and all his information for you. All he and Lily ever wanted was for you to be safe and happy. Me too."

Slowly, one by one, the realizations are creeping into my brain. I look at Trinity and croak out, "So you're really my sister." And maybe that's why I've always felt this inexplicable closeness to her.

"Uh, huh. That's why you can't leave." Tears streak Trinity's face, sprinkled with freckles, just like mine.

Frankie is staring into the distance, contemplative. Finally, she says, "I did what I had to do, and I'd do it again."

"I can't believe any of this." Owen puts the heel of his hand to his eye.

"Don't worry, Owen." Trinity pats his shoulder. "I still love you the same. But I love Willow too. And she needs me. She needs family."

I manage a weak laugh through my tears. "I do."

Frankie's mouth curves. "We need her, too."

Owen nods. "Yes, we do."

"I love you, Frankie." I pull her into a hug, even though I know she hates them, and she hugs me back. "And I forgive you. Thank you for all the sacrifices you made for me."

Family is everything, but they're not always those who share our blood.

"So, what are you gonna do now, Willow?" Trinity asks.

I hesitate, thinking about what I should say, what I could say. Then I realize none of it matters because I know what I have to say. "My life is here. My family is here. And my heart is here. That's all I know right now, but I have that, so the rest will fall into place."

"Sounds like you're sure." Frankie's lips quirk up.

"I am. In fact, I'm more sure than I've ever been about anything in my entire life." This should be the hardest decision I've ever made, but somehow, it's the easiest.

"Welcome to the family, Willow Dawson." Emotion breaks around Owen's words.

I run a finger across his cheek, then I march over to the tree and yank that godforsaken cross from the ground.

Epilogue

I spent the three weeks in New York listing my apartment, getting moved out, and doing all the final prep work for selling Revita-Home to the Klein Brothers. They needed my team for the restoration division of their home-building business—and buying me out was a great way to expand. In the contract Roy drew up, Natanya's stated as the head of the restoration division.

She's thrilled.

And I'm thrilled because with the money I got, I'm able to pay back the loan on Bo's Château *and* have enough to build it all over again.

This time, since the place is no longer historic, it's going to be just for me. However, I'm dedicating my job and my life to restoring the other historic sites of Violet Moon. This way, I can still bring the town something they all want so very much. I do, too.

So, I'm back here for good, and right now, I'm blindfolded as Owen ushers me somewhere. I don't know where, but I can tell by the sounds and the terrain that we're on my property. Aren't we? I must be confused because we step on something that feels like a grate. "This is getting creepy," I tease, making a scared face.

"Don't worry. But do hang on." Owen directs my hand to a bar. Then we're moving upward with the wind blowing on my face, and I'm trying not to get *actually* scared.

Then we step off the grate onto a wooden floor. Or a plank? We're clearly higher up because the wind is stronger on my cheeks. And up here, the sounds of birds chirping, waves lapping, and frogs croaking are pure and clear.

"Where *are* we?" I say.

"You're about to find out." He ushers me further into whatever we're standing on before he finally says, "Ready?"

"Yep."

He slips the blindfold off and I'm standing at a railing with a view of the lake below. We're at our lookout spot, except I'm on some sort of roof.

It hits me.

"This is the barn I designed." My eyes pan around, scanning the railing, the woodwork, and the structure below me with the accordion glass doors on two sides. "It's my dream barn—and we're standing on it!"

"Is it as nice as you hoped?"

"Way, *way* nicer." I can't believe how majestic the view is from up here. Shock numbs me as joy overwhelms me. "Thank you, Owen!" I pull him into a hug before planting a big kiss on his cheek. When I step away, I ask, "How did you do it?"

"You can get a lot done quickly when a whole town comes together to finish something." He points at the boom lift that got us up here.

I put a hand over my mouth. "Amazing."

"Yup. Come with me." He guides me to a railing that leads to a spiral staircase.

"There are my stairs. No way!"

"Yup. Premade. Just like you said."

Before I step down, I take in the view. *My* view. "I still can't believe you did this. It's something out of a dream."

"It is, isn't it?"

Once I've stepped into the barn's open loft, I hear a jumble of voices from below yell, "Surprise!"

I turn and blink, not trusting my own eyes. I'm inside the barn, and there's a zillion people here—Owen's family, Dakota, Jeb, Sissy, Gertie, Roy, Owen's nurses, work crews, and every other person from Violet Moon who's touched my life.

"Happy birthday, Willow." Owen's smile glows.

I shoot him a puzzled look. "It's not my birthday."

"Yes, it is."

Huh? "Oh, yeah. Today's my *real* birthday," I utter, thinking back to when I found my baby bracelet. I'd told Owen that day we remodeled the bathroom. "I can't believe you remembered."

"Of course I remembered."

"Only you." I put my arm around him as my eyes roam the beautiful, open space. It has a tall wooden-beamed ceiling, rustic beer barrels as cocktail tables, a stocked bar, and a counter of solid oak. Then I see the stunning two-story fireplace. "That's gorgeous."

Owen shrugs. "I may not be good at painting or color, but I am good with stone. And maybe I had a little help." He nods to Jeb, who gives him a thumbs up.

"Thank you, Jeb and Owen. I absolutely love it."

Once I'm in the crowd mingling, Dakota walks up and nudges me with her elbow. "Looks like we both have a wedding venue now. Wink-wink."

"We do! Any update on that front?"

"Bennett's moving here in the next six to nine months." She lets out a squeal. "So, put us on the schedule. After you, of course."

"On, no. You first."

Trinity appears holding a cake, which might be the ugliest thing I've ever seen. I study it, and I think it's supposed to be a cat and a goat? Or is that a mouse and a bull? Trinity chimes in. "That's Sir Fig A Lot and Demon playing. I made it!"

"It's the best cake ever." And I mean that. I put my arm around her. "Love you, Trin."

Roy approaches me, leaning into my ear and whispering, "I found out more about Blake's sentence. No probation. No parole. He'll serve out his sentence."

I let out a silent stream of air. Annie may not have been able to catch Blake, but that's the thing about criminals. They keep committing crimes, getting bolder and sloppier as their egos grow, and often, get caught eventually. Roy found out that Blake's served three years of his twenty-year sentence in an Ontario, Canada federal prison for a list of felony offenses. It's no surprise one of them is assault with a deadly weapon. "Glad justice has been served."

"Better late than never." Roy pats my shoulder.

"Thanks for everything. You know, Roy, not all heroes wear capes."

"Pfft." He bats his hand as he drifts into the crowd.

My eyes wander to the mantle where a display catches my eye. I wander over and get a close look at all the framed pictures. Owen joins me and says, "Figured we could make this place home until we get the house finished."

Tears well in my eyes as I run my finger over the photo of me and Dakota sitting at the Malted Moon Brewery together, smiling. Or the picture of me and Owen in the middle of the restoration job, sweaty but happy. Then there's one with Trinity, me, Demon, and Sir Fig A Lot, who looks quite dashing, I might add.

My lips quiver when I say, "This is the nicest thing anyone's ever done for me."

"It's what families do for each other." Owen puts his arm around me and squeezes.

Right. I have a family now. I lean in and whisper, "You know I love you, right?"

"You know I love you too."

Sir Fig A Lot approaches us, and there's a set of newly minted keys labeled "barn" hanging on the horns he recently sprouted. I take them and jangle them in the air with a smile on my face.

The crowd breaks out into an off-key rendition of Happy Birthday, and I've never had this many people sing to me. It's terribly goofy, and oh, so awkward, but I don't care. It's painfully wonderful.

Even Levi joins in on the singing, standing in the corner, alone, like he does. But he doesn't mean anyone harm. He's a good kid, always staying late on the farm to make sure everything's tidied up. As it turns out, the night of the fire, he rushed away from Owen and me because he was embarrassed to be working so late.

I look around at the smiling faces, the waving hands, and the bottles of beer tipped in my direction. The warmth and love are palpable. I never could've imagined I'd end up here forever, after coming to this strange town under stranger circumstances.

This barn was executed exactly to my specs—the charming spiral stairwell, the rustic fixtures, the stony two-story fireplace, and the open accordion doors, where a cool breeze carries in the smell of fall with its sweet-decaying leaves. On the lake outside, the dipping sun casts a twinkling shade of saffron along the water. It's more beautiful here than the day I arrived, and even then, I knew I was home.

I own this estate officially now, but what makes it mine isn't any of those things. It's the people gathered here for me.

The very place I belong.

Don't Go Quite Yet!

Want more of Buried Roots? How about a bonus story that tells you about Willow and Owen's wedding, plus introduces Violet Moon Book Two?

https://www.terraweiss.com/free-stories

Want my free novelettes, bonus content, short stories, and special giveaways?
https://www.terraweiss.com/free-stories

Books by Terra Weiss

Finding Yesterday, Blue Vine Book One

I hightail it into a wine cellar instead of down the aisle, my caterer, famous bad boy chef, Jack Brady, provides a bottle opener and a listening ear. But buried secrets could send our dreams up in flames.

Cutting Chords, Blue Vine Book Two

Eight years ago, I had two loves: music and the awkward yet brilliant guitarist Will Evans. When he ghosted me, I lost both. Now, Will's back, but I have a secret of my own that could close Will's heart forever.

Restoring Hearts, Blue Vine Book Three

When my dead husband's best friend, Grant Bresser III, comes to town to win the auction on my grandfather's mountaintop estate, the bombshell lie my husband took to the grave threatens to leave our lives in ruins.

Buried Roots, Violet Moon Book One

I might've found my own grave. But a perfect stranger willed me his fifty-acre farm, and this New Yorker is swamped taking care of it. My hot neighbor Owen Brooks helps out, but danger intensifies as my buried roots surface. I must confront that grave...and my bombshell family secret.

Wingmom, A Rom Com Mystery

Forget helicopter parenting: my mother is the hovering, UFO type. When she and my new hot CEO become BFFs, I start to fall for him. But that could destroy everything.

Storybook Christmas, A Rom Com Holiday Novella

Stripper. Work Nemesis. My fake holi-date? Yes, I drooled over Finn Hayes last weekend as he gyrated in a sparkly fuchsia thong. So what if he's my new co-worker?

About Terra Weiss

As a lover of books with mystery, witty banter, family-friend dynamics, and all the feels, I do my best to provide each in my stories. I work to steer away from cookie-cutter formulas and focus on how real-life people find real-life love.

When I'm not spilling the tea on what happens in the big and small towns that live in my heart, you'll find me with my spunky daughter, mad scientist husband, wacky and wonderful mother, and the two six-pound dogs that run my house. I enjoy jogging at a snail's pace, reading from my iPhone, and piling bright orange mountains of squeezy cheese on my crackers.

Stay Connected!

TerraWeiss.com

Newsletter

Instagram

Facebook

TikTok

Goodreads

Bookbub

Thank Yous

Buried Roots came to me on a phone call with my friend and critique partner, Deena Short. I wandered in the backyard, and I may have been in my robe, as she and I discussed the idea of a more intense romantic mystery than I'd tried before. We'd decided that Willow had to find her own grave, and we'd work backward from there. Thanks to Deena's badassery, I was able to create the book I'd always wanted to read but never quite found. So many books with a mystery end up being a little too intense, bloody, and dark for my taste. So, this is for you readers who want a big dose of mystery without too much grit.

As always, thank you to my husband, whose big huge brain helps me make better scenes and story summaries. Also, for his dialogue help with statements like, "Who says that? No one says that." Hey, he's blunt, but he's right. Bigger than that though, a huge thanks to him for being here for me, every day, year after year, supporting me a million and one percent. Dave, you are my biggest cheerleader, and I really don't know how I would do it without you pulling me through this, even on the toughest days. To my daughter. Thank you for making me a mother, and being by far and away the greatest thing I have ever done. You are seriously the best kid ever, and I'm not just saying that because I'm your mom. You rock, empirically. All my love and thanks to my writing and brainstorming partner, my biggest fan, and my example—Mom. Thank you for all your help dialing up the suspense and endless ideas on how to handle scenes. Many thank yous to Dad, who's always there via text, cheering me on. To Terry Ann, my step-mother, who encourages and supports me. And a big thanks goes to my mother in law, Philippa Strum, who's encouragement and editing on all my books have helped bring them to the world. Thank you to my in-laws, Herbert and Sevana, who are always rooting for me, ready to step in to help when needed. To my sisters, Christina, and Paris who cheer me along.

To Deena Short who helped with everything (and do I mean everything) in this book, but especially for plotting, dialing up the mystery and tension, and making the characters come to life. Deena, I dedicated this book to you because there's no one who will reading through my endless pages, countless times, more times than anyone should, like you. Thank you for treating my books like your own. Thank you for calling me and the time and talking me through all things books, but life too. You really are a superhero.

To Deb Lacativa, Brenda Lowder, and Jill Cobb. Deb, thank you for read every single dingle page, making sure my characters sound realistic and genuine and catching some critical things about horses, historical restorations. Also, for cheering me on! Brenda, who helped me figure out the end of this book. Thank you, Brenda, that was a brilliant day with a brilliant friend! Thanks to Jill, who told me with honesty that my original chapter one had to go, and she was right.

To Eliza Peake, for kicking my butt into gear with marketing. You help me daily, encourage me, and inspire me, and you're kicking butt. To Tory Bunce, who helped me with the initial idea of this book, talking me through how to make it work. Ten years of friendship, baby! Thank you for always being there with your marketing genius to help me kick off each new book. To Grace Wynter, thank you for being there with all your advice and emotional support. Always! To Kim

Conrey for sharing ideas and helping me maneuver this wild wacky world of self publishing. To Ciara Knight, for her expert self-publishing and marketing knowledge that she so generously shares not just with me, but the entire writing community.

Thank you to Tenesha Curtis and George Weinstein, who support me and the entire metro Atlanta writing community.

A gigantic thank you to my wonderful and amazing editors, Reina from Rickrack Books, and Marcia Migacz from Final Edit.

Many thank yous to my beta readers and advanced readers who champion through one book after another of mine, and help me get my words into the hands of more readers. I couldn't do this without you!

To you, my reader, who makes this all possible. Thank you for making my dreams come true.

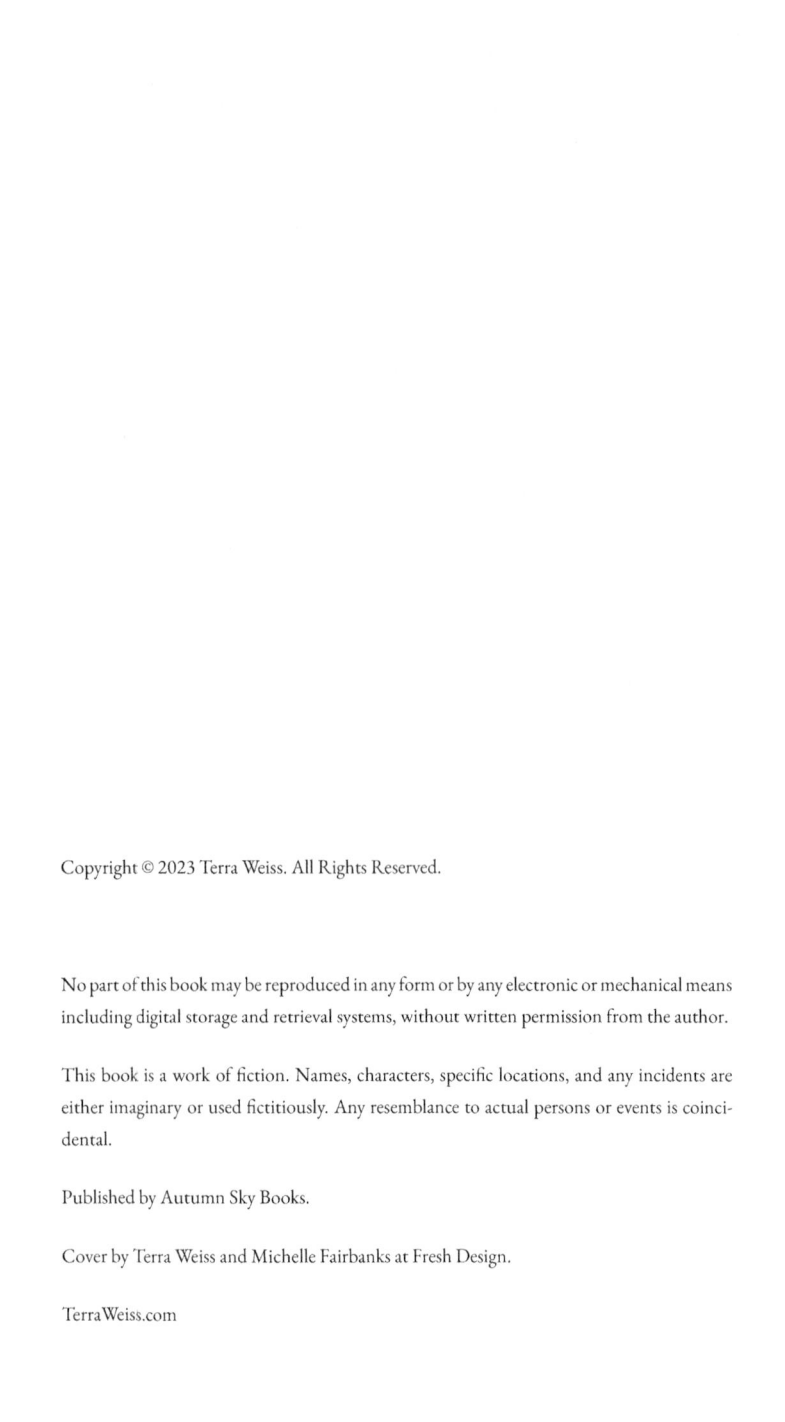

Copyright © 2023 Terra Weiss. All Rights Reserved.

No part of this book may be reproduced in any form or by any electronic or mechanical means including digital storage and retrieval systems, without written permission from the author.

This book is a work of fiction. Names, characters, specific locations, and any incidents are either imaginary or used fictitiously. Any resemblance to actual persons or events is coincidental.

Published by Autumn Sky Books.

Cover by Terra Weiss and Michelle Fairbanks at Fresh Design.

TerraWeiss.com

Printed in Great Britain
by Amazon